A Rustle of Silk

Alys Clare is the pseudonym of Elizabeth Harris,
who studied archaeology at the University of Kent.
lizabeth also writes the much-loved Hawkenlye and
Aelf Fen series. *A Rustle of Silk* is the first in her
gripping Gabriel Taverner series.

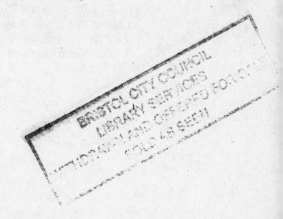

Also by Alys Clare

The Hawkenlye Series

The Paths of the Air
The Joys of My Life
The Rose of the World
The Song of the Nightingale
The Winter King
A Shadowed Evil

The Norman Aelf Fen Series

Out of The Dawn Light
Mist Over the Water
Music of the Distant Stars
The Way Between the Worlds
Land of the Silver Dragon
Blood of the South
The Night Wanderer

A Rustle of Silk

ALYS CLARE

BLACKTHORN

First published in Great Britain, the USA and Canada in 2019
by Black Thorn, an imprint of Canongate Books Ltd,
14 High Street, Edinburgh EH1 1TE

Distributed in the USA by Publishers Group West and in Canada by
Publishers Group Canada

First published in 2016 by Severn House Publishers Ltd,
Eardley House, 4 Uxbridge Street, London W8 7SY

blackthornbooks.com

1

British Library Cataloguing in Publication Data
A catalogue record for this book is available on request from the
British Library

ISBN 978 1 78689 479 3

Typeset by Palimpsest Book Production Ltd, Falkirk,
Stirlingshire, Scotland

Printed and bound in Great Britain by Clays Ltd, Elcograf S.p.A.

PART ONE

ONE

April 1603

'So, Doctor Gabriel, we're to get that Scots Mary's lad, just like they predicted,' Sallie said. She had her back to me, her wide rump swaying to the rhythm of her vigorous polishing of the sideboard.

Very slowly and quietly, I bent forward and banged my head several times on the gleaming surface of my oak table. It was at least the fifth remark of this sort that my housekeeper had made since she came into my study to 'tidy up', as she would have it. I had been hoping to have a peaceful morning of hard work – I had so much to learn – but I wasn't going to be allowed that dubious pleasure until I had made some sort of response.

'Yes,' I agreed.

It wasn't much of a reply, but even the single word was sufficient to open the gates and allow Sallie's spring tide of garrulousness to surge forth.

'Well, like I've said all along, it's a mystery to me,' she began, stopping her polishing as suddenly as if she'd been turned to stone and, leaning her backside comfortably against my table, fixing me with a stern look. 'Twenty-five years back, and the Queen – God rest her – was sending the order to have the young fellow's mother's head cut off! Not that I blame her for that, mind,' she added hurriedly – the late Queen Elizabeth had been her idol. 'Now she's named this green boy as her successor! What are we to make of it, Doctor?'

She had taken to referring to me thus. While it is perfectly correct – the reward for three of the most mentally demanding years of my life – nevertheless, I wished she wouldn't. I sounded like a stranger to myself.

I gathered my thoughts to form an answer. 'James can hardly be described as a boy,' I said mildly, 'since he is thirty-seven years old, and if by green you mean inexperienced, he's not that either since he's already King of Scotland and has been for thirty years and more. Besides,' I added, trying to sound as if I was firmly concluding the conversation, 'he is the only male blood relation that the late Queen had.'

Elizabeth had said, so the tale went, *who but a prince should follow a prince?* Enigmatic right to the end, those close to her had interpreted her meaning correctly – or so we all supposed – and now James VI of Scotland was to become James I of England, and our new monarch. How he would make out, attempting to fill the huge boots of his charismatic, infuriating, powerful, feeble, contradictory, loved, hated predecessor, we waited, in some trepidation, to discover.

Sallie was still chattering on, and now we were far down the tunnel of memory and back in the golden days of Queen Elizabeth, when Gloriana had been worshipped as a red-haired goddess whose dainty feet danced the Volta while her shrewd, clever brain – she was, after all, her father's child – plotted ceaselessly, ruthlessly and, for the most part, efficiently.

I stopped listening.

Suddenly Sallie's eyes happened to light on the book lying open on my table. Belatedly I covered the illustration with a blank sheet of vellum, but Sallie's open mouth, and the fact that she stopped talking in mid-sentence, suggested the damage was done.

She gave me a very odd look, then, without another word, picked up her dusters, her broom and her beeswax and lavender polish, and swept out of the room. As her footsteps trotted away up the passage, I distinctly heard her loud, judge-mental sniff.

I couldn't blame her for the reaction. I was studying the female reproductive system and even if Sallie might not be very good at reading the words, she would have understood the diagrams. I sighed. I'd have to find a way of making it right with her, or else I would suffer a week of my least favourite foods served up, half cold like as not, for my supper.

Resolutely I dragged my thoughts away from King James, Sallie and the prospect of seven days of pallid and unappetizing meals featuring salt cod, and applied myself to my studies.

I have spent the greater part of my life at sea, latterly as a ship's surgeon. Land-bound these six years, I had hoped to set up as a sawbones, barber surgeon – whatever you prefer to call it – in Plymouth, the closest busy town to my home. The numerous existing sawbones and barber surgeons, however, had other ideas. Medicine being all that I knew, all that I could do or wanted to do, hurriedly I reviewed my options, and made the difficult decision to go to London and gain a qualification as a physician. I achieved my aim – just about – and now I was trying to establish my practice.

Which was why, that sunny morning in early April, I was studying the female body. My life on board the late Queen's ships had taught me a great deal, and I knew as much as any surgeon about broken limbs, amputation, sewing up deep wounds, preventing infection in the lashed back of a flogged sailor, how to recognize a variety of diseases and do what I could for the poor sufferer, how to treat the wide variety of injuries to which men on a sailing ship were prone. But my life at sea had left a vast gap in my knowledge and experience: I knew next to nothing about women. My recent years of training had naturally gone some way towards redressing the balance, although I knew I still had a long way to go. Since a doctor could scarcely call himself by the name if his expertise only extended to half the human race – not even that, for I also had yet to experience at first hand the mysteries of most of the wide range of childhood maladies – I was determined to study as hard as I must until I felt fully confident.

The bright day passed. I worked on, my concentration so intense that I was only vaguely aware of goings-on around me. The sweet smells of spring floated in through the open study window, briefly interrupted by a richer, riper and less fragrant aroma as Tock, the dim-witted lad who carries out the more straightforward of the outdoor tasks, carted another load of dung out to the vegetable patch. Dipping my quill into the ink horn yet again, I paused briefly: Tock needed someone brighter to order his days, and Samuel, most reliable of men and equipped with an inexhaustible fund of patience when it comes to Tock, had gone to market. Tock is willing and he has strong arms and broad shoulders, but he is totally lacking in initiative. Order him to take a load of dung from the midden to the vegetable garden and he'll do just that: take one load. Then, unless somebody notices, he'll sit beside the empty cart gazing into space for the remainder of the daylight. I put down my quill, about to go outside and gently but firmly encourage Tock to go back for another load, but Sallie beat me to it. As I returned to my books, I heard her shrill voice screeching at him to get back to work as that dung wasn't going to grow legs and walk to the vegetable patch by itself.

I have no idea what Tock's real name is, and very possibly he hasn't either. He must have been orphaned young, and he first came to my family's notice when he began hanging around my grandfather's forge, blue-tipped hands spread to the warmth, refusing to go away even when various objects were hurled at him along with the imprecations. He'd have been seven or eight then, filthy, lice-ridden, starving, clad in rags and with his bones standing out so that you could have traced his entire skeleton under the blotched and scabby skin. My grandmother took pity on the boy, and persuaded my grandfather to put him to work in the smithy. Tock would sit for hours, tapping a hammer against the huge old anvil and murmuring 'Tock'. It was the only word he spoke – and tapping his hammer purposelessly on the anvil the only activity he did – for almost two years. But my grandparents refused to give up, and Tock has been with one or other member of the family ever since.

I heard Sallie come bustling back into the house and cross the hall below me, muttering not quite under her breath about being far too busy to worry about stupid clot-heads who hadn't the wits to carry a task to its fulfilment, and how was she expected to get the spring cleaning done when she was interrupted every few minutes and nobody had done anything about her perfectly reasonable request for a new goose-wing duster, and *where* she was going to find the time to gather the tansy for the springtime vermifuge she *didn't* know . . .

I shut Sallie firmly out of my mind and went back to the seemingly endless list of reasons why a woman fails to conceive.

*   *   *

My peace was abruptly ruptured by a shriek from below. The hall of my house is wide and high-ceilinged, and has a fine echo. Sallie's scream was still resonating as I leapt up and ran from my study – which is on the upper floor – to see what had happened.

She was standing in the entry porch, leaning against one wall, her hands up to her pale face, fingers pressed against her mouth as if to prevent vomit flying out. Indeed, the stench was such that the precaution seemed sensible. I caught a brief glimpse of blood, gristle, severed vessels . . .

A big black shape came pounding up and I was almost knocked off my feet. With a curse, I caught hold of my dog by the scruff of his neck and shut him in the front parlour. Then, hurrying back to Sallie, I patted her shoulder, muttering some vague reassurance. 'I'll see to it,' I added, 'you go and sit in the kitchen and have a restorative drink with a big spoonful of honey.' She didn't move.

With an inward sigh, I stepped out on to the front step to have a closer look. Wide eyes following my every movement, Sallie removed her hand and muttered, 'It's too much, really it is! The other things I could deal with, but this! It is *too* much!'

I crouched down. Sallie stood close behind me. I could feel her hot, agitated breathing on my neck.

On my doorstep lay a mess of semi-putrefied flesh. Uterus, cervix, vagina and vulva, neatly and precisely cut from the body. Embryos in their enclosing membranes could be seen through a deep cut in the flesh. The raw, bloodied edges had attracted flies; soon their eggs would be hatching.

I poked at it briefly, then, pushing Sallie before me, retreated to the back of the house to fetch a spade on which to pick up the stinking thing and take it away for decent burial, and a mop and bucket to wash the step.

'They've gone too far this time,' Sallie said. She had been repeating variations on this theme since I had escorted her into her kitchen and sat her down with a small glass of brandy. (Alcohol, she had told me firmly, was better for shock than the honey in hot water which had been my suggested remedy.)

'Faeces, dead mice, the square of linen soaked in blood, the rotting calf's foot alive with maggots, even that headless rat, I could deal with. I'm not saying I *liked* the clearing up' – as if anyone would, I thought – 'but I managed it with not a word of complaint.' In fact there had been quite a lot of words of complaint, especially about the rat and the pile of dog shit, but I didn't think now was the moment to point that out. 'But this, this is something different altogether. That *thing*,' – she pointed a trembling finger in the direction of the front step – 'that's nothing short of criminal!' Her voice throbbed dramatically with outrage. 'Now they, whoever they are, have stooped to violating human bodies and, for all we know, possibly they killed the victim too, and it is too much.' She glared up at me. 'It must stop, Doctor, or else – or else—' I would have sworn she was about to say, *or else I leave*, but, happily for both of us, she must have thought better of it.

I knelt down before her on the cool flags of the floor and took hold of her hand. To my surprise – perhaps it was the shock – she didn't pull away. 'Sallie, those were not the reproductive organs of a woman,' I said gently.

Her eyes flew to mine. 'Not . . . But I saw the cunny and the womb!' Only her distress allowed the blunt words to escape her habitually prudish lips. 'I *saw* them!'

'Yes, you did,' I agreed, still in the same soft voice. 'But they came from a pig. A sow, to be exact, and one which had been about four weeks pregnant.' I squeezed Sallie's hand. 'I expect you saw the little embryos?' She nodded. 'Well, for one thing, no woman ever produces that many, and, for another, they were housed in a differently shaped womb from that of a human. In a sow, the uterus is formed from two structures that resemble horns, which act both as a conduit for the boar's sperm and also house the growing foetuses. The—'

Sallie extracted her hand and waved it feebly. 'Yes, thank you, Doctor, I understand.'

Embarrassed, I stopped. Bodies, both animal and human, have fascinated me since I was a child, and I frequently forget that others are not at ease discussing the more intimate aspects as freely and casually as I do.

I pulled up a chair and sat down beside her. 'I expect

somebody was slaughtering their sow and, seeing the' – Sallie gave me a sharp look as if daring me to repeat the coarse words she herself had used – 'seeing the insides,' I said instead, 'decided to extract them and play a trick. Or perhaps whoever had killed the pig had thrown the detritus away, and our joker came across the – er, the organs and decided he had a use for them. Not a very pleasant thing to do,' I added as Sallie, face full of indignation, opened her mouth to protest – 'but harmless.'

'It wasn't harmless for the pig,' Sallie pointed out with ruthless logic.

'No, indeed not,' I agreed. 'But she'd have been dead anyway, Sallie. Dead, and her flesh now on the way to some-one's smokehouse.'

Sallie gave a sniff and reached for her brandy, rather ostentatiously draining the little glass. Observing her, I decided she was recovering well enough and deemed it prudent not to offer more. Her complexion had resumed its normal ruddy glow and she was no longer shaking. Soon, I would creep away and return to my study, leaving her to get back to work.

Fortunately, the shock appeared to have made her overlook the obvious: pigs were slaughtered in the autumn, after they had been fattened up on the last of what nature provided and let loose, where possible, to forage in the woods and the forests on the acorns and the beech mast. April was no time to slaughter any pig, especially a pregnant sow.

Whoever had deposited those gruesome, pathetic remains at my door was no country joker, coming by chance across unwanted bits of carcass and deciding to provoke me with the bloody gore. The latest and most horrific of the offerings that had been left, it was possible that the pig uterus represented nothing more than an escalation of the unpleasantness.

Back in the peace of my study, I tried to convince myself of this. But Sallie's words kept echoing in my mind: *this is something different altogether.*

I had a nasty feeling she was right.

My name is Gabriel Taverner. I was born and raised in Devon, in a beautiful old house situated to the north of Plymouth on the banks of the Tavy River. My paternal grandmother Graice

Oldreive had a copy of the Geneva Bible: a book which she treated with such awed reverence that it might as well have been made of solid gold. If the family tree she carefully inscribed inside its front cover is to be believed, all the many bloodlines which united over the centuries to make me had their roots in the good, rich, red Devon soil.

I have no idea whether Grandmother Oldreive's tree is accurate. Since she was a woman of scrupulous honesty, I am inclined to think it probably is. Her account of my ancestry begins with her four times great-grandfather Gelbert Oldreive, under whose name is inscribed, in my grandmother's clear hand, *of Brocktavy Wood*, followed by the magical words *fought at Agincourt*.

Before you ask yourself why my father's mother should be called Oldreive and not Taverner, I should explain that, although she was married to my grandfather Taverner for forty-four years, Grandmother Oldreive chose always to be distinguished by the family name of her forefathers. Possibly she considered that the high-born Oldreives outranked the Taverners.

As far as I know, it didn't raise any eyebrows since everybody knew full well that she was married to him. A woman of such irreproachable, iron-clad morality and rock-hard faith would have let no man near her until she had the wedding ring on her finger.

Grandmother Oldreive was fiercely intelligent, with a rebellious spirit and a questing mind. As a young woman, she utterly refused to accept the opinion of the day, which held that woman was a weak, feeble vessel ruled by her womb and her emotions, given to fits of hysteria and likely to faint at the least provocation, undoubtedly incapable of taking any decision for herself more important than what to wear, even then with the proviso that sometimes a man's opinion might be needed. Graice Oldreive insisted that she knew her own mind when it came to the choice of a husband, firmly rejecting the suitors paraded before her by her anxious parents and repeating over and over again that the only man for her was Ralfe Taverner, an emphatically masculine, dark-haired, ripplingmuscled and very handsome young man who was the son of the village blacksmith and learning the craft himself.

Graice Oldreive got her own way. She usually did. She and Ralfe produced four children, the youngest of whom was my father, Benedict Taverner. He had set out to be a smith, like his father, grandfather and elder brother, but then he fell in love with Frances Gillard and everything changed.

My mother was the eldest of her siblings. She had a younger sister, Thomasina, and two little brothers, neither of whom survived infancy. Accordingly, it was she who inherited her wealthy father's farm, and her new husband – my father – gave up learning to be a smith and instead became a farmer.

I was their second child, born on 10 June 1572, three years after my brother Nathaniel. After my birth my mother produced two little girls, both of whom died at or soon after birth, and then she had a series of miscarriages and stillbirths. Finally, when I was nine years old, my sister Celia was born. All of us were born – and some of us died – in my mother's ancestral home, the lovely old farmhouse known as Fernycombe.

I knew from early on that I didn't want to be a farmer. Blacksmithing interested me greatly in one particular respect, and I used to spend hours with my grandfather Ralfe, at first only allowed to observe from a safe distance while he transmuted metal with fire and ground blades to a lethal sharpness on his granite: 'Finest sharpening stone in the whole of Devon, this is,' he used to say, winking at me as I stood wide-eyed watching the sparks fly.

Then, as I grew older and more responsible, Grandfather Ralfe began to teach me how to put an edge on a blade. In the course of his long life he had amassed a collection of axes, knives and sundry other ironmongery, and he was only too eager to explain how to get the best out of each and every tool. Because he was so skilled, all the barber surgeons and the sawbones of the area came to him, and from him I learned how to take a knife, a scalpel, an axe or any other of the horribly stained implements that emerged from the surgeons' leather bags, and restore it to clean, precise, ruthless efficiency.

'Blade's got to be keen, see,' one crusty and white-bearded old ship's surgeon told me. 'You got a sailor writhing in agony, arm or a leg mangled beyond saving, and you gotta lop that limb off him afore the infection spreads and kills him. Also, see, you've got your captain screaming at you because he needs his wounded men back at their posts soon as yesterday, and the quicker you amputate, quicker the sailor starts to recover. Unless he dies, of course,' he added, 'which is much the more likely outcome. Speed, though, speed is the sawbones' watchword, see, because when it's gotta be done, best do it quickly, and the sharper the blade, the swifter the cut.'

I couldn't claim it was that particular old salt who led me to take the path that I followed. It *was* him; but it was also all the others who came to my grandfather's forge, with their cruel instruments made marginally less agonizing by the provision of a sharp edge. They told their stories of shipboard life, and from the time of my first understanding I wanted to hear more. I realized, as I matured, that all I wanted was to go to sea, and when I was twelve years old I went to Plymouth and signed on aboard Queen Elizabeth's ship *Nightbird*. The Queen's navy was not an outfit to let a lad's talents go to waste, and quite soon my knowledge of blades was spotted and I was put to work with the ship's surgeon.

My years at sea were exciting, terrifying, arduous, exacting and at times magical, and I wouldn't have missed them for the world. I explored lonely islands in seas the colour of sapphires under suns that burned like Grandfather Ralfe's furnace. I saw men like giants, men no bigger than a child, men with yellow skins and men with black skins. I saw, in the words of the playwright, the ambitious ocean swell and rage and foam. I fought with Drake's fleet and we routed the Armada. In the company of the Sea Dogs I helped take Spanish ships laden with gold and I was awarded my share of the prizes. I observed, took notes, conducted experiments, tried again when I failed. I read everything I could get my hands on that other men in my particular field wrote, sometimes with fierce interest, sometimes, in the case of the most outlandish proposals, with scepticism and scathing laughter. I sat with village healers and wise women, with witch doctors; with tiny black men living so deep in the great river basins of the southern continents that often mine was the first white face they'd ever seen. I watched what they did: I took careful note of what worked and what didn't and, once I had managed to put my arrogance at what I first thought to be their naive stupidity firmly in my pocket, I learned to respect and envy their access to the deep pool of ancient knowledge passed down through countless generations. I began, slowly and painfully, to be of use to the men whose care and well-being lay in my hands.

This life came to an abrupt end in the Caribbean when a careless sailor supervising the loading of supplies let a rope slip, so that a very heavy box hit me on the side of the head, just behind my right ear. They thought I was dead. When I came round, after two days and on the voyage back to England, I wished I was: for the first time since the early days of finding my sea legs, I was seasick. And not just once or twice but continuously, relentlessly, violently, my head swimming with vertigo and my stomach heaving up yellow bile that burned as it came out. Had it not been for my captain, who forced me to eat and drink even though I tried feebly to fight him off, I would have died. 'Drink, you fucking idiot!' Captain Zeke yelled at me over and over again, forcing the cup to my lips. 'Drink all you can, even if it comes straight back up again, for it's your only hope!'

I thought it was a temporary state. I thought the effects of the blow to the head and the two days of unconsciousness would pass. After the nightmare of the journey back across the Atlantic – we hit bad weather and it took almost eight weeks, Captain Zeke's beloved *Falco* bucking and rearing under us like a terrified horse – I thought a few days ashore would see me right. They didn't. When I tried a brief trip back on the old *Falco*, Captain Zeke watching like a hawk even though he pretended not to, I was sick all over again, as I was the next ten times I tried.

Deeply anxious and profoundly depressed, I sank into self-pity and began to drink. Seriously and determinedly, possibly with the aim of drinking myself to death. Captain Zeke – his real name was Ezekiel Colt – sought me out. He drank with me, measure for measure, and wouldn't leave me alone. When finally I managed to confess my fears, he said, 'You have to ask yourself, Gabe, if this has happened for a reason.' He leaned closer, lowering his voice, his expression furtive, almost embarrassed. 'Way I see it, there you are, doing a good job at sea, hacking and patching, saving lives, thinking things through, happy enough, so why would it be any sort of a good idea to move you on?' He suppressed an alcoholic burp, not altogether successfully. It was a question, I reflected miserably, that I'd frequently asked myself, although not in those words: the voice that yelled and raged inside my own head tended to say things like *why the fuck did it have to happen to me?* 'It's my belief,' Captain Zeke went on sonorously, 'that you've been guided, young Gabe.' He nodded solemnly. 'I believe some power up there' – he jerked a thumb towards the filthy ceiling of the dockside dive we were drinking in – 'has noticed you and singled you out for something better than sewing up sailors.' Then he gave me a thunderous bollocking, told me to pull myself together and stop feeling so sorry for myself. 'You have a gift!' he yelled in the sort of voice that drowns out a storm at sea. 'Use it! You're a born healer, so get on with it!'

So I left the sea and the life I loved more than my own soul.

When I emerged from my misery, I wondered what to do next. I tried to set up as a surgeon in Plymouth, but it was already an overcrowded occupation and there was no room for a newcomer. So I took myself off to London, where I enrolled in the King's College of Physicians in order to learn how to be a doctor. Once qualified – and it would prove to be the hardest task I've ever faced – I would return to Devon and begin touting for business.

My years at sea had left me a reasonably wealthy man. I had saved most of what I earned, there being little to spend money on when on board a ship for most of each year. And I had earned very well: Queen Elizabeth had given her captains licence to take the ships of other nations – specifically those of the old enemy, Spain – and help themselves to the contents. Since most of these huge, cumbersome Spanish galleons were lumbering home from the New World laden with purloined silver and gold, it didn't occur to any of us that we were doing anything wrong. For one thing, the treasure didn't belong to the Spanish. They had stolen it – ruthlessly and with unbeliev- able cruelty – and now we in our turn were stealing it from them. And we didn't slaughter whole villages of men, women and children as we did so. Yes, we slaughtered Spanish sailors, but they killed plenty of us, too, and anyway we were at war, even if nobody actually said so.

I used a portion of my hoard to purchase a place to live. My parents had offered me a home with them at Fernycombe, but, sore, maudlin, bristling every time I saw the pity in my mother's eyes, I rejected their kindness. I thought about moving right away, but Devon is in my very blood and I found I couldn't. After a few desultory weeks during which I inspected perhaps a dozen possible dwellings and found something wrong with every one, I was riding back to Fernycombe one day when I came across Rosewyke.

It was an early evening in midsummer. I was cross, I had a band of pain radiating from the site of my injury right round my head, and more than anything I felt like shouting at someone. I was drawing close to the small village of Tavy St Luke, and perhaps six or seven miles from Fernycombe, when I noticed a track on my left that wound away towards the river. Sweaty and hot, my head bursting, I thought all at once how pleasant it would be to ride down to the water and let my tired horse drink his fill while I took off my boots and soaked my feet in the cool water.

The track took its time, turning this way and that, going always gently downwards. It was narrow and bordered with vegetation thick with summer flowers and foliage. I smelt honeysuckle, and my weary eyes were dazzled by the pale pink of the wild roses that grew on both sides of the green tunnel. Slowly a quiet contentment stole over me, and my headache eased. *There's no hurry*, I remember thinking. *I will reach the river bank eventually.*

The bosky tunnel came to an end and I found myself emerging on to a strip of pebbled shore. The river flowed past, silent, smooth, powerful. I dismounted and let go of the reins. My horse, perhaps affected by the same languor that was enchanting me, walked slowly on to the water, lowered his head and began to drink. I heeled off my boots and waded into the river.

I don't know how long I stood there: long enough for dusk to fall and the first bats to emerge, wheeling and diving around me but never once touching. Stars were starting to appear in the deep blue sky: idly I located the three bright summer stars, Altair, Deneb and Vega. In the west the sun had gone down below the horizon, although it was still close enough to produce a vivid wash of gold and orange.

I reached for my boots, took my horse's reins and we set off back up the path. I was in a dream, I think: outside myself. Halfway back to the road, I spotted another track, leading off to the left. *Why not follow it?* I thought.

This smaller track was steeper, its verdant walls pressing closer. It was as well I was not mounted, for there was scant headroom. After quite a climb, the path abruptly ended and I stepped out into the soft, golden light. The last of the sunset, over to my left, painted red streaks across the sky.

Before me stood a house. It was built of small reddish bricks and it was in the shape of the letter E, with protruding wings on the left and right and a shallower one in the middle, in which there was a porch. To the left was a tangle of fruit bushes, wildly overgrown: I made out redcurrant, white currant, gooseberry, raspberry. I moved over to them, picking a handful of deep red, succulently juicy raspberries and cramming them in my mouth. On the other side of the house, furthest away from the river, I could see a thick, unruly hedge, behind which I could just make out the shadowy shapes of outbuildings.

The house was deserted. That was suggested from the state of the grounds and confirmed when I approached the big old wooden door, which hung from only one of its original three hinges and succumbed readily to the pressure of my shoulder.

I stepped into the hall.

It was wide and high. On the far side, a staircase wound its way to the upper storey. To right and left, arched doorways opened into further rooms: small parlour, kitchen and servant's room to the right, two larger rooms – library and a second parlour, perhaps – to the left. I wandered on, mounting the stairs. They were old, stained, covered in dust and sundry animal and bird droppings, but they were sturdy and sound. Upstairs was a long gallery to the rear, off which led a large, central bed chamber and an arrangement of smaller ones.

Thoughtfully I descended again and stood, silent and still, in the hall. I stood there some time. I think my deep, inner mind knew the moment my eyes first lit on this house that it would be mine and in the course of that time – long, short, I don't really know – the message reached my consciousness.

I was very late returning to Fernycombe and my mother had been worried. I took her in my arms and gave her the sort of hug I hadn't seemed capable of since the accident had taken away my life as I'd known it. I felt her shock and surprise; she gave a soft little moan and I heard her whisper, 'Oh, Gabriel. Oh, my son.'

I went on holding her. 'I'm sorry,' I said softly. We both knew I was apologizing for a great deal more than just being late for dinner. 'It's going to be all right now.'

In the morning I set out early and began my enquiries. Less than a fortnight later, Rosewyke was mine.

It crept gently into its permanent place in my heart quite quickly, so that it was a wrench when I had to leave to go to London and begin my studies. But the pain of leaving a beloved place is rewarded by a corresponding joy upon returning, and so it was with me, when I quit my lodgings – in a tall, narrow house near St Paul's – for the last time and came home.

I keep a small staff: Sallie is my housekeeper, and she calls on a couple of sturdy girls from Tavy St Luke whenever she has need of extra hands. Samuel looks after the livestock and grounds: he is a solemn, reserved countryman, no doubt in the mould of his forefathers through countless generations, and never ventures two words if one will do. I have no idea if I like him or not; it is not relevant to our respective positions and, indeed, how can you determine your feelings for a man who holds his entire being within himself? Samuel is efficient and he works hard, and that suffices. Tock – poor, simple Tock – is a cross we all have to bear; the main burden falls upon Samuel's narrow shoulders, but I do not hear him complain.

To the rear of the house the yard is surrounded by fruit trees, and a more extensive orchard of apple, pear and medlar shelters the property from the northerly winds. To the right of the yard there is a hedge concealing the privies and the midden. Within the yard there are the dairy, the bake house, the well, Samuel and Tock's modest quarters, store rooms and a stable. We have chickens and a house cow. I have a sturdy black gelding called Hal and a large black dog with ginger patches over his eyes that I named Flynn, after an Irish sailor I once sailed with who had violently orange eyebrows and a fiery temper to match.

I took up my permanent place in this rural idyll some eighteen months or so back. Since then I'd been getting on all right; I had attracted several patients, not a few of whom are wealthy and able to treat their doctor well in the hope that by so doing he will always come as soon as he is summoned. Life had been tentatively and steadily improving, except for one thing: it had become uncomfortably obvious that the new physician in the area was poaching on someone else's patch and treading on their toes.

The succession of little gifts left on my doorstep began relatively innocuously, and had never been sufficient to cause my stalwart Sallie more than a tut or two and a bit of a moan. Today, however, the offering was more gruesome: whoever it was that resented my presence and my growing doctor's practice had stepped up their efforts quite dramatically.

I sat in my study that night, long after my servants had retired. I had finally given up the struggle to persevere with my studies, accepting that my powers of concentration had temporarily deserted me.

I also had to accept something else: I couldn't go on pretending this ongoing, insidious attack on me and my household was not happening. Much as I disliked the thought, I was going to have to do something to stop it.

Wearily I stood up, made a desultory attempt to put my books and papers into order and blew out my candle. By the gentle glow of the moonlight I took Flynn outside so that both

he and I could empty our bladders. I watched as he padded
off to his straw-stuffed sack in the corner by the kitchen hearth
and turned round a dozen times to make himself comfortable,
then I went to bed.

TWO

My resolution to begin a subtle investigation into who might be responsible for the series of little surprises left at my door had to be postponed. In the morning of the next day, Samuel summoned me with what for him passed for a state of urgent anxiety: the house cow and her calf had forced a way out through a weak place in the fence and he needed more intelligent help than Tock could provide to persuade the beasts to return to their pasture and then to effect a repair to the fence.

And then, early in the warm, still afternoon, I heard the sound of a horse's hooves in the open space in front of the house and a voice called out my name. I knew that voice, and as I hurried through the house to the door, all thoughts of pursuing my persecutor pushed to the back of my mind, I was already smiling.

My sister Celia gave me a regal wave. She was mounted on a rather fine grey mare, and she rode astride. *She's won that battle, then*, I thought.

At least two of the men in Celia's life – her husband and our father – considered it unseemly for women to ride in any fashion other than side saddle. But Celia liked to ride fast, and far, and, whenever she was allowed to, alone. As she had frequently pointed out, sitting on a side saddle with your feet on a little ledge was only efficient – only safe – if you rode at a walk and a groom or other attendant led your horse. You had no contact with your horse, and therefore no control.

She was wearing a sumptuous silk gown in a deep red shade, puffed out by layers of underskirts, with a fitted velvet jacket of the same colour. Her long fair hair was braided, covered with a light and almost transparent veil and wound up under a pretty little hat. I crossed the yard and held my hands out to her. She slid her feet out of the stirrups, swung her right leg over the pommel and flung herself into my arms. As my hands closed round her waist, firmly held in the embrace of stiff buckram, she winced, drawing in a sharp breath, and just for an instant she leaned against me. Or, at least, I thought she did . . . I guessed she'd turned an ankle as she landed.

But I must have been mistaken, for now she had extricated herself from my embrace and stood looking up at me, light blue-green eyes dancing and a bright smile on her lovely face.

'You have absolutely no idea if you're expecting me or not,' she declared. 'You're horrified in case you invited me and have forgotten all about it, or if I'm the first out of a whole band of guests who imagine they are coming to dine with you.'

Oh, Lord. Was she teasing, or was there really some function I was meant to be hosting that had slipped my mind?

'Er . . .' I began.

'And here you are looking like a field hand and in no fit state whatsoever to entertain guests,' she went on, eyeing me critically, 'dressed in your oldest hose, a stained shirt and that scarred leather jerkin that you cling to as if it were a second skin. You're in need of a haircut' – she raised her voice over the start of my objections – 'and you're *still* wearing your earring!' She shook her head as if despairing of me. 'Do you *want* all the wealthy sick people hereabouts to think you're nothing better than a pirate and take their custom to some conservative type who dresses as a doctor should?'

'I never was a pirate,' I protested. *And,* I might have added, *my earring will stay in my ear till I'm in my grave and beyond, if I have any say in the matter.*

I wear it in memory of a very important day in my young life. I was serving on the *Mandragora*, under Captain Pemberthy, and we were engaged by an attacking fleet of Spaniards in a brief but very fierce action. *Mandragora* was a lumbering old craft and we were at a distinct disadvantage, so Captain Pemberthy encouraged us by offering a series of rewards. I killed my first man that day, and the captain gave me a solid gold doubloon to celebrate the fact. He told me it had been minted in Nueva Granada from plundered treasure and I had it made into a heavy earring by a clever, nimble-fingered Jewish jeweller in Havana. It is the size of a broad wedding band and it took me a month to get used to its weight.

My sister took pity on me. 'No, I know you weren't.' Taking my hands in hers, she said with a laugh, 'And there's no need to look so horrified, Gabriel. You haven't forgotten about my visit because I didn't tell you I was coming and, since I'm planning to enjoy a long, uninterrupted chat with my favourite brother, I'm hoping as fervently as you are that you're not expecting anyone else.'

'I'm delighted to see you, you're always welcome under my roof for as long as you wish to stay, and I'm pretty sure Sallie would have told me days ago if I was expecting company,' I said. 'Come in. I'll summon Tock to see to your horse.' I reached up to the big, strangely shaped leather pack tied behind the saddle, already unbuckling the restraining straps.

'*Don't touch that!*'

I stepped away from the mare, mildly surprised at Celia's sharp tone.

'I'm not staying so I won't need my pack,' my sister went on with a sweet smile. 'I'm on my way back home to Ferrars – I've been home to Fernycombe to see the family.'

We went into the parlour and Sallie brought refreshments. Very adequate refreshments: Sallie grumbles frequently and repetitively that the house needs a mistress's touch, and in the absence of any sign that I might be about to marry or even courting, she gives a particularly fulsome welcome to my sister, my mother and any other female friend or relation who calls. Dainty lace-edged cloths were spread on two little tables, and Sallie laid out a variety of pretty sweetmeats in small glass dishes and a selection of tartlets, the cheesecake filling flavoured with rosewater or honey. To drink there was Sallie's own home-brewed ale, its somewhat mundane nature offset by being served in fine pewter goblets. When everything was arranged to her satisfaction, Sallie bobbed a curtsey to my sister – she never did that for me – and left us alone.

Celia caught my eye. 'Phew!' she exclaimed.

I grinned. 'She isn't usually like that. She wants to impress the lady visitor, but she doesn't bother when it's just me.'

'I imagine she knows you wouldn't notice,' my sister said crushingly.

I asked after my parents and my elder brother Nathaniel, and Celia brought me up to date regarding my family's doings. Mother and Father were well, Nathaniel – who in effect ran the farm now, although my father had not been persuaded of the fact – was, as usual, grumbling about the livestock, or the crops, or bullfinches attacking his apple blossom, or it might have been the pears. 'I confess I don't pay much attention,' she concluded. 'Nathaniel's always moaning about something, but everyone knows he wouldn't have any other life but that of a farmer.'

I nodded. Then I said, 'And how is Jeromy?'

Celia married Jeromy Palfrey two and a half years ago, while I was still in London learning to be a physician. She was nineteen, her bridegroom twenty-eight. I hadn't witnessed their courtship, but apparently Celia had been besotted by the handsome, flamboyant and wealthy man who had come to woo her. Although nobody had ever said so, I had the impression that my parents – my father, to be exact – had entertained one or two reservations about Jeromy. According to my brother Nathaniel, Celia had threatened all sorts of reprisals if she didn't get her own way, and she'd shouted at my father that she was *nineteen* and far too old to be unmarried and unwanted.

My father gave in. The September wedding was at Fernycombe, and I'm told the bride wore flowers in her hair and a gown of aquamarine silk specially chosen to match her light sea-coloured eyes. The bridegroom – elegant and sophisticated in deep crimson silk and rich purple velvet and, according to my brother Nathaniel, looking like some wily, flamboyant courtier – bore his new wife off to his beautiful, richly furnished old house near to the river, high on a rise above a slow bend where once a ferry used to operate. There they had been ever since, living, as far as anyone could tell, in lavish comfort and connubial delight.

'Jeromy is well, thank you,' Celia said. 'Busy, as always.' She flashed me a smile. 'A trip to Exeter, then, two or three weeks after he comes home, another to Dartmouth. His work necessitates so much travel, as you know, but he says that is less of a hardship now he has the new gelding.' She bent forward, brushing a tiny drop of liquid from her beautiful silk skirt, and I could no longer see her face. I could imagine her expression well enough, however. I'd often noticed how, when speaking or thinking about Jeromy, she seemed to go off into a trance. It was as if, just for a few moments, she absented herself and withdrew to the space within that she shared with him. That was, I surmised, what a great love did to you. It was quite moving, really.

Jeromy was a merchant. Perhaps it is more accurate to say he was in the employ of a merchant. Nicolaus Quinlie was known throughout the county and far beyond – even as far as London – for he imported silk. He was hugely wealthy and a shrewd and successful businessman with very good contacts and highly placed patrons; he was reputed to have supplied the late Queen Elizabeth, and wild tales were flying around to the effect that he was already in negotiation with the new King's staff regarding the provision of fabrics for the coronation. Quinlie silk, as Jeromy often said, was the best.

Nicolaus Quinlie's speciality was not the everyday stuff but the finest, most luxurious Venetian fabric known as *seta reale*, or true silk, that resulted when the cocoon of silk was placed in hot water and unwound intact, producing a long, strong, continuous thread. I knew quite a lot about silk, for my brother-in-law, having taken on too much of my father's brandy one Christmas, had lectured me for what felt like most of the afternoon.

I had a sudden, vivid image of that day. It had been the Christmas before last; the penultimate, as it turned out, of Elizabeth's long and glittering reign . . .

'Of course, Nicholas can afford to pick and choose when it comes to customers,' Jeromy said in my memory. He wore a scarlet doublet and a pure white silk shirt, its extravagant cuffs and neck ruffles spilling out and moving with a life of their own, beneath a strange sort of half-cloak which covered only one shoulder and was tied with heavy gold cords under the opposite arm. He sat on the settle by my father's hearth, one arm around my sister's delicate waist, the other clasping the heavy-based, stemmed glass, green-tinged, in which my father habitually served brandy. 'Not that any but the wealthiest and most important of men can afford our prices!' He laughed, turning to drop a tender kiss on Celia's cheek. She smiled, resting her head on his shoulder. Eyeing her gorgeous gown – she too was dressed in silk; violet silk, the sleeves cleverly shaped so that a little puff of fabric stood up on the shoulders – I reflected that a considerable yardage of the wares in which Jeromy traded had found its way home.

My father had overheard. Shooting Jeromy a frowning look, he said, 'Only the wealthiest and important would want it.' His eyes moved to the generous folds of Celia's violet gown, then, taking on a look of disdain, to Jeromy's silly little cloak. 'Hardly practical, that stuff, for anyone with a day's work to get through.'

'The best silk is actually surprisingly durable,' Jeromy said equably. He smiled up at his father-in-law.

'For *proper* work? For ploughing? For muck-spreading? For shoeing a restless horse? For sweating in the forge all day beside the furnace?' my father returned sharply.

Celia roused herself from her post-prandial semi-stupor. 'Oh, Father, when did you last spread muck?'

'I've done my share!' my father countered. 'And—'

But just then my mother came to stand beside him. Leaning close, she whispered something in his ear, and whatever it was seemed to have the desired effect. I watched, amused, as my father's better nature struggled to control his urge to have the last, crushing word. His better nature won: with a very obvious effort, he forced a smile and said, through painfully obviously gritted teeth, 'Well, the silk looks very fine on the pair of you.'

Then he shrugged off my mother's hand and went to fill up his glass.

He'd been right, I thought now, about Celia and her husband looking good in the expensive silk. My sister would look lovely in a sack, or so I've always thought. As for Jeromy, he was handsome, charismatic, charming and sophisticated; born, or so it would seem, for costly fabrics. Not above average height, he was slim – he gave the impression of a man who took good care of his elegant body – and moved like a dancer. He was almost androgynous in appearance and he presented himself

immaculately. He had silky, well-styled hair in a shade of pale
brown and light blue eyes, and was always most beautifully,
expensively, fragrantly and stylishly dressed in the height of
fashion. He was, in short, a wonderfully attractive, walking
advertisement for Nicolaus Quinlie's wares.

I sometimes wondered why else Nicolaus Quinlie needed
Jeromy, for, despite his superficial charms and his undoubted
good looks, he lacked wisdom and he wasn't very intelligent.
I'd concluded that it was for Jeromy's connections with the
world of the rich and influential: the men and women who
were Quinlie's potential customers. Jeromy came from old
money and a long, well-established family, and the doors of
the best houses in the county were always open to him.

Now, the afternoon sunshine flooding the parlour, I studied
my sister. She was pale, I observed, and her lovely eyes
were shadowed in grey. 'You must miss him when he's away,'
I said. 'Ferrars is an isolated house, and you have no one
but servants for company.' This, no doubt, was why she'd
been staying at Fernycombe with our parents.

'I don't mind!' she said quickly. She flashed a glance at
me, smiling. 'In truth, life is so hectic when Jeromy is home,
you have no idea. We entertain a great deal, you know, for
Ferrars has become a showplace for the stuff in which Nicolaus
and Jeromy deal, and he – Nicolaus – says that seeing it in
place, in the form of upholstery, curtains and, naturally,
garments, is the best way to display fine silk, so that everybody
who sees it is mad to purchase some for themselves. Ferrars
has silk *everywhere*, although I'm not complaining, I love the
very luxury of it.' She gave a little laugh. 'Why, when Jeromy
is travelling, I am in truth quite glad of the respite!' She
laughed again, as if to demonstrate the absurdity of the very
idea of being glad for any reason that her husband was absent.

I went on looking at her. 'Are you well?' I asked.

She gave a brief sound of exasperation. '*Yes*, Gabriel. Please
don't act like a doctor with me.'

'I *am* a doctor.'

'Only just,' she flashed back, 'and you're not my doctor.'
She drew a breath. 'Anyway, it annoys me. I've *told* you.'

'You look a little pale,' I persisted.

She sighed gustily. She's done that since we were children but, back then, this expression of her irritation with me was usually followed by a hard thump. 'What do you expect when I've just come from a few days at Fernycombe!' she exclaimed. 'You know how it is – they put such rich food on the table, and in such quantities, and Mother persists in telling you to eat up, and then she ladles even more on your plate, and it's so delicious that you find yourself gobbling it up. I have a touch of dyspepsia, if you must know.'

I studied her critically. Now she mentioned it, she looked a little plump; the inevitable aftermath of a succession of meals taken at my mother's table. I opened my mouth to say so, but managed just in time to hold back. I've never met a woman yet who receives the comment *you've got fatter* with any sort of pleasure.

It occurred to me that she might be with child. Married more than two years, and still no baby? It happened, of course it did, and, as Celia had just said, Jeromy was often absent from home. But no: I recalled the firm, hard feel of her stomacher as I'd helped her down from her horse. No woman, surely, would constrict her body so tightly if it housed a developing foetus. On the other hand, though, it mattered a great deal to Celia to look good, so perhaps that was just what she had done . . .

There was silence between us for a while. I raked around to think of some other comment that would allow Celia to speak of her husband – she never seemed to tire of the subject – but, since I did not know my brother-in-law all that well, and, to speak the truth, wasn't over-impressed by what I did know, I raked in vain. We chatted about the weather, about my work, about what, if any, effects the accession of a new monarch would have on our quiet life in Devon. Then Celia stood up, reached for her gloves and announced she ought to be on her way.

I accompanied her outside into the yard, calling Tock to fetch her mare. She thanked him prettily, then, looking round, asked, 'Where's Samuel? I ought to say goodbye to Samuel.'

I couldn't really see why, but nevertheless I sent Tock to find him, and watched as my sister bid him farewell. 'I always enjoy staying here at Rosewyke so much,' she added, 'and you all make me feel very welcome.'

Samuel looked a little puzzled. Tock just stood there with his mouth hanging open, bafflement written all over his face. Bafflement, however, was his usual expression. I was about to point out that she hadn't actually stayed, although she'd certainly done so in the past and was always welcome to do so again, but she brushed me aside and reached for the reins.

As I gave her a leg-up her wide silk skirts caught the breeze and I noticed her riding boots. They were of soft chestnut leather, well-worn but highly polished, obviously cared for. 'Those, I believe, are mine,' I observed.

She gave me her winning smile. 'I know. But admit, Gabriel, it's years and years since you wore them! You'd never get your great feet into them now, so I thought I might as well have them. Shame to see a good pair of boots go to waste, and there's plenty of wear in them.'

I wondered what else of mine she had helped herself to while staying at our parents' house. Suddenly I understood why she had been so anxious not to have me handle her odd-shaped pack: I might well have felt through the soft leather the remembered outline of other possessions I'd left in my mother's care at Fernycombe.

I looked up at Celia, shielding my eyes against the westering sun. I didn't begrudge her my boots; as she pointed out, they were no more use to me. I'd taken everything I wanted when I moved out and she was welcome to anything of mine that I'd left behind.

For some reason, I was filled with sudden, profound affection for my sister.

'Shall I ride with you?' I suggested. 'It'll be getting dark soon, and—'

'No. Thank you,' she added.

'Are you sure? I could drop in and say good evening to Jeromy, and perhaps—'

'He won't be there – I *told* you, he's gone to Exeter – and I'm going to have an early night,' she said firmly.

'But he'll be back soon?' Still I felt uneasy.

'Yes, dear Gabriel, probably tomorrow.' Some expression

flashed in her eyes briefly – excitement? passion? – and I wondered at the power of her love for him, that the very thought of his homecoming could elate her so.

She must see something in him that the rest of us had missed . . .

She reached down and kissed me. 'Goodbye, Gabriel. Please thank Sallie for the refreshments and tell her the tartlets were especially delicious.'

'I will,' I said absently. 'Celia, stay,' I added impulsively. 'You will be returning to an empty house, and—'

'It's not empty,' she replied with a touch of hauteur. 'You forget, we have plenty of servants.' She raised her chin, a proud light in her eyes, and I could hear the unspoken comment: *better ones than you see fit to engage, despite Sallie's tartlets*.

But perhaps I did my sister an injustice, for her face softened into a loving smile. 'Thank you all the same,' she said. 'I'll come and stay again soon, I promise.' Then she touched her heels to the mare's sides and the horse sprang into a brisk walk, then a lively trot.

I watched my sister ride away. Then I turned and went back inside the house.

The days gradually lengthened. Sallie finally finished her spring cleaning and we broached a new barrel of beer to celebrate. Tock reached the bottom of the midden, and the vegetable plot now steamed and reeked gently under the strong sun.

I acquired a new patient.

I was working in my study one morning towards the end of the month when I was summoned to the door. A farm labourer stood there, cap twisted in his hands, blood soaking the front of his jerkin and hose. 'Can you come quick, Doctor?'

I grabbed my bag, which stands ready in the hall. 'Yes. But if you're injured I should examine you here and now, for delay can—'

'Ain't me, it's Master,' the man said succinctly.

I followed him out of the house, matching his pace as he hurried off down the track. 'Is it far? I can fetch my horse but it'll take time.' Hal was out in the field, almost certainly right over on the far side where the trees on the river bank gave shade.

'No. This side of the village.'

We ran on.

He was right, it wasn't far. After less than a quarter of a mile the man turned right, off the main track and up a narrower path that wound up a slight rise. Before us, Tavy St Luke spread out in the hollow over to the right. I could make out the church spire, and some figures dotted on the village green. Our destination, though – and presumably my bleeding patient – was ahead.

We turned a final bend and came to a small hamlet of five or six dwellings and a collection of outbuildings. One house was larger than the rest and apparently a small farmhouse. The door was open and from inside I heard someone wailing; a high, continuous note like an animal in a trap.

Dear Lord.

My companion read my mind. 'That ain't Master, that's her. Young Mistress. Hysterical, like. Hates the sight of blood.'

She wasn't going to make much of a farmer's wife if she threw a fit at the sight of blood.

I went inside.

A young man lay on the floor before the fireplace. Two indoor servants hovered around him and a woman with flying brown hair – loose and wild, as if she had been tearing at it – crouched over his rigid body. He was cradling his left arm to his chest, gritting his teeth to hold back the cries. Just as well, as his wife was making enough noise for both of them. I took hold of her shoulder, gently but firmly. 'Come away now, Mistress,' I said. 'I'm the doctor. Let me see the injury.'

She wheeled round, her hands flying out as wildly as her hair. One of them caught me across the mouth. It hurt. 'He's going to lose his arm!' she shrieked, right in my face. 'Oh, *oh, OH*, what will become of us?'

I met the eyes of the elder female servant, indicating the shrieking woman with an inclination of the head. 'Get her away,' I muttered. 'Hot, sweet drink of some sort, and clean her up.' Like the man who had summoned me, the young wife was soaked in blood.

At last, I had my patient to myself.

He was conscious, but barely. His face was deathly pale, brown eyes huge. I said calmly, 'I am going to remove your clothes. I will be as swift as I can.'

I pulled away the tunic and tore away the undershirt. The wound opened up before me like a gaping red mouth. It was above the main upper-arm muscle, but through the mess of blood I could see the ends of severed tendons and vessels.

I thought at first I would have to remove the arm. Then, beginning to wash away the blood with the cloth and pail of hot water that the man who had fetched me had helpfully placed beside me, I saw that it might be salvageable.

I knew exactly what I had to do. It was a procedure I'd done countless times before in my years at sea, where the risks already inherent in a sailor's life – disease, poor nutrition, hazardous work – had been greatly increased by the development of the new weapons. You don't have to have much imagination to visualize what sort of harm two crews can bestow on each other when their ships fight at close quarters and they are trying to blast each other to bits with cannon and musket fire. The poor sods working the cannon were as vulnerable to harm from their own weapons, given a cannon's tendency to hurl itself backwards when fired and demolish any limb in its path.

This young farmer's arm hadn't been almost hacked off by some vicious fragment of red-hot metal produced by naval weaponry, but it didn't make any difference. The injury was almost identical, whatever had caused it, and I reckoned I could help him.

My patient opened his eyes and stared up at me. 'Will you have to cauterize it?' he whispered. I saw the deep fear and the panic begin to take hold.

'No,' I said gently. 'I am not in favour of the hot oil method.' I patted his uninjured arm reassuringly. Then, looking up at the younger of the female servants, I gave my orders.

I first came across this novel treatment for amputations and severe cuts in a publication called *The Method of Curing Wounds Caused by Arquebus and Firearms*, written by a French army doctor named Ambroise Paré. Horrified at both the agony suffered by, and the mortality rate of, patients treated by the cauterization method, he had taken advantage of a situation where the oil had run out to experiment with something else.

The new treatment worked. It was what I was going to use now.

The woman had brought me egg yolks, rose water and turpentine. The wound, washed as clean as I could make it, was ready. I gave my patient a mouthpiece to bite down on, then began to put the severed blood vessels back together. I applied clamps called *becs de corbin* – another Paré invention: translated it means crows' beaks – and slowly the flesh came together again. Then I applied a thick, cool poultice, wrapping the whole of the upper arm in a length of clean white linen.

My patient – who had passed out during the ligature phase – now opened his eyes. 'Have you finished?' he muttered through chewed and bloody lips. He had long ago spat out the mouthpiece.

'I have.' I smiled down at him. 'You still have your arm.'

He twisted his head, looking wide-eyed at the large bandage. 'It feels . . . it feels cool,' he said.

'Let's hope and pray it stays that way.' I got up, stretching my aching back. 'Send for me the instant you feel any heat in the wound.' I looked at the woman who had served as my nurse. She seemed sensible and capable. 'You too – keep asking him, keep feeling the flesh for heat.'

She nodded.

I wanted to leave, but I supposed I should reassure the panicky wife first. I straightened my shoulders and went through into the small, stone-flagged kitchen. She was sitting on a stool beside the table. The older servant was busy at a sink in the far corner of the room.

But she hadn't left the young wife to look after herself. A slender, fair-haired man dressed in black, about my own age or maybe a few years older, stood at her side. His position and his protective attitude were strongly suggestive of a guardian angel.

'I heard you say we should pray for young William,' he said in a pleasant, mellifluous voice. His 's' sounds were slightly sibilant. 'Katharine and I have already been doing so.' He stepped forward, holding out his hand. 'Jonathan Carew. I am the vicar of St Luke's, Tavy St Luke.'

I took his hand. 'Gabriel Taverner.'

He nodded. 'Yes, I know. So, the arm has stayed on?'

'Yes.' For now, I might have added, but I decided it was overly pessimistic.

'I'm impressed,' said Jonathan Carew. 'I saw what happened. He had been chopping wood, fell over his own feet and landed on the axe blade. I didn't think there would be any option but to amputate.'

The young woman – Katharine – gave a groan and laid her head down on her arms, folded on the table.

'I used to be a ship's surgeon,' I said.

Jonathan Carew nodded his understanding. 'How very fortunate for William, then, that you were the doctor summoned to his aid.' He glanced down at Katharine's bent head, the wild hair spread on the table top like a rich blanket. There was an expression of faint distaste in his lean face, as if he privately thought she ought to have done better. 'I do not believe there is any more I can do here,' he went on. 'May I ride home with you?'

'I'm at Rosewyke,' I said. 'It's the other direction from Tavy St Luke.'

'I know.' I wasn't sure if he meant he knew our roads lay in opposite directions, or that he was aware of where I lived. 'I would still like to ride with you.'

'I'm on foot.' I felt awkward; as if I were giving every reason to avoid him. 'I'm sorry,' I added impulsively, 'I must sound very grudging and rude. I would welcome your company, if you don't mind leading your horse.'

'Not in the least.' He caught the servant's eye, raised his eyebrows and jerked his head in the direction of the prostrate figure lying across the table. The woman nodded: whatever silent order he had given, she understood and would carry it out.

Jonathan Carew turned to me. For the first time, he smiled. I'd rarely seen a lightening of the expression so change a man's appearance.

As we left the farmhouse, I decided I was looking forward to his acquaintance.

'I would have called upon you when you took up permanent residence at Rosewyke,' Jonathan Carew said as we set off down the winding path, 'only it was my understanding that you worship elsewhere.'

'Yes,' I agreed. I felt vaguely apologetic. 'I was born in the area – the house is called Fernycombe, and is situated near the river to the north-east of here. When I left the navy I stayed there with my parents for some time and got back into the habit of attending church with them.'

'I quite see how someone in your position might feel the call to return to the church, and perhaps also the priest, he had known as a boy.' It was a generous remark. I wondered, however, quite what the vicar meant: did he know about the accident that had brought my naval career to such an abrupt and unwelcome end?

'I suppose I could—' I began.

But Jonathan Carew held up a well-shaped, well-cared-for hand. 'If you were about to say you could change your habits to attend St Luke's instead, please let me forestall you.' He gave me that smile again. 'Whilst the recusancy laws oblige us all to attend Protestant services, as yet the legislation does not specify where that worship must take place.' His tone was neutral; carefully so, I thought. He glanced at me out of intelligent eyes; they were a particular shade of deep, blue-tinged green. 'Pray where you will, Doctor Taverner.'

We walked on, momentarily in silence. He had been considerate in giving me every reason not to attend his church but, nevertheless, I had the feeling I was going to. There was something about the man that intrigued me.

'Have you been the incumbent at St Luke's for long?' I asked presently. 'Forgive me for not knowing.'

'Of course,' he replied. 'No, not long.'

I waited for him to continue but he didn't. Wondering if I was being discourteous in pursuing my questioning, I said, 'And before that?'

He paused for so long that I wondered if he wasn't going

to answer, or perhaps had simply not heard. But then he said, 'Before St Luke's I was briefly in London, and prior to that, at Cambridge.'

I wasn't sure I'd heard: had he said *at* Cambridge or *in* Cambridge? The two had rather different meanings. 'At college?' I asked.

'Trinity Hall. Canon law.' All at once he had become as unforthcoming as the farm hand who earlier had fetched me. Then the strange green eyes met mine in an intense look. 'I was to have entered the law, but various influences and pressures steered my steps instead into the priesthood. The study of canon law, I suppose, began as a compromise.'

He fell silent. I was quite glad of it, for my thoughts were racing. This man was clearly an intellectual – his very demeanour shouted that, never mind the years of study at Trinity Hall – and he had been destined, surely, for some position a great deal more elevated than vicar of a tiny village parish in the wilds of Devon.

Had something happened? Had something gone amiss with the potentially illustrious career? Had some figure of power high up in the church hierarchy taken grave offence, and shoved Jonathan Carew right out of the light and into the out-of-the-way darkness of Tavy St Luke's?

I hoped, as I shot a surreptitious glance at my companion, that I was going to find out.

THREE

Jonathan Carew and I parted company at the end of the track leading up to Rosewyke. I offered refreshments, for I was enjoying the challenge of his company, but he politely declined. Then he mounted his horse – a bay cob gelding with a broad blaze – and set off back the way we had just come.

I walked on thoughtfully to my door. So thoughtfully, indeed, that I missed what lay across the step until I had all but stepped on it.

I stopped dead.

'It is the bright day that brings forth the adder,' I said aloud.

It wasn't an adder but a blindworm, well over a foot long, fat and glossy, which barred the way. I knew the creature was harmless but seeing it there was unexpected, to say the least. Thinking I'd better remove it before Sallie found it, I bent down to pick it up, planning to deposit it back in the grass.

My fingers closed on its upper body, just behind the head. As I straightened up, holding the worm's smooth shape firmly, the head remained on the ground.

With a soft curse, I crouched down for a closer look.

The head had been bitten cleanly off, probably by a buzzard or a fox. And it had not happened there on my doorstep: someone must have found the blindworm, very recently dead, and, shooing away whatever predator had killed it, picked it up to reassemble it where I could not fail to find it.

It wasn't a pretty sight, and I had to admit that I'd been mildly shocked to find the creature had been decapitated. Nevertheless, this latest offering wasn't in the same class as a sow's internal reproductive organs.

What was happening? Had my nemesis regretted being so harsh and crude with the pig's uterus, and now decided to revert to milder items?

I didn't know.

But I resolved there and then to increase my efforts to find out.

I strode through the hall, calling out to Sallie that I was home, and ran upstairs to my study. Pulling towards me a sheet of vellum and reaching for my quill and ink, I set out to list all the medical practitioners – doctors and barber surgeons – in the immediate vicinity. I knew the names of quite a few of the latter, having been made aware of their presence (quite forcefully in some instances) on trying to become one of their number when I first came home. Whilst I could well believe that some of them – the raven-bearded shaven-headed giant with the ruddy cheeks and swaggering walk who haunted the Plymouth quays looking for patients off the ships, for instance – were more than capable of taking action against me, I thought it more likely that this would have taken the form of a direct confrontation, probably involving his fist and my nose. Besides, I wasn't in competition with him, or with any of his fellow practitioners. They weren't doctors.

Still, I listed all the names I could recall. Then I went down to the kitchen to find Sallie and asked her if she could add any more.

She looked at me, a calculating expression in her narrowed eyes. 'Why do you want to know?'

I hesitated. Should I explain? Might it alarm her, to know that I thought some disgruntled medical man resented my presence and was trying to scare me off? But then the doorstep offerings were well known to her – especially since it had been she who had cleared most of them up – so, in truth, she had a right to know.

So I told her.

She pulled out a stool from under the table and sank down on it. 'I've been thinking the same thing,' she said calmly. 'It's logical, really. Who else would want rid of you except someone who feared you'd steal their business?'

She had it in essence, so I didn't bother to point out the difference between a surgeon and a physician. 'Well?' I demanded.

She thought for a while. She repeated some of the names I already had, most of them in Plymouth, and added a couple I didn't, from up towards Tavistock. Then, frowning, she fell silent.

'Oh, and there's Black Carlotta,' she added after a moment.

'Black Carlotta?'

Sallie waved a vague hand. 'She's a witch.' The wandering hand flew to cover her mouth and her eyes widened in horror. *'No she's not!'* she squeaked. 'Of course she isn't, how could I possibly have said that!' She had gone quite pale.

I reached out and patted her shoulder. 'It's all right,' I said softly. 'There's only you and me here, and I won't tell anyone what you said.'

She nodded her thanks, clearly unable to speak.

I understood her distress. You never refer to anyone as a witch, even your worst enemy. The consequences for them, should someone overhear and decide it's up to them to do something about it, are just too dreadful.

'So, Black Carlotta,' I prompted, after waiting what I thought was long enough for Sallie to collect herself. 'A wise woman? A herbalist?'

Sallie nodded. 'She treats people for nothing, or, maybe, for what they can give her,' she said. 'She's good. Kind, too. She's calm and reassuring with women in childbirth, and she's trained other women in her ways.' She met my glance. 'Please don't do anything that might bring danger to her door,' she whispered.

'Of course I won't.'

I meant what I said. Country people needed women like this Black Carlotta. Besides, I very much doubted that it was she who had been menacing me.

On the other hand – an idea struck me – she might have a good idea who was behind the offerings . . .

'Do you think Black Carlotta would see me?' I asked Sallie.

'Why? What do you want with her?' she demanded.

I met her suspicious eyes. 'I'd like to ask for her help.'

Black Carlotta did not appear to have a regular home, or not, at least, one that anyone knew about. When I had finally persuaded Sallie to give me a hint, at least, of where I might find the woman, she would do no more than give a few locations where Carlotta had been known to treat people. Accordingly, later that day I saddled Hal, whistled for Flynn and set off to find the places. Most of them were in out-of-the-way spots – one right up on the edge of the moor – and appeared to be deserted.

Tired and frustrated, I turned for home.

My road took me past Tavy St Luke's, and I decided to check up on my young farmer before I went back to Rosewyke. I tethered Hal, left Flynn panting in the shade, tapped on the door and went inside.

William lay on a pallet, propped up by cushions. Katharine crouched beside him, her hair now restored to order under a prim headdress and her expression a great deal more tranquil than it had been this morning. That tranquillity, however, shattered as she saw who her visitor was.

'Oh! Oh, *no!*' she whispered.

Then, before I could even try to reassure her, she had leapt to her feet and scurried out to the kitchen, from where I could hear the sounds of water splashing, as if someone was thoroughly washing their hands.

William, hampered by his injury from a similar escape, looked up at me ruefully.

'This is rather embarrassing, doctor,' he began. He gazed imploringly at me, clearly inviting a response. I held my peace. 'Er – it was her idea.' He jerked his head towards the door through which his wife had just fled. 'She's worried about the money, you see. We'll pay you for this morning, of course we will, and please don't think I'm not grateful because I am, more than I can say, but, you see, she's a lot cheaper and if there's going to be the need of continuing care, she – Katharine – says we can afford her more readily than we can you.'

I thought I understood.

I knelt down beside him. 'Of course I need to be paid,' I said quietly, 'since, just like everyone else, I have to eat, and food doesn't come free. But you won't find me unreasonable.' It was not my policy to set one level of charges and demand them from every man, whatever his means.

William blushed, and turned his face away. 'My apologies, doctor.'

'Accepted.' I stood up again. 'Now I think, don't you, that it's time I met my successor.'

Without waiting for his response, I strode out to the kitchen.

Katharine was standing in the middle of the room. At my abrupt entry, she took two rapid steps away from me, half-concealing herself behind the figure in the far corner, who was facing away and wiping dripping hands on a grubby length of linen.

'Am I addressing Black Carlotta?' I asked.

The figure turned to face me.

She was old. Quite amazingly old, with strands of pure white hair escaping from under the elaborate and voluminous black headdress and a face browned by countless suns to the colour of a chestnut, deeply lined and wrinkled. The eyes, however, were ageless: pale grey, the whites as clear as a child's.

'You are,' she replied. 'What can I do for you?'

I hesitated. *Stop treating my patient* was the obvious answer, but I had just spent half a day looking for the woman and it didn't seem sensible to antagonize her. 'I'd like your advice.'

She raised one eyebrow. Then, neatly folding the piece of linen and depositing it by the sink, she said, 'Let's walk together, then.'

She nodded to Katharine, took one last look at William and then led the way out of the house. As she strode on, I untied Hal's reins, clicked my fingers to Flynn and, leading my horse, hurried after her. Then, for the second time in a day, I found myself talking to a new acquaintance as I headed for home.

'You mustn't mind Katharine,' said Black Carlotta. 'She lost a baby only a few months after she and William were wed, and, try as they might, she can't conceive another.' She flashed me a swift glance. 'Desperate, she is. It's turned her mind, although, way I see it, she'll come back to herself once there's a baby in the cradle.'

I nodded thoughtfully. 'Any reason why she slipped the foetus?'

'None that I could detect.' Another glance, and this time there was a glint of something – amusement? – in the ancient eyes. 'You'd maybe know better, being a navy surgeon.' *And having all that experience of gravid women*, hung unspoken on the air.

'I've trained in London as a physician since leaving the sea,' I said mildly, determined not to rise to her dangling bait, 'although I'd be the first to admit that when it comes to women in general and not just the pregnant ones, I have a great deal still to learn.'

She nodded once, a quick, curt action. As if in confirmation, she muttered, 'It's the beginning of wisdom when you recognize all that you don't know.' I felt I'd passed some test. 'Liked what you did for young William,' she added. 'Not seen such a treatment before. Works, does it?'

'More often than not.'

She nodded again, and I had the distinct impression that an egg, turpentine and rose-water poultice had just been added to the long list of remedies she stored in her old head. Not that I minded: it hadn't been my idea in the first place, and I was fully in favour of the spread of new, improved methods.

'What advice did you want from me?' she asked presently.

I told her. It didn't even occur to me to hedge, or prevaricate, or disguise my question with subterfuges. She was an honest woman; that was as plain as the spring sunlight on the young green leaves. In my experience, honesty demands honesty.

She walked on for quite a long way. Then she said, 'Know Josiah Thorn, from over by Buckland?'

'No. Should I?'

'Maybe you should. He's a doctor – a *physician*' – she gently mocked my use of the word – 'only I don't reckon he ever had any fancy London training.' She pronounced it *Lunnon*.

My senses sprang to the alert. 'You think it could be him?'

She held up her hand, swiftly, firmly. 'I don't think any such thing. I'm just asking, do you know him?'

'As I said, no.'

She stopped, turning to look me full in the face. 'Maybe you should. Now, I'll bid you good day.'

And she was gone. Gathering up the long, flowing black skirts, hitching the battered old pack higher on her back, she

leapt nimbly over the ditch running beside the track and scamp-
ered off up the shallow bank like a startled deer. I tried to
follow her progress and see which way she went but she was
too fast for me, dipping behind a small spinney of young oaks
and vanishing from sight.

I mounted Hal and rode on home.

The days went by. April went out in a week of violent weather:
heavy rain, at times turning to sleet, and a south-westerly gale
blowing hard from the western approaches, driving swathes
of sea waters up the Tamar and washing high tides even as
far as the Tavy. I did not forget about searching for Josiah
Thorn and, indeed, before the storms hit I ventured up to
Buckland and on towards Tavistock, enquiring here and there
for him, but met with no success.

I was deeply engaged in a challenging project. While in
London learning my craft as a physician I had been one of a
small group of like-minded men who, well away from the
lecture halls and the ever-alert eyes and ears of our teachers,
sought answers to the great medical questions of the day by
a method which, we very well knew, would have been frowned
upon by our superiors; probably to the extent of having us
dismissed from the college and banned from any chance of
further tuition. We called ourselves, with an inflated sense
of our own importance, the Symposium. What we were doing
amounted to medical heresy, for we were attempting to peer
through the obscuring veil that stated unequivocally that
Disease A must be treated by Remedy B and asking ourselves,
what if we were to try something different? Something – and
the word was surely anathema to the medical world – *new*?

Once our studies were complete and we went our separate
ways, I lost touch with many of the group. If they now felt
ashamed of their rebellious attitude and opted to blend in
smoothly with established medical practice, I didn't blame
them. Life was tough, and money hard to come by. No matter
what your profession, as a general rule it was easier – safer
– to toe the line and not upset people. But two of the men felt
as I did; like me, they were unwed, and without dependents;
this gave us the freedom, I believe, to take a few risks. The

three of us were in regular contact, sharing our thoughts, laboriously copying out the documents on which we worked and dispatching them for comment and contributions. We tried to meet when we could; one man lived in Bristol, the other had stayed in London, so such meetings were not as frequent as we could wish. We were planning to get together later in the year, in London, and already I was excited at the prospect. I loved my life in Devon, but sometimes the longing for like minds with which to converse – and to argue – became overwhelming.

My field of interest then was the matter of the humoral theory: that long-held, unquestionable doctrine that we all contained the four humours – black and yellow bile, phlegm and blood – and that each related to a particular type of person – melancholic, choleric, philosophical and sanguine respectively, although that is gross over-simplification. Any sort of sickness was regarded as an imbalance between the humours, probably caused by a blockage, and the usual remedy was to relieve this blockage. Bowels would be purged by the administration of a strong laxative; the stomach emptied by an emetic; poisons encouraged out of the body by powerful diaphoretics to encourage sweating; too much hot blood flowing through the body by bleeding. Everyone believed this was the right – the only – way. They had been believing it since the golden days of Classical Greece.

In my early days as a ship's surgeon I had been as unquestioningly accepting as everyone else. But, as the years passed and my carefully kept record of patients, their treatments, my observations on the effectiveness of these treatments and the eventual outcome steadily grew to the size of a small library, I began to wonder. In my work at sea I dealt with more than my share of terrible wounds, as I have said. Now the accepted treatment for a man who had lost a vast amount of blood and was weak, pale, sweating and feverish was to bleed him and keep on bleeding him.

The trouble was that it didn't work.

Sometimes nothing else worked, either. But, just occasionally, it did. I once tended a sailor who had lost half his hand, neatly removed by a huge splinter of wood torn out of the side of the ship by an incoming cannon ball. We put in to a port on the mouth of the River Plate and, as the crew tucked into ruby-red beef fresh from the cow and fresh, dark green vegetables, I persuaded my patient to eat up. At first he refused, for he was nauseous, in pain, hectic with fever. But I wouldn't give up, and in the end – probably because he knew it was the only way I'd leave him alone and allow him to sleep – he gave in. Appetite comes with eating, as the old saying goes, and soon my patient was stuffing himself as fast as food could be brought.

He recovered.

I had been wondering ever since *why* he recovered. If, as I believed, some substance in the good, fresh food had somehow *fed* his blood, then the truth was that bleeding such a patient was the very last thing a doctor ought to do. And that was alarming, to say the least. But I would not abandon my research and, when my colleagues in London evolved the idea of each of us pursuing secret studies of our own, my choice of topic seemed to have been made for me.

So now, spurred on by the prospect of meeting my fellow Symposium members later in the year, I had once more thrown myself into the theory of the four humours.

It would have been good to have shut myself up in my study and lost myself in my work while the present foul weather persisted, but it was not to be. A bout of fever broke out on the Plymouth waterside and one of the less hostile sawbones down there sent word to me, on the off chance that the malady was one with which I was familiar from my travels. It shared many of the characteristics of tropical fevers: very high temperature, blinding headache, rash, haemorrhage, stools running like brown water, eruptions in the skin; and for a while both the sawbones and I feared we were witnessing the start of a serious outbreak. Fortunately for Plymouth, however, whatever fever it was turned out to be largely non-fatal (only two deaths out of seven victims, both of them weary old sailors who had probably been nearing the end of their days in any case) and not very contagious.

May announced herself with brilliant blue skies and long, sunny days. My household and I went up to Tavy St Luke's

for the May Day celebration, a rambunctious affair which
lasted from noon until well after dark and, to judge by various
abruptly suppressed cries and furtive rustlings in the undergrowth clearly audible as I finally staggered home, would lead
to a crop of babies around February.

It was a lush time. The grass in the pastures grew so quickly
that you felt you could see it, and the milk produced by the
house cow turned rich, abundant and creamy. Sallie was busy
in the dairy, utilizing the bounty to make butter and cheese,
sporadically helped by a large, round-faced and singularly
plain girl called Dorcas, who lived in Tavy St Luke and was
some distant relative of Sallie's. It occurred to me to wonder
who, out of Tock and Dorcas, was the brighter. There wasn't
a lot in it.

I was standing at my study window one morning soon after
the start of the month, stretching my back after too long bent
over a treatise on the treatment of bronchial disease in infants,
when I spotted a man on a horse turn into the track and ride
up to the house. Sallie was scrubbing out the dairy, and I
knew she hated to be seen by 'company' when she was sweaty,
flushed and dishevelled. Samuel and Tock were somewhere
outside, but it wasn't their job to answer the door. So I went
down myself.

I opened my heavy oak door just as the man, dismounted,
raised a hand to knock.

He was a large man; taller than average, broad in the
shoulder, long-limbed and with the sort of girth that suggested
he enjoyed his food. He was dressed in a well-worn doublet
over hose and good boots, over which he wore an ankle-length,
sleeveless garment in fine black wool. This, together with the
vaguely scholarly black cap he had just swept off, gave him
an air of authority. His hair – short, thick and standing up as
if he'd been running his hands through it – was sandy fair,
his beard had highlights of ginger, and his eyes were a clear,
brilliant blue with not a hint of green or grey.

He was about to speak when I forestalled him.

'Julius Caesar,' I said with a grin.

A slight frown briefly replaced his smile of greeting but

then it cleared. 'The man from Devon!' he exclaimed. 'Well met, my friend!'

During my time of study in London I had taken to visiting the Globe theatre. I enjoyed the writing of William Shakespeare in particular, and, from the way he described the country and his clear love of it, I'd taken him for a Devon man till someone said he came from Stratford. One of the last plays I'd seen was *Julius Caesar*. In an early scene – just after the soothsayer issued his warning about the ides of March – the emperor declaimed, 'Let me have men about me that are fat!', adding some remark to the effect that he found lean and hungry-looking men dangerous. A big fellow standing right at the front of the groundlings had said – a little too loudly – 'I'm your man, Caesar!', making the crowd around him burst into laughter and momentarily stopping the action. The actor playing Caesar hadn't looked at all pleased, but everyone else had loved it. Afterwards, enjoying a few mugs of beer in a Southwark tavern, I'd come across the man, and the discovery that we were both Devonians had been all the prompting we needed to have several more mugs of beer. We'd ended the evening singing dirty songs and holding each other up as we staggered along the river, trying to find a craft to ferry us back to the north bank and our lodgings.

I hadn't expected to meet my friend again.

But now he stood on my doorstep.

I threw the door wide open. 'How good it is to see you again! Come in – there's beer in the kitchen, cool and refreshing, and—'

The big man interrupted me. 'Thank you, but we must save our celebrations for another time, for I am here in my official capacity.' His expression grew serious, and it seemed to me that he drew himself up straighter, as if coming to attention. 'My name is Theophilus Davey, I am the coroner, and I have come in search of Doctor Gabriel Taverner.' The humour flashed again, just for an instant. 'Unless you are an intruder, I would say that you are he?'

Our previous acquaintance hadn't been the sort to encourage a man to vouchsafe his name and station: as far as appellations had been necessary, we had called each other

'Julius' and 'Devon'. Silly maybe, but it was that sort of evening.

'Yes,' I said now. 'I'm Gabriel Taverner. What can I do for you?'

'I'd like you to come and look at a body,' said Theophilus Davey. 'It's at Old Ferry Quay, down on the Tavy and not far from here. I understand that you are the nearest doctor, which is why I have sought you out.'

I knew the place. Old Ferry Quay was on the river to the south-west of Rosewyke, a few miles north of where the Tavy meets the Tamar and their conjoined waters tumble on down to Plymouth. Once it was busy with small craft going to and fro across the river, but now it had fallen into disuse. There was a wooden landing stage, a huddle of tumbledown sheds and deserted dwellings and a tavern that barely warranted the name, being the sort of filthy, sordid place that is the last resort of those far gone in addiction. There they sell gut-rot spirits whose only advantage is their cheapness. I very much doubted that this was the first time one of its desperate clientele had been a victim of the ultimate violence. Unless, of course, the poor soul had finally succumbed to the poison of the cheap alcohol, or fallen in the water and drowned.

'I suppose you want me to come with you to confirm death?' I asked the coroner.

He grinned briefly, that quick flash of humour once again lighting up his sombre expression. 'Not much doubt he's dead, doctor. The rats have eaten quite a lot of his face.'

'Ah. I see.' I thought quickly: what would I need? Were the right tools and equipment in my bag? Yes. 'Wait here – I'll fetch my horse.'

Shortly afterwards, we set off. Reaching the end of the track, I went to turn left, towards the road that runs roughly south-west, following the course of the river but on higher ground – but Theophilus Davey stopped me. 'There's a short cut we can take, avoiding quite a long detour,' he said. 'I just came up that way. It's a bit of a scramble in places, but it'll save time.'

I was going to say that surely a few minutes here or there didn't make much difference since the man was dead, but stopped myself. Perhaps coroners were duty-bound to act always as swiftly as they could. 'Lead on,' I said instead.

We took a narrow track leading down to a lower level, our mounts treading carefully as we followed its bends and curves, hugging the contours of the river bank. In a couple of places the path descended right down to the water, only to climb up again, sometimes very steeply, until once again we rode close to the summit of the bank. Then, after perhaps three or four miles, we made a final descent, emerging on to the foreshore where once a fully operational wooden quay had stood. Four men stood together by the water, heads together, quietly muttering. They greeted the coroner with a touch of the forelock. On the ground behind them lay a stretcher on which there were two folded blankets. The men, undoubtedly, were there to take the body away.

We had arrived.

The place was much as I remembered it, although now even more dilapidated. The end dwellings on the ancient row of habitations had collapsed into a pile of wood and plaster. The quay had lost some more of its structure. The tavern seemed to be hiding away in shame, huddled into the bank, its walls stained with mould and green streaks where rain water had leaked from broken gutters, and it gave the appearance of having been deliberately camouflaged. It seemed to be deserted: at some time, someone had broken the door down and now it sagged against the entrance to the dark little passage beyond. A couple of planks had been nailed across the doorway, although quite why anyone would have taken the trouble thus to deter intruders, I couldn't have said.

The coroner dismounted, and so did I. We tethered our horses – he rode a thick-set, heavy-bodied bay mare with sturdy legs and a luxuriant black tail – and I followed as he led the way towards the row of tumbledown houses.

The corpse was propped up against the ruins of the last hovel still standing. It leaned on the rear wall, facing into the river bank so close behind, and was not visible until we had walked round the end of the row. 'How was it found?' I

murmured to Theophilus Davey. 'He's well-hidden here.'
Having just noticed the sex of the corpse, I quickly changed
from the impersonal *it* to *he*. 'Did someone smell him?'

'They did,' the coroner agreed shortly. 'A fisherman came
down to the foreshore to gut and clean his catch and had an
unpleasant surprise.'

I took a step closer to the body. As Theophilus Davey had
warned me, the cheeks had been eaten clean away. The eyes
were mere bony sockets, and the flesh of the lips had been
nibbled. The damage had been done by rats, certainly, but
also by maggots. Blowflies are attracted to the blood when a
corpse has an open wound: here, they had colonized the body
and laid eggs in the nostrils, eyes and mouth, and these
eggs had hatched and instantly begun eating. The rats had
joined the banquet, eating the exposed flesh of face and hands
and one bare foot.

I had initially judged that the body was that of a man by
the prominent brow ridges and the generally heavier build;
he had not been a large man, but, even so, few women were
as broad in the shoulder. Now that I looked more closely, I
saw that the rags of clothing – animals and insects had been
busy there, too – looked like a man's. Hose, one tall leather
riding boot – heaven knew where the other one was: in the
river, likely as not – and what could once have been a doublet
or tunic, now so matted with bird and animal faeces, mud
and blood that it was impossible to tell the colour.

There was no mystery as to how the man had died.

The body was in a sitting position, the head with its thatch
of dirty, tangled hair reaching to just below the narrow sill of
a mean little window. There was a blade of some sort thrust
deep into the belly, and the corpse's hands – what was left of
them – were clasped around the weapon's broken-off shaft.

I straightened up and stood back, gazing down at the body.
Theophilus Davey, standing a little apart as if giving me the
space in which to inspect and think, kept his silence. I realized
I was glad of his company: he had a presence, there was no
denying it, and all at once, in that dark, sinister place and
facing a body dead by violence, I knew I was very glad not
to be alone.

'Dead, as you already knew,' I said eventually, 'and it happened perhaps as much as a week ago.' Blowfly eggs hatch in a day, but even a big swarm of maggots takes time to strip the flesh off a body. 'The cause of death is obvious.' I pointed to the blade, driven in at an upward angle, under the ribs and towards the heart. 'And, from the way the hands are clutching the weapon, it looks very much like suicide.'

FOUR

Theophilus Davey and I stood watching as the four men picked up the corpse and placed it, still in its hunched position, on its side on the stretcher. One of them turned away to vomit. I didn't blame him. As the body had separated from the ground there was an unpleasant squelching sound. Where the buttocks had rested there was a seething pit of maggots. It was a relief to all six of us when the hideous sight of what had been a man was finally covered with the blankets.

The coroner turned to me. 'I shall take the corpse back to my house, which, for your information because sooner or later you'll need to know, is also the place from which I carry out my official duties. It's at Withybere, which as you undoubtedly know is this side of Plymouth, and I'm between the village and Warleigh Point.' He hesitated, and I thought his expression was asking something of me.

'Do you wish me to come with you?'

He shook his head. 'No need for the present.' He smiled briefly. 'I just wanted to make sure you knew where to find me if I have cause to summon you.'

'I'll be happy to come,' I said truthfully. 'Any time.'

I realized that I liked Theophilus Davey.

He held out his hand. 'Farewell for now, Doctor Taverner.'

I took his hand. 'Goodbye, Coroner Davey. My name's Gabriel,' I added.

'Not Devon?' His grin widened. 'And my friends call me Theo.'

Then he mounted his big bay mare and rode off up the winding path to the top of the bank.

I would have gone with him willingly if he'd asked, for I was sure there was more that the body could tell me about how the man had met his death. I was, however, relieved that he hadn't asked, for I had a different and quite pressing errand.

From the place where the path leading up the river bank met the main track, it was no great distance to Ferrars. I didn't really fear for my sister's safety, because I reckoned Jeromy would be home now, and, as well as him, there were the servants. Nevertheless, the fact remained that a dead body had been found in the vicinity, and, even though it looked very much like death by suicide, I knew I wouldn't be reassured until I'd paid my sister and her husband a visit.

Although I tried not to, I couldn't help thinking that there were an awful lot of men I'd prefer to have by my side when danger threatened than Jeromy Palfrey. Virtually every adult male I'd ever met, in fact.

The other pressing reason for a swift visit to my sister's house was that my hands stank of rotting meat.

As I rode along the track above the river, I distracted my mind from the stench by thinking about a subject I had studied during my years at sea: namely, the effect of dirt on open wounds. I didn't understand the reasons, but my lengthy experiments had led me to believe that dirt made cut flesh more liable to the redness, swelling, accumulation of pus and, finally, dark red streaks and bad smell that always lead to amputation. On the last of the Queen's ships on which I sailed, where my seniority was sufficient for me to have the captain's ear, I imposed a particularly ruthless routine of swabbing decks, washing both blankets and clothing and regular sea bathing that had the grumbling crew in a perpetual state of resentment. They weren't so recalcitrant, however, after we'd been into action. We had a high number of wounded, and the marked difference in healing between those who'd gone along with my dictates and those who hadn't was enough to convince the dirty ones – those among them who survived their infections – that perhaps the ship's surgeon was right. The captain thereafter made it a rule that sailors going into action had to don a clean shirt.

I rode into the stable yard behind the flamboyantly impressive house where my brother-in-law had installed his wife. I can't say I liked Ferrars: it was built of brash red brick, with turrets on the three towers that rose up at either end and in the middle of the long central wing, and whoever had built it hadn't missed one opportunity to elaborate and over-decorate. The plain lines, as a consequence, were smudged and complicated by too much fussiness, and the whole building seemed to be shouting, *Look at me! I was built by a very rich man with money to burn!*

A groom busy in the stables came out to greet me, and showed me where to wash. He didn't ask what on earth I'd been doing and I didn't tell him. He led Hal away to give him a drink and a rub-down, and I went on into the house.

I found my sister peacefully sewing by an open window, the sun making highlights in her smooth fair hair. She smiled in greeting, depositing her sewing to get up and give me a hug.

'Where's Jeromy?' I asked as we sat down. 'I thought you said when I last saw you that he'd be at home by now?'

'He *was* home,' Celia said. 'I said – as you've clearly forgotten – that he was *about* to come home but then was going away again.'

'Ah.' She was quite right; I had forgotten.

'He's gone to Dartmouth to receive a consignment of *very* valuable silk,' my sister said importantly. 'Apparently it's something really special: a new line fresh from Venice, with some wonderfully rich colours and patterns, that Nicolaus Quinlie hopes will prove irresistible. Because it's so costly, however, he wants to try it out by acquiring only a limited amount to start with.'

'So that the outlay is not too great in the case of its not selling.' I nodded. 'Well, he's a businessman. He doesn't like to lose money.'

Celia ignored that. I'd noticed that she didn't like to hear criticism of her husband's employer. 'We shall have some of it here,' she said. I glanced at her, for I didn't detect the usual note of excited anticipation normally present in her voice when she spoke of improvements to her house. Getting up and pacing around – there were new hangings at the windows since my last visit, and Celia wore yet another gown I hadn't seen before – it occurred to me that perhaps the joy of even the most sumptuous silk in the world paled when you were the person who had to turn it into furnishings and garments.

'When do you expect him home?' I asked after a moment, stopping my pacing.

She paused in her stitching, raising her head and looking out of the window. 'I'm not sure.' She turned to me. 'Often he's unable to say how long he'll be absent.' She gave me a teasing smile. 'Ships take their own good time reaching port, Gabriel, as you're surely the first to appreciate.'

I sat down beside her on the window seat – heavy pale-green silk, the colour of the finest jade, so smooth to the touch that you could feel the sheen with your fingertips – and studied her surreptitiously. She had lost the slight plumpness she'd gained after her visit to our parents; a natural concomitant to having ceased to pack away our mother's gargantuan meals, no doubt. She still looked pale, and also a little strained, I thought.

'Your servants take good care of you?' I asked.

'Yes, indeed they do.' She carried on sewing.

'And . . .' This was delicate: I wanted to make quite sure she was well protected, with some strong, reliable male servant to check all the doors and windows were securely fastened at night, but without alarming her by telling her I'd just found a dead body down by the quay not half a mile from her house. 'And you feel safe here alone?'

She dropped her sewing in her lap with what I thought was unnecessary violence. 'Gabriel, I've just said the servants look after me! That includes a twilight ritual of bolting doors and barring windows that at times makes me feel like a prisoner in my own home! Yes, I feel perfectly safe. Thank you,' she added. I could hear the effort it took.

I stood up and resumed my pacing. She endured it for a short time, then said, 'What *is* the matter with you? You're like a – a – a cat with piles. Can't you sit still for five minutes?'

I grinned. I had never studied a cat with haemorrhoids, and I doubted Celia had either, although it seemed likely such a creature would be reluctant to sit down. It was reassuring to hear my sister resort to the crude language of our childhood, however; sometimes it seemed that her marriage to Jeromy had taken away for ever the little girl with the smutty face and the dirty knees who used to tuck her skirts out of the way so that she could pretend she was a boy and join in her brothers' games. It still rankles with Nathaniel, I know quite well, that Celia was a better shot with a catapult than either of us. If I'm honest, it still rankles with me, too.

'I should be on my way,' I said. 'I only came to make sure you—' I caught sight of her expression and stopped. 'Er, because I was passing and I haven't seen you for a few weeks,' I said instead. 'I won't disturb you further.' I went to kiss her goodbye.

She grabbed hold of my hand and, just for a moment, held on hard. 'You don't disturb me,' she said very quietly. 'I'm always pleased to see you.' Then she raised her head, gave me a bright smile and let me go.

Still I couldn't leave well alone. 'If Jeromy should be delayed and you feel like company, come and stay at Rosewyke,' I said. I felt anxious about her although I couldn't have said why. Trying to disguise any sign of it that might have crept into my voice, I added, 'Since Sallie seems to be on a crusade to prove to you what a fine cook she is, I get far better food when you're staying so you'd be doing me a service.'

She smiled. 'Thank you, Gabriel,' she said. 'If I get lonely, I'll come.'

It was, I felt, the best I was going to get. I took my leave and set off for home.

Theophilus Davey said to himself, *If I don't find a name for that blasted, stinking, disgusting, rotting thing in the next few days, I'm going to bury it anyway and sod the consequences.*

It was almost a week later, and he had had no luck in identifying the dead body in the cellar of the building that served both as coroner's office and his own private residence. The house was large, and built on three storeys above the extensive stone cellar that was the oldest part of the building. The ground floor and cellar formed Theo's official headquarters and the top two floors were his private residence, which he shared with his wife and three young children, each of whom had been taught from their days of earliest understanding that visiting their father while he was at work was as strictly forbidden as one of the Ten Commandments, transgression being highly likely to be punished as harshly and certainly more swiftly. Both Theo and his comely but strong-minded wife knew only too well that the matters regularly discussed in Theo's office were not for childish ears.

His children, wide-eyed in fascinated horror, were already asking about the funny smell. As for his wife . . .

Deliberately he put from his mind the outraged tirade she had inflicted upon him that very morning. She was quite right to complain, and he didn't blame her for it, but couldn't she see he was doing his best?

Despite extensive and persistent enquiries in the vicinity of Old Ferry Quay, nobody had anything useful to say. A couple of locals had verified that nobody used the tavern any more. The innkeeper had died, apparently, and no one had felt up to the depressing task of replacing him. Some of those known to have formerly frequented the place said they didn't know of anybody who had gone missing, all their small band of companions in adversity being accounted for. Or so they said.

Theo swore under his breath. Nobody was admitting to knowing anything about the dead man, and the fisherman who reported the corpse had himself gone missing. Too much time was being wasted, and Theo could think of a dozen tasks on which his small band of men would be far more profitably employed.

His stomach rumbled. It must be time for the midday meal. He was about to set off for the tavern where he usually ate when two of his men came through the door, one holding a piece of rag up to his bloody nose.

'Trouble?' Theo asked.

The other man shrugged. 'Not really. Bit of a to-do down by the quay. We were asking around for news of your missing fisherman and we heard a fight break out. Tomas here' – he nudged his bleeding companion – 'decided it was his job to sort it out, and caught a flying fist for his trouble.'

'I hink by dose is broken,' Tomas mumbled.

Theo suppressed a grin. 'What was the fight about, Matthew?'

'Some of the lads who work for that rich bugger with the huge warehouse down at the end of the west quay were arguing. Something about one of the others not turning up when he was meant to, and someone else getting a bollocking because he was supposed to do the job instead of the missing man and didn't. Sounded to me as if there was a lot of blame-shifting going on.' Matthew nodded sagely.

One of the others not turning up when he was meant to . . .

Forgetting his growling stomach and the fact that it was time for dinner, Theo picked up his cap and strode out of the house.

The coroner was a familiar figure on the Plymouth quays. It was his duty to investigate unnatural, sudden and suspicious death, and it was quite surprising how often unexplained corpses turned up along the waterfront. As Theo made his way along to the large warehouse at the end of the quay, he responded to the respectful greetings of half a dozen men.

The disturbance that Matthew and Tomas had encountered seemed to have settled down, although a group of young men were still standing muttering crossly to one another. On seeing Theo approach, as one they melted away. Putting on a turn of speed unexpected in such a big man, Theo sprinted after the slowest of the young men and caught him by the collar.

'I hear you lads were fighting,' he said conversationally. 'Perhaps you might tell me what it was about. One of your number gone missing?'

The young man tried to reply but all that came out was a strangled gasp. Theo loosened his grip a little.

'Yes, sir, yes, that's it,' the young man agreed with pathetic eagerness. 'He was sent to meet a ship over in Dartmouth, and when he didn't come back we didn't think anything of it at first, guessing the ship had been delayed by bad weather or something. But then the master, he finds out the ship reached harbour almost a week ago, and he was furious, beside himself, because he'd a very valuable cargo on that ship and he was afraid someone had helped themselves.'

'He suspected his own employee?' Theo demanded. Rich merchants were avaricious bastards, he reflected. What sort of revenge would such a one exact on an employee who had tried to cheat him?

The youth shook his head. 'Couldn't say, sir. He wouldn't reveal his thoughts to the likes of us.'

The words had the ring of truth. Theo let go of the lad's collar and he scuttled off after his companions.

Theo walked on the short distance to the big warehouse at the end of the quay.

After being made to wait for quite some while, he was ushered into the man's presence. Now Theo decided to take his time, too, strolling across the room as if he had all the hours of the day at his disposal.

He studied Nicolaus Quinlie. He was a tall, cadaverous man, aged perhaps in his late forties or early fifties. His colourless face – the pallor exaggerated by the unrelieved black of his sumptuous silk robes – was utterly devoid of humour. *He looks like a snake*, Theo thought. *He has the ruthless air of a man who would enjoy inflicting pain. Who would kill without compunction.*

Quinlie had been standing by the window, leaning against the wall and gazing down upon the busy scene below. Disconcerted perhaps by Theo's silence, he turned to face him.

'I hear one of your employees is missing,' Theo said. 'Possibly with a valuable consignment.'

'You hear right,' Quinlie replied with a scowl, 'although my goods are safe, thank God.' The scowl deepened, as if the very thought of goods going missing caused him actual pain. 'Young fool was meant to be in Dartmouth, to meet a ship and bring back my cargo from Venice. He never turned up, and the captain sent word asking what I wanted him to do with my silk. I had to send one of my other men, at considerable annoyance to both the fellow and me.' Abruptly his expression changed, to one of suspicion. 'What has this to do with you?'

'You know who I am?' Theo asked.

Quintile nodded. 'I do. You wouldn't have been admitted into my presence if I didn't.' His supercilious sneer suggested he had better things to do with his valuable time than answer a humble coroner's enquiries.

Theo decided not to reply to Quinlie's question. Instead he said, 'What is the name of your missing man?'

Quinlie leaned towards him, narrow face pinched as he drew in his lips. 'Why do you want to know? I've got my silk, and it's just as well I have. I have valued customers impatient for my goods, you know. It doesn't do to keep them waiting.'

'The man's name, please,' Theo repeated patiently.

Quinlie threw up his hands in disgust. 'Oh, very well. If it's what it takes to get rid of you and permit me to get on with my work, I'll tell you.' He glared at Theo. 'He's called Jeromy Palfrey.'

FIVE

Back at his wide oak desk, Theo sharpened his quill to a fresh, sharp point with the little silver penknife that had belonged to his grandfather. Then, inserting it between two back molars, he poked around till he had extracted the piece of gristle left over from his midday meal of chops. Then he sat quite still for some moments, thinking.

Then he got up, went outside to where one of his officers sat bent over a ledger and said, 'Is Jarman about?'

'Out the back,' the man said without looking up.

Theo sighed. 'Go and fetch him, please.'

Some time, he reflected, he was going to have to have a word with his underlings about discipline and respect . . .

He went back to his room and sat down. Presently the door opened again and a slimmish man of medium height came in, quietly closing the door after him. He had removed his soft cap, and now stood quite still before Theo, holding it in his hands.

Everything about Jarman Hodge was medium, Theo thought, studying the man. Mid-brown hair, nondescript eyes of a sort of hazel shade, clean-shaven, plainly dressed, and, in his manner, modest and quiet. Only a few people – Theo among them – knew that behind that unassuming, almost self-effacing exterior there was a razor-sharp brain fed by very sharp ears and ever-observant eyes.

'I have a job for you, Hodge,' Theo said without preamble. 'I have a body and the name of a missing man, and I wish to ascertain if they are a match.'

Jarman Hodge nodded. 'The corpse down there.' He jerked his head towards the steps leading down to the cellar and its unsavoury contents. 'Making his presence felt, poor bugger.'

'Indeed he is,' Theo agreed. 'The man who's missing is a merchant's agent. He was meant to collect a consignment from a ship making port at Dartmouth but he never turned up.'

Hodge thought for a while. 'The body was found down on the river.'

'Yes. Old Ferry Quay.'

'Nasty spot to end your days,' Hodge remarked. 'Especially by your own hand.'

'Quite.'

Hodge thought some more. 'Could be your missing merchant's man has snuggled up with a Dartmouth doxy and a couple of bottles of brandy.'

'Could be,' Theo agreed.

'Was that the consignment? Good French brandy?'

'No. It was silk. Very exquisite and very expensive silk.'

Hodge nodded. 'Want me to go to Dartmouth?'

'Yes.'

He nodded again. 'Since the cargo was silk I imagine the merchant is Nicolaus Quinlie.'

'You imagine right,' Theo agreed.

Hodge shook his head, a brief, succinct movement. 'Not a man I would care to anger. I hope that, if I do locate his missing man, the fellow has a good excuse for failing to do as he was ordered.'

'Me too.'

Hodge turned to go. 'The man's name?'

'Jeromy Palfrey.'

Hodge repeated it to himself a couple of times then, with a nod to Theo, left as quietly as he'd arrived.

Theo had little hope that Jarman Hodge would return with a shame-faced, hungover Jeromy Palfrey, quaking in his boots for fear of what his employer was going to do to punish him for his dereliction of duty. Theo had a bad feeling that he already knew the name attached to the corpse slowly rotting in the cellar.

He used the couple of days of Hodge's absence to pursue enquiries of his own. He had a good memory for faces, and had no trouble in locating the bunch of young men who had been brawling at the end of the quay, close to Nicolaus Quinlie's warehouse. They were in one of the meaner taverns, and at least two of them were already the worse for drink, even though it wasn't long after sunset.

Theo bought himself a tankard of beer and went to join them.

'I'm debating with myself,' he said pleasantly as he shoved a thin youth along the bench so that he could sit down, 'whether I want to be here less than you want me here, or the other way round. Best thing for you lads' – he smiled round at them in a friendly way – 'is to tell me what I want to know as quickly as you can, and, if I'm satisfied, I'll leave you alone.' He paused, considering. 'If I'm totally satisfied, I might even reward you with the price of another round of beers.' He jingled the coin purse tucked out of sight under his robe.

The young men looked worriedly at each other. Then one who looked older than the rest spoke up. 'We work for Nicolaus Quinlie,' he said self-importantly. 'He doesn't like us talking to outsiders about his business affairs.'

'That's all right, then,' Theo said, 'since I'm not here to ask about his business. I want to hear everything you can tell me concerning Jeromy Palfrey.'

Again, the youths glanced swiftly at each other. Then the one who had spoken up before said, 'He's gone missing.'

'I know.' *Dear Lord, give me strength.* 'That's why I'm asking about him.'

Now the young men put their heads together, muttering softly. Theo waited. They were going to help him: he was sure of it.

Eventually the whispering ceased. The spokesman turned to Theo and said, 'Jeromy's a showy sod. He has a very pretty wife, a costly house, he rides a fine horse and he's always dressed in the height of fashion. Obviously, he earns a great deal more than the rest of us, and he never hesitates to remind us of the fact. He lords it over us, giving us orders and getting us to do the dirty work he clearly feels is beneath him.' He stopped. He was red in the face, slightly breathless. He looked vaguely astonished, as if his venom had taken him by surprise.

'I see,' Theo said. 'Your comments suggest that he was given the more responsible tasks, perhaps?' The young men nodded. 'So it was normal for him to have been the one sent to Dartmouth to receive the consignment of very valuable silk?'

'How do you know—' one of the others began. A sharp dig in the ribs from the lad sitting next to him silenced him.

'Yes, it's the kind of job he mostly does,' the spokesman said. 'That, and tout for new business. He's the sort of man that the rich welcome into their fine houses, being acquainted with or related to most of them. Or that's what he tells us, anyway.'

Theo nodded. He thought for a short while. He had learned more about Jeromy Palfrey than he had expected. He now had more questions, but ones to which he didn't think these young men could provide answers.

One thing, however, he reckoned they might help with.

'You said he likes fine clothes,' he reminded the spokesman. 'Describe what style of dress he usually wears. What, for example, was he wearing when you last saw him?'

'Er . . .' said the spokesman doubtfully.

One of the others spoke up; a younger man, scarcely more than a boy, with red hair and a pimply chin.

'He had a new doublet,' he said eagerly. 'Beautiful reddish-brown, heavy silk, and the sleeves were slashed so that the finer silk beneath showed through, and that was a sort of golden yellow shade. He had fine wool hose, and they were brown too, and good leather boots of a chestnut colour, very shiny. He always kept them shiny. He favoured high boots, said they were more comfortable for riding.'

Theo grinned at him. 'Thanks, that's very helpful.' He noticed some of the other lads nudging one another and murmuring, sending mocking glances towards the redhead. 'It's rare,' Theo went on, raising his voice a little, 'to find a young man so observant. You'll go far, lad.'

The jeering and the murmuring stopped.

Theo drained his tankard and got up. He took a few coins out of his purse, putting them on the table between the main spokesman and the youthful redhead. 'You two have earned this,' he said to them. 'You can share it with the others or not, as you choose.' Then he raised a hand to tip his cap and left them.

*   *   *

Theo took a deep breath, opened the low door giving on to the cellar steps and descended into the dank, stinking darkness. He reached the last step and set out across the stone-flagged floor, holding the lantern high to light his way. Then, trying to quash the disgust – the thing curled up on its left side on the trestle table had once been a man – he folded back the covering sheet and leaned forward over the corpse.

He began with the boots. *Boot*, he amended: one was missing. The remaining one was a high, close-fitting riding boot. Theo had brought some bits of rag with him, and now he used one to rub away at the carapace of mud. A large, crusty chunk fell off. Theo spat on the cloth and rubbed again, revealing a patch of fine, soft leather, chestnut-coloured.

Boots: correct, he said to himself.

Next he studied the bent legs, clad in supple, costly wool. He scrunched up a fistful of the fabric, removing some of the dirt. Brown. *Hose: correct.*

But many men, after all, wore brown hose and chestnut leather boots.

Now he held his lantern low over the doublet, with its slashed sleeves. How on earth was he to determine the original colours of the filthy silk? A thought struck him. Gingerly he raised the corpse's right arm. A shower of maggots tumbled out of some hidden cavity in the chest. Theo swallowed the vomit that rose up at the back of his throat and forced himself to concentrate.

He peered under the arm, right up into the armpit; a sweaty armpit, he noticed, automatically leaning away from the stench. Surely that was unexpected in someone so fastidious about his clothing? Perhaps he'd been running hard, or doing some other sort of energetic activity, just before he killed himself? But then, as Theo had hoped, he noticed there was a cleaner, brighter patch of silk. It was reddish-brown.

Suddenly eager, Theo grabbed at the lacings that fastened the front of the doublet and wrenched open a small gap. The lighter silk of the lining could now be seen. It was a deep, golden yellow.

'Doublet: correct,' he said aloud.

Theo put his lantern down on the trestle beside the corpse's head. Then, carefully, respectfully, he tidied the doublet, drew up the laces and re-fastened them. Finally he pulled the sheet right up over the head and the ruined face.

'Jeromy Palfrey,' he murmured. 'Jarman Hodge has been sent on a pointless mission, for I have found you.' He paused, thinking. 'Now, I have to decide why you took your own life.' He gazed down at the hump of the shoulder, swelling the covering sheet. 'And I believe I may have the very beginnings of an answer.'

I was on my way home from a long walk. I was on foot, Flynn panting by my side, my falcon Morgana on my wrist. I'd been flying her up on the fringes of the moor. She had brought down a pigeon and I was going to gut it and hang it until it was ripe for eating.

Flynn knew we had a visitor before I did. He stopped, ginger eyebrows twitching, long black nose scenting up the track towards the house, and gave one deep bark. I put my hand down and patted his back. 'Thank you, Flynn. It'd be good if you could put a name to whoever comes calling, but maybe that is asking too much.'

He gave a slightly disgruntled 'Hnff,' and trotted on up the track.

I recognized the big bay with the long, swishing tail before I made out the man. I hurried on and, as soon as we were in hailing distance, called out a greeting.

'Come inside and have a drink,' I added. It was, I realized, good to see him. 'And a bite to eat, if you have the time. I've—'

'No. Thank you,' Theophilus Davey interrupted. Then I saw that he wasn't returning my smile of welcome. 'I'm sorry, but I have bad news.'

He had found out the name of Jeromy Palfrey's wife, and that name had led him to me. Rather than rush straight to Celia and break the news that her husband wasn't coming home and she must prepare herself for widowhood and a life without him, instead he had first sought me out. 'It's not that I'm being cowardly,' he assured me, his earnest expression suggesting he really wanted me to trust that he spoke the truth. 'Believe me, I've broken such news many times. Far too many times,' he muttered bitterly. 'But as soon as I knew she was your sister, I decided it'd be better – better for her, I mean – to have the devastating tidings broken when you were there too. To help her afterwards, in case she faints, or falls into a crying fit,' he added, as if I might have missed the point.

'She won't do either of those things,' I said softly.

At least, I didn't think she would.

Theo was moving towards the door. I stayed where I was. Turning, he looked at me questioningly. 'Are you coming?' he asked.

I realized what he meant. 'I'll go alone,' I said.

His bright blue eyes fixed me with a penetrating stare. Then he asked simply, 'Why?'

Because my sister is a proud woman, I could have said, *and if she does break down when I tell her, she would rather a stranger was not there to witness it.*

I wasn't sure I could tell a coroner such a thing.

'I think she would prefer it that way,' I said instead.

But he understood anyway. He nodded. 'She won't want me to see her weep.' His voice was full of sympathy.

'I will go immediately,' I said. We walked together out on to the wide space in front of the house, to where his horse stood tethered. I watched him mount up and prepare to ride away. 'Is there anything more I should know?'

He considered. 'I believe I told you everything relevant just now,' he said. 'He was meant to go to meet a ship in Dartmouth, and his absence was discovered when a message was sent by the ship's captain to the merchant – Nicolaus Quinlie – demanding what he was meant to do with the consignment of silk, Jeromy Palfrey not having turned up to collect it. The rest you know, since you came with me to view the body.'

'Why did he do it?' I asked. 'Is Nicolaus Quinlie such a terrifying employer, for a man to kill himself rather than face his wrath?'

Theo shook his head. 'I do not believe that to be the case. I'm thinking he was dead before even he set out for Dartmouth,

and that fear of punishment for not obeying Quinlie's orders
was not relevant.'

'Then why—'

Theo held up his hand. 'I have a theory, but' – he smiled
apologetically – 'if you will forgive me, I need to ascertain
rather more information before I share it.'

I looked up at him. It came as a slight surprise – after all,
our acquaintance had been brief, and I didn't know him well
– to discover that I trusted him.

I returned his smile. 'I look forward to that,' I said.

I watched him ride away, then went for my horse.

I set out straight away. I'd have taken Flynn with me – I
really didn't want to be alone – but he'd run for miles already
today and so I left him by the hearth in the kitchen, looking
up at Sallie with longing eyes as she went about preparing
food for the evening meal. I reckoned his hope was in vain.
I'd just told Sallie the dreadful news, and she wasn't in any
mood to respond to the pleading of a dog. I'd suggested
gently not to bother about supper since it wasn't likely
anybody would have much of an appetite, but she appeared
to have ignored me.

I wished the journey from Rosewyke to Ferrars was longer. I
needed time, both to decide how to tell Celia and to think
about how to deal with her reaction. Would she want to stay
in her home? Probably not, at least for the first few awful
days as she tried to absorb the fact that she'd lost him. Would
she prefer to go to our parents, or come and stay with me?

I tried to keep my mind on such practical matters but without
success. I kept picturing her beautiful, smiling face, lit up with
a variety of vivid emotions, all of them inspired by Jeromy:
excitement, laughter . . . sheer happiness. As I've said, I could
never understand what she saw in the man, but that wasn't
really relevant. Celia had chosen him; she had known she
would be happy with him, and she'd been right. Admittedly I
hadn't seen much of her as a married woman, at first because
I'd been away in London, and lately because – well, if I was
being honest, I had to admit it was because I didn't really like
her husband.

I considered Jeromy Palfrey to be a bit of a fool: a pretty, overgrown boy who was over-fond of his silks, his velvets and the sickly, richly scented pomade he ladled on to his hair. He was shallow, self-centred and vain, and I'd always resented the fact that he seemed too in awe of his own beauty to appreciate fully my sister's. But on the other hand – I forced myself to be fair as the distance between me and my sister's impending pain inexorably lessened – he had provided her with a very beautiful home, dressed her in the finest silks and allowed – perhaps even encouraged – her to live a life of pampered luxury in which the hardest work she'd be called upon to do was decide what to sew next and thread up her needles.

If I was distressed by the spoilt little pet of a woman she'd become, and lamented the loss of the vigorous, rude, outspoken child she'd once been, that was nobody's problem but mine.

And I had to admit that she loved him. Privately, I thought she'd been taken in by his charm, his wealth and his handsome face, but whatever had attracted her to him seemed still to be working. The marriage was clearly a success, and I had to conclude that there might be more to my brother-in-law than I'd suspected.

I had reached Ferrars.

Now I had to go and tell my sister that her husband was dead.

She barely said a word.

I told her to sit down because I had the worst possible news. I took her little hands and said, as gently as I could – but how can the telling of such appalling things ever be gentle? – that Jeromy's body had been found and that it seemed he had died by his own hand.

I couldn't bring myself to recount the details. Why should poor Celia be forced to share the horror?

She went very pale. She sat so still that I feared she might have gone into some sort of trance. After a while, very worried about her, I said, 'It seems he never went to Dartmouth. At least, he didn't turn up to collect the cargo from Venice.' She nodded. Just once, but it proved she was hearing my words.

'He must have gone off by himself to a quiet spot,' I went on, answering the questions she hadn't asked. 'I think he really meant it.'

I wondered if she'd understood. It's been my experience that people sometimes make a half-hearted attempt on their own lives as a means of telling their family and friends how very unhappy they are, sending out the message *Now please do something about it.* There had been nothing half-hearted about that great blade thrust up behind Jeromy's ribs. And besides, if he'd wanted to be brought back from the brink he'd have done it somewhere where he'd have been swiftly found.

I wanted to ask so much more. Such as, *Did you realize he was so desperate?* And, perhaps more crucially, *Why was he so desperate?* But I wondered if she would be able to give me any answers.

We sat for what seemed a long time. Then I disengaged my hands and went to seek her servants. I came back with brandy, which obediently she sipped, and a warm, soft blanket, which I spread over her legs. A slight pink flush returned to her cheeks.

'Come back with me to Rosewyke,' I said, taking the empty glass from her. 'I know you always say your servants take good care of you when—' Oh, God. I'd almost said, *when Jeromy is away.* 'I know you're well cared for here,' I hurried on, 'but I think you should be with your family. And I won't fuss over you like Mother would,' I added, trying to make her smile.

The tiniest of twitches curled the end of her mouth.

'I'll come tomorrow.' She had spoken so softly that I barely heard.

'Tomorrow? But why not return with me right now?' I demanded. Too forcefully: she shrank away from me. Instantly I knelt down before her, taking her hands again. 'I'm sorry,' I muttered. 'I'm so very sorry. I so want to help you, but I don't really know how.' I bowed my head.

I felt a soft touch on the top of my crown as she gently

kissed me. 'I know, Gabriel,' she whispered. 'But I don't want to leave the house just yet.'

'I'll stay here, then,' I said quickly. 'I could—'

'No, my dear.' She kissed me again. 'Just now, you can help me best by leaving me alone. Please don't be hurt. I need you, more than I can say, and I will come to Rosewyke tomorrow.'

I got to my feet and stood looking down at her. Then I said, 'Very well. If you change your mind, come straight over. Any time, day or night.'

Then I left her.

I spoke at length with the senior household servants – a round-faced, maternal woman called Ruth who appeared to be the housekeeper and the stiff-backed man who habitually answered the door – and when finally I left, I felt slightly better about deserting her. Her housekeeper was almost as distressed as Celia, and more demonstrative in her grief and shock, but she gave me her solemn promise to look after her mistress until she came to join me at Rosewyke. 'I won't leave her in the hands of that empty-headed little maid of hers,' she confided quietly to me, jerking her head in the direction of the fair-haired young woman huddled in the corner, weeping into her apron. Her face sombre, she added quietly, 'You have to have experienced grief to know how to deal with it.'

For now, Celia was in safe hands.

There was nothing left for me to do but go home.

Early in the morning I had a visitor.

I'd been awake since first light and, for want of anything better to do, I was out in the stables giving Hal the sort of grooming nobody usually had time for. Hearing the sound of hoofbeats, I turned round, shading my eyes against the low sun. I watched as Jonathan Carew rode into the yard.

We greeted each other and I invited him to dismount and come inside for refreshment.

'Nothing to eat or drink, thank you,' he said as he followed me into the small morning parlour. 'This is not a social call.'

'No, I guessed as much.' I indicated the settle beside the

fireplace, and he sat down. I drew up a chair and sat opposite him. 'Has Theophilus Davey told you the news?'

'He has. I went late yesterday afternoon to see Mistress Palfrey, who I learned from the coroner is your sister, to give my condolences and to offer any assistance I can.'

'Thank you,' I muttered.

He shrugged, smiling faintly. 'It is what I do,' he said gently. Then, his expression growing serious, he said, 'She was distraught. At times during our brief conversation, I had the sense that she was not truly present.'

'It's hardly surprising!' I said before I could stop myself. 'She'd just learned that her husband is dead.'

'She told me she will be coming here, to stay with you,' Jonathan Carew continued, as if I hadn't interrupted. His strange green eyes met mine. 'I admit I was relieved to hear it. I do not believe she should be alone.'

'Neither do I.' I paused. 'Did she ask you about the funeral?'

Now it was his turn to pause. 'I regret that our discussion did not reach that point.'

'What do you mean? Surely it would have been one of the first things she asked?'

'She was overcome,' Jonathan admitted. 'She was swooning, desperate in her grief, and the old housekeeper took her off to her bed.'

'But—'

He put up a hand to stop me. 'It is my experience,' he said softly, 'that grieving cannot pursue its natural course until after interment. It is as if' – he paused to think – 'as if the placing of the body in its final resting place is required, to mark the definitive end of its time on earth.'

'I see,' I said, although I wasn't sure I did. 'So you're saying it will be a comfort for her, then, to have the funeral as soon as possible.'

'The burial cannot go ahead.'

'Cannot – *what?*'

'There are two difficulties,' Carew went on neutrally. 'The first is that the coroner will not release the body.'

'Why not?' There was one very good reason, and I found

myself desperately praying it wasn't relevant in the demise of my late brother-in-law.

But it was.

'Theophilus Davey does not believe this was a natural death,' Jonathan Carew said, his face expressionless.

'Of course it wasn't!' I said. 'He was found with the blade that killed him still inside him.'

He nodded slowly. 'Quite.'

Then, startling me and making me jump sharply, he said, 'What do you think? You saw the body.'

I shook my head. 'I did, but the maggot and vermin damage was extensive, and—'

And I'd done no more than confirm death before hurrying away, I could have added.

Something about the Reverend Jonathan Carew's steely expression stopped me.

And all at once I understood what he meant.

But, perhaps imagining I was still confused, he told me anyway. 'Under certain circumstances,' he said, and I was sure I detected a note of regret in his tone, 'I cannot bury a man in consecrated ground. The excommunicated; those possessed by the devil, such as lunatics; unbaptized babies.' He stared at me. 'And someone who has taken his own life, for that act disobeys God's commandment, *you shall not kill*. It is the ultimate act of despair, for by it a man indicates his belief that his own evil is too great for divine goodness and forgiveness.'

I heard his voice but I was no longer taking in the words he spoke.

I was deafened, blinded, to everything but images of my sister. I heard her distress as she wept, I saw it in the face wrecked by her tears. Her husband was dead; he had driven a blade into his own heart. Now, his body lay alone in some bleak cellar, and it seemed it was going to have to stay there.

What in heaven's name was I going to do?

SIX

I went over to fetch her.

As soon as Jonathan Carew had ridden off – swiftly, as if perhaps he wanted to hurry away from the place where he had just delivered such devastating news – I saddled Hal and rode straight to Ferrars.

I found her sitting on her window seat, in the place where she habitually settled to sew. She had a small piece of gaily coloured fabric on her lap – silk, of course – but I doubted very much that she had sewn even a stitch. Ruth sat beside her, her kindly old face creased into anxious lines as she vainly tried to encourage Celia to sip from whatever warming drink had been prepared down in the extensive kitchens of Ferrars. As I came into the room Ruth looked up, her expression full of relief, and said to Celia, 'Ah, now, my dear, here's your brother the doctor, come to see how you are.' Out of my sister's line of sight, the old woman made a face and shook her head, mouthing something that I thought was *She won't take even a sip*.

I went forward and knelt before Celia, taking hold of her hands. They were very cold. 'You said you'd like to come and stay at Rosewyke,' I reminded her. 'Will you come with me now?'

She raised her eyes and met mine. She nodded.

'Good, that's very good,' I said gently. 'Have you prepared a pack?'

'I've seen to that, Doctor Gabriel,' Ruth said quietly. 'It's set ready by the door, and her horse can be saddled and bridled in a moment.'

'Thank you.' I kept my eyes on Celia. 'Shall we leave straight away?'

Now Celia looked up. Her eyes roamed right round the room, lighting on a chair by the fireplace, an ornate china tobacco jar on the mantelshelf, a pair of soft leather house shoes set down just inside the door. Jeromy's things. My heart aching for her, I watched her as she bore yet another wave of her overriding grief.

I stood up and held out my hand. 'Come on,' I said.

She put down her sewing, carefully folding the bright cloth, and got to her feet. Then she turned to Ruth and gave her a brief, intense hug. The old woman tried unsuccessfully to suppress a sob. 'I'll see about that horse,' she muttered as Celia let her go, and hurried out of the room.

I led my sister out into the wide hall, its brilliant, expensive hangings and furnishings far too colourful for this house of mourning. There were several cloaks hanging on pegs by the door, and I selected a warm one with a deep hood that I'd seen Celia wear in bad weather. The morning was bright and sunny, but she was so cold: shock, I'd observed before, tended to make people shiver and shudder.

Then we were outside in the yard, and a groom was bringing her dainty grey mare. I stowed her pack behind the saddle, then helped her to mount. She came back to herself a little once she was settled – perhaps the very familiar sensation of being in the saddle was some sort of comfort – and, after one long look back at her house and at the old woman and the groom, she turned away.

She didn't utter a word all the way back to Rosewyke.

'I've asked Sallie to prepare your room,' I said as I led my sister across the hall and up the stairs. 'It's the front bedroom on the right, where you've stayed before' – for a ghastly moment I thought I'd been unthinkingly tactless, but then I realized it was all right: Celia had certainly stayed under my roof before, but never with her husband – 'and I thought you might like to use the little anteroom as a private sitting room?' She didn't answer, but then I hadn't really expected her to. 'You may find you feel like being on your own sometimes,' I went on, 'and Sallie's made it welcoming, with a nice bowl of early roses.'

I heard the echo of my voice and thought how fatuous I sounded. As if a bowl of roses was going to do anything to assuage Celia's agony of sorrow.

Understandably, she didn't reply.

I hurried ahead up the stairs, turning to the right at the top and on to the long gallery that ran right across the back of the upper storey. It jinked left and then right, ending in the doorway into the simply furnished anteroom that gave on to the bedroom. The bed had been made up with crisp linen sheets and a prettily embroidered pillowcase, and there was a subtle smell of lavender. Unlike my own bedchamber next door, whose walls were panelled and in which my huge four-poster bed loomed like some dozing animal, this room had white-painted walls and a general feeling of airy spaciousness. Sallie, I reflected, had done an excellent job in getting it ready, and I resolved to thank her when I had the chance.

Celia stood in the middle of the room, staring around her as if she'd never seen the place before. She touched the bedspread with gentle fingers, then moved over to look out of the window. I waited. After what seemed a very long time, she reached up a hand and unfastened her cloak. She turned to me. 'Where's my travelling bag?'

'Here!' I said, far too brightly.

The tiny glimmer of a smile. 'I'll unpack,' she said.

'I'll send Sallie up to help you, she's—'

'No.' The single word rang out harshly. 'I can manage,' Celia added more softly. 'I did not bring much.'

I watched as she unfastened her pack and began withdrawing the contents: a soft shawl, a gown, soft little slippers, what looked like a nightgown. I had never felt more useless. 'I'll wait for you down in the morning parlour,' I said, backing out of the room.

It was unworthy and uncharitable, but just at that moment I couldn't wait to get away from her.

Sallie was waiting for me in the hall, her face a picture of anxious solicitude. 'How is she?' she whispered.

'As you would expect,' I replied. Then, relenting, I added, 'You've made the rooms very welcoming, Sallie. Thank you. The roses were a thoughtful touch.'

'Did she like them? I thought she would.'

It would have been unkind to say *she didn't notice them*,

so I didn't. 'She's unpacking now – no, she doesn't need any help – and presently she'll come down and join me in the morning parlour.'

'That's right,' Sallie said approvingly, 'a nice bit of early sunshine will do her good. I'll listen out,' she added, hurrying off in the direction of the kitchen, 'and bring hot drinks and a bite to eat when I hear her come down.'

I went into the sun-filled morning parlour and sank down on the wooden settle. It was still only mid-morning, and already this day felt ages long.

Celia and I made little impression on the generous tray of food that Sallie brought in. I could have demolished most of it on my own, but it seemed insensitive to wolf my way through the little pies and tarts when my poor sister sat there, white-faced, hollow-eyed, picking disinterestedly at the tiniest of the cakes and making less progress than a sickly mouse.

I studied her. I wanted to bombard her with questions. What will you do? How will you manage? Have you access to Jeromy's money? Will you remain in that huge, showy and extravagant house, or sell it and purchase something more discreet and tasteful? I kept my mouth shut. These weren't matters for now, the first of all the days that Celia would have to live without him, and they could wait.

One matter, however, could not.

I had to tell her that Jeromy could not be buried in hallowed ground.

I said, 'Celia, I have had a visit from Jonathan Carew, the vicar of St Luke's.'

She nodded. She had given up on the tray of sweetmeats and pastries and gone to stand by the window. She was idly fingering the fabric of the curtain, perhaps unconsciously comparing its plain, robust practicality with the luxury of Ferrars. 'Yes, I know who he is,' she said, her voice low. 'Ferrars falls within his parish, although Jeromy likes us to attend services at St Mary's because that is where Nicolaus Quinlie worships.'

Likes. How long, I wondered, did it take for a widow to speak of her dead husband in the past tense?

But I was prevaricating. I made myself go on.

'I'm afraid I have bad news.'

She was standing with her back to me, staring out through the window on to the sunny garden below. She had been holding herself stiffly, her carriage very upright, almost as if she had to keep her body tense in order not to collapse. As I said the terrible words 'A suicide is not permitted in consecrated ground,' I saw her slump.

Her iron self-control had given way at last.

I hurried forward and took her in my arms before she could fall.

I studied her closely over the next few hours and days. She was in a strange mood: distracted, distraught, frightened, almost in dread, jumping at shadows, and my hopes that at last whatever was holding back her tears had broken proved premature. After that brief collapse when I told her there could be no burial in hallowed ground, I didn't see her weep. It was probable, I decided, that she preferred to do so in the privacy of her own quarters. She'd always been proud, and reluctant to give any sign that she was in pain or distress; no doubt it came from having two older brothers.

I wondered if my house was really the right place for her. Would she fare better with our mother to fuss over her and our father to advise her on her future? I suggested it, in a roundabout way – I didn't want her to feel she was unwelcome at Rosewyke, so I asked her if she'd prefer a busier household, with more family activities going on to take her mind off her grief – but she understood exactly what I meant. 'No, Gabriel, I don't want to go to stay at Fernycombe. Mother would drive me out of my mind.'

She didn't elaborate. I believed I knew, though, what she meant. I had sent word to Rosewyke informing our parents of Jeromy's death, and Mother had sent Samuel back with a long letter to Celia, presumably expressing her shock and distress. Knowing our mother, however, I was pretty sure she had also included several pages of sound, sensible advice.

I doubted that Celia would have read it. I didn't think she was ready for advice just yet.

As the endless days went on, her continuing silence began to worry me. She answered if I asked her a direct question, and once or twice she managed a soft 'Thank you' when Sallie performed some little service for her, but otherwise she barely said a word. She didn't do anything: she sat for hours, hands folded in her lap, eyes gazing into the middle distance, and each evening she retired to her bedchamber as early as she could, saying merely that she was tired.

I would have been willing to bet, however, that she didn't sleep.

It was not healthy, this suppression of her grief, and I tried constantly to work out how best to help her out of the stone cell in which she seemed to have imprisoned herself. In most cases, as Jonathan Carew had remarked, the pain of bereavement appears to be eased by the formal ceremony of the funeral; it is as if interment marks the moment when those who grieve know they must pick themselves up and walk on. But there could be no traditional funeral for poor Jeromy. I didn't know what happened in the case of those who died by their own hand: I ought to have asked Carew, but at the time it hadn't occurred to me. I had something in my mind about suicides being buried at crossroads, but somehow I couldn't see the intellectual mind of the vicar of St Luke's endorsing such a practice.

The more I thought about it, the more likely it seemed that Celia's prolonged silence and withdrawal were, in part at least, because she could not move out of the terrible grey state of having lost her husband yet not having buried him. Under other circumstances, she might now be throwing herself into arranging the funeral service – which would undoubtedly be something in keeping with Jeromy's wealth and position, perhaps in the big church where Nicolaus Quinlie and his rich friends worshipped – and making sure all those well-fed, important and influential people knew the precise date and time. Then there would be the funeral feast to prepare, with Ferrars buffed and polished till it shone and every room filled with the smell of lilies.

I arrested my imaginings. I wasn't being fair to my sister

and she didn't deserve my criticism, even if it remained unspoken. She hadn't asked to be in this awful position.

If only Jeromy hadn't killed himself.

Then I thought, *I am a doctor. A medical man.* What would happen if I were to throw doubt on the verdict of suicide? And just how much doubt would be required? Would Jonathan Carew relent and bury my late brother-in-law at the mere suggestion that he might not have died by his own hand, even if I wasn't able to prove it beyond question?

It was surely worth the attempt.

Theophilus Davey leaned back in his chair – it creaked in protest – and drew in a deep breath. Ah, sweet air! He knew he shouldn't have moved the corpse, strictly speaking, but, faced with imminent revolt from his staff, not to mention his wife, he felt he'd been left with no alternative. When it had been brought to his notice (by the resourceful Jarman Hodge, who had complained longer and louder than anybody about the stink) that there was a cool crypt with a stout, lockable door in an empty property on the edge of the village, and that the owner of that property was willing, for a considera-tion, to allow its temporary use as a morgue, it had seemed like a gift from heaven. Accordingly, yesterday evening Theo had ordered four of his men to cover the corpse and transport it to its new resting place. Then he had himself cleaned the cellar, rolling up his sleeves and scrubbing away at the trestle on which the body had lain so long until all but the worst of the stains had gone. Then he had scattered bunches of herbs – lavender, sage, rosemary – and lit a fire in a small brazier, on which he burned pieces of wood soaked in fragrant oils. The stench was still detectable if you went right into the cellar and sniffed hard, but who in their right mind was going to do that?

The relief was unspeakable. Theo eased his conscience by reminding himself that no imminent end to the situation had been in sight; he had had a visit from the vicar of St Luke's Church, Tavy St Luke's, who, when Theo had informed him of the cause of death, explained the church's stand on suicides, which seemed to Theo to be depressingly firm. What with Theo's reluctance to release the body – which had been rapidly lessening, he admitted to himself, as putrefaction had advanced – and the vicar's stand on burying it, the corpse of that poor man looked likely to be around for a while yet.

It was strange, he reflected briefly a moment later, that he had just been thinking about the dead man when his visitor was announced . . .

'Someone to see you, Master Davey,' Tomas yelled from the outer office.

'Who is—?' Theo began.

But before he could complete the query, Gabriel Taverner strode into the room.

Mildly surprised at how pleased he was to see the man, Theo said, 'Good morning, doctor. What can I do for you?'

He decided to keep to himself his musings on the odd co-incidence of Gabriel's having arrived at precisely the moment when his own thoughts had been on the corpse of the late brother-in-law. It wouldn't do for a coroner to acquire a reputation as a man given to fey fancies. It wouldn't do at all.

Gabriel stood over him, hands resting on Theo's desk, a frown on his face. 'I think you'd better sit down,' Theo added mildly. 'You have the air of a man with something on his mind.' *You also look rather threatening, looming over me*, he might have added. Gabriel Taverner was a broad-shouldered man, heavily built, quite tall; the shoulder-length hair and the heavy gold earring enhanced the impression that this wasn't a man to tangle with. There was something wild about him; as if he couldn't be relied upon to be totally civilized . . .

Gabriel pulled up a chair and flung himself into it. Briefly he rubbed his hands over his face, quite vigorously, as if he was washing, then looked Theo straight in the eyes and said, 'My sister can't bury her late husband as she would wish because he's a suicide and the church won't permit it.'

'So I understand,' Theo remarked.

Gabriel nodded. 'No doubt you have had other such cases.'

Theo considered. 'I'm not sure that I have,' he said. 'However, the vicar of St Luke's has been to see me.'

'Ah.'

'You know him?'

'I've met him, yes. He—'

'He is only doing his job,' Theo said gently. 'He cannot do other than follow his church's ruling, and if you have come to ask me to intervene and try to change his mind, I cannot do so.'

'No, I know,' Gabriel replied quickly. 'And I too understand that Jonathan Carew has no choice.' He paused, and Theo thought he could detect some struggle going on in his mind.

'So,' he prompted after a while, 'why *have* you come to see me?'

Again, the frank look. Then Gabriel said, 'I only saw the body briefly. It looked as if Jeromy had killed himself, but, under the circumstances, it is surely right to make absolutely sure.'

Theo nodded. 'Because, if there is the smallest room for doubt, then a good, Christian man such as Jonathan Carew would surely be charitable and come down on the side of compassion, and permit your sister to bury her husband with due pomp and ceremony.'

'Er – yes, precisely so,' Gabriel agreed.

Theo thought. Then he said, 'Two things I must tell you. Firstly, that I asked a local barber surgeon his opinion, and he agreed with your assessment.'

'But I only—' Gabriel began hotly.

Theo held up a hand, and Gabriel fell silent,

'Secondly, you should not, strictly speaking, be any further involved in this matter, the deceased having been a relative by marriage.'

'But I'm already involved!' Gabriel protested. 'You yourself involved me when you came to my door asking me to view the corpse!'

'Ah, but then neither I nor you knew who he was,' Theo countered.

'I – I—'

It was quite painful, Theo decided, watching Gabriel fumble around for counter-arguments. He decided to put the doctor out of his misery.

'If you are asking what I believe you're asking,' he said with a faint smile, 'then the answer is yes.'

'Yes,' Gabriel echoed. He was eyeing Theo warily.

'The body has been removed, as no doubt you've guessed by the pleasant air of my house,' Theo went on. 'Since I don't really want there to be any witness to our clandestine excursion, I suggest you present yourself back here at nightfall.'

Comprehension dawned on the doctor. 'You'll take me to see the body?'

'I will.'

I really hadn't anticipated Theophilus Davey agreeing to my request. Not so readily, anyway, although when I made my careful way under cover of the growing darkness to his house, I certainly wasn't going to start questioning his decision.

He must have been looking out for me, because he had the gate on to his yard open as I rode up. 'Leave your horse here,' he said softly. 'It's quite a short walk, and we're less likely to be seen on foot.'

I dismounted and led Hal into the yard. There was a row of three stables on the left, and Theo's bay mare put her head enquiringly over one of the half-doors as I tethered my horse in the adjoining, empty stall. Theo and I hurried out of the yard and he fastened the gates behind us. I glanced up at the house, and noticed a light shining from an open window in the upper storey. Had Theo a wife? Family? Now wasn't the time to ask, but, if so, then they must have been overwhelmingly relieved when the dead body was removed out of the house.

But just then there came the sound of a singularly sweet and pure voice, singing an ancient lullaby. I had turned away but now spun round, looking up at the window again.

Noticing, Theo said softly, 'My youngest has a touch of colic and my wife is trying to soothe him into sleep.'

'She sings most beautifully,' I remarked. 'What a lovely voice!'

Theo grinned. 'It's not always so pleasing to the ear,' he said. 'Elaine can bellow like a sailor when the children are unruly.'

I caught a glimpse of his expression as he stared up at his house. His wife, I guessed, could bellow all she liked and he would not think the less of her. He was, it seemed, a man very content in his marriage.

We set off out of the village, going westwards towards the last of the light in the sky. I could smell the salt and seaweed of the sea, and part of my mind registered that the tide must be coming in. Warleigh Point was only a mile or so ahead, I calculated, so we weren't far from the river.

After a short while Theo muttered, 'That's the place,' pointing to a large stone house that stood back several yards from the road, its hedges high and unkempt, its roof sagging and in need of repair.

'Does nobody live there?' I asked.

'No. The man who owns it inherited it from an elderly uncle and is trying to decide if the price he might eventually get for it is worth the expenditure of having it made fit for sale.'

We went in through the gate – leaning sideways and attached by a broken hinge and a length of twine – and walked up the path to the front door. Theo produced a key, and we were inside. Theo struck a flint and lit a lantern hanging inside the door, indicating for me to do the same with its pair. Then he led the way along the stone-floored hall to a low archway giving on to stairs leading down. The stairs were stone, like the floor, and steep and narrow. I grasped a rope attached to the wall with my free hand, not wanting to slip and fall on top of Theo.

The stench wafted up the steps to greet us.

Theo found two more lanterns, which he lit from the one he carried and placed on the trestle on which the body lay. A glow of golden light illuminated the small crypt, giving plenty of light for me to work by. There was no excuse not to begin.

I unwound the layers of cloth covering the corpse. It lay with the right side uppermost, legs bent towards the chest, hands still clasping the weapon that had ended life. Apart from the fact that it was lying on its side rather than sitting up, it looked as if the body was in exactly the same position as when the blade had gone in.

'You have preserved the evidence very carefully,' I remarked.

'I have,' Theo agreed. 'I had a feeling we hadn't heard the last of this one.'

I inspected the chest and the abdomen, moving the garments aside so that I could study the bare flesh. The weapon had pierced the skin just below the ribs on the left side, driven in at an upward angle. The blade was still held in the putrefying flesh, although the firm grip was weakening as the flesh began to disintegrate. Then I pushed the doublet and shirt down off the shoulders so that I could look at the corpse's back. Just under the shoulder blade, the tip of the weapon was sticking out, surrounded by a crust of dried blood.

It looked very much as it had done at first sight: as if Jeromy Palfrey had driven the blade in himself, especially as his dead hands were still clasping the weapon's handle.

But then something occurred to me.

'I need your help,' I said to Theo. 'We need to move the body into the position in which it was found. The *exact* position, mind.'

He didn't protest, although the task must surely have been repellent. 'It wasn't I who found him,' he said as we began, 'but I reckon I can put him as he was when I first saw him.'

'Which is presumably how he was when you and I arrived on the scene?'

'Yes.'

We sat the body on the floor of the crypt, leaning against the damp stone wall as it had leaned against the dilapidated building at Old Ferry Quay. The head lolled as it had done then, and the hands retained their grip on the weapon handle: I guessed they had been effectively glued to it by blood and other bodily fluids.

I stood gazing down at the corpse. Then I said, 'Did you speak to the fisherman?'

'Fisherman?'

'You said he'd been found by a fisherman who'd gone to the shore to clean his catch.'

'I did, I did,' Theo agreed. 'At first the man couldn't be found, and I was beginning to wonder about him, but then one of my men located him. It doesn't look as if he was involved, other than finding the body.'

'Is he local?'

'He is. Keeps his boat at Warleigh Point.'

'Could he be fetched?'

I thought I heard Theo sigh, and I didn't blame him. 'Is it important?' he asked.

'It is.'

'Very well.'

He stomped off up the steps, and I heard his heavy tread cross the hall above. Then the door opened and closed. I anticipated a long wait and so, shortly after Theo had gone, I followed him upstairs and went outside into the night air.

He was back quite quickly, and with him was a thin man with a weathered face and strongly muscled arms. The man looked awed, even frightened. 'I've told him there's nothing to worry about,' Theo muttered as we entered the house and headed for the steps down to the crypt, 'but he doesn't seem to believe me.'

I smiled to myself. Nothing to worry about other than the prospect of being in close proximity to a corpse that must surely be around two weeks old by now. It was no wonder the fisherman was apprehensive.

Once we had assembled around the body, I said to the man, 'I would like you to tell me, if you can, if this is how the body was when you first came across it.' I didn't say any more: it was crucial not to prejudice the fisherman.

'Let me see now,' the man muttered. He swallowed a couple of times, and there were beads of sweat on his brow and upper lip. I hoped he wasn't about to be sick. Then he straightened up, nodded to himself and said, 'The dead man was sitting leaning against the ruined wall of a house, legs out in front of him and just a little bent, hands on the end of the weapon's shaft. The shaft's broken off, see? It was like that when I found him.'

He fell silent. He seemed to understand the importance of what he was being asked. He took his time, looking first from the right side then from the left, finally crouching right down and staring up at the chest and shoulders from beneath. Then, standing up again, he nodded again and said, 'Reckon it's about right.'

'The hands are placed as you remember?' I asked.

'Yes,' he said firmly. 'He was holding on to that weapon like it was a lifeline, which is odd considering it was the very opposite.' He leaned forward, pointing. 'The right hand's just at the top of the handle, see, with the left immediately beneath it, and I recall thinking to myself that if he'd held it any higher up, he'd have sliced into his hands. That looks sharp, that does.' Again he made the confirming nod.

I was thinking very hard. After a moment Theo cleared his throat and said quietly, 'Is there anything else, doctor?'

I waved a hand. 'No, no.'

I was only vaguely aware of Theo telling the fisherman he could go, of the man's footsteps as he hurried away.

After a while I said, 'It wasn't suicide.'

'How do you know?' Theo asked quietly.

'Look.' I pointed, just as the fisherman had done. 'Jeromy's hands were on the weapon's shaft, clutched round it.'

'So how can you—' Theo began.

'He couldn't have reached the handle. The blade is at least the length of his forearms, perhaps more, as we can readily tell because its tip is sticking through the flesh of his back. So, before it was thrust inside his body, the handle would have been a forearm's length further away. See?'

A new light shone in Theophilus Davey's clear blue eyes. He said slowly, 'Oh, yes. Indeed I do.'

'His hands—' I began.

But, full of the heady pleasure of realization, Theo forestalled me. 'His hands were carefully wrapped round the weapon's shaft *after* it had been used to kill him.'

SEVEN

I rode home to Rosewyke, very eager to see Celia and bring her the news. I was sure in my own mind that being permitted after all to arrange Jeromy's funeral would mark the start of her healing. I had suggested to Theo that I call upon Jonathan Carew as soon as I could to tell him what we had discovered about the body, but Theo said that really ought to be his job, promising to see to it first thing in the morning.

'I shall tell him that I am now satisfied as to how Jeromy Palfrey died, which was not by suicide but by unlawful killing at the hands of another,' he said solemnly. 'I'm now prepared to release the body.'

'Thank you,' I replied. 'You will have my sister's gratitude.'

He gave me a brief and piercing look. 'I rather think she should bestow it on you.'

I could hear Tock's snores bouncing off the courtyard walls as I rode in through the gates, but Samuel was still up, and came out to greet me.

'All well, doctor?' he enquired as I dismounted and handed him Hal's reins.

'Oh, very well, thank you, Samuel.'

Sallie had retired for the night – no light showed under the door to her room leading off the kitchen – so I lit one of the candles set ready on the table and tiptoed across the flags, still damp from their last swab of the day, hoping not to wake her. I hurried through the hall and up the stairs. I didn't doubt, as I raised a hand to tap on the door to Celia's little anteroom, that she would still be awake, for I was sure insomnia was adding to her low state.

But there was no soft call of 'Come in'.

I tried again, this time saying quietly, 'Celia?'

Still no answer.

I raised the latch and opened the door, just far enough to

peer into the room. I held up the candle. All was orderly, with her sewing folded and placed on the small table beside the settle. There were fresh roses in the bowl.

The door to the bedroom was ajar. I stepped forward.

Moonlight flooded the room, and I saw my sister, curled up in her bed, fair hair spread over the pillows, her face soft and relaxed. She was fast asleep.

Very quietly I backed away, closing the anteroom door as I left.

My good news would have to wait till morning. I felt absurdly disappointed.

'And so you'll be able to bury Jeromy exactly where he should be buried, in the graveyard of St Luke's, and Jonathan Carew will officiate,' I concluded.

It was early the next day, and Celia had just joined me in the morning parlour. Anticipating that relief would sharpen her appetite, I'd asked Sallie to bring us a decent breakfast, which was now spread out on the table in the window.

Celia hadn't spoken.

'Don't you see, my dear?' I asked gently, going to stand beside her and reaching for her hand. 'Now you can plan his funeral feast, and all his friends and business associates can be invited, and his name will be honoured in death as it was in life.' I wondered if that was going a little far, but then she had loved him, and undoubtedly saw qualities in him that others did not. Well, *I* didn't see them. 'There won't be the scandal of suicide attached to him now,' I went on, 'and you'll be able to—'

I felt her slump against me as she fainted.

Fool! Dolt! I reproved myself, supporting her as I helped her across the room to the chair beside the hearth. I draped a blanket over her, then knelt in front of her, chafing her icy hands. I was furious with myself, for, in my relief at being able to break the news that Jeromy hadn't killed himself, I'd entirely overlooked the corollary: if he hadn't, then his loving, grieving wife had to face the terrible fact that somebody else had.

Because one thing was certain. That great blade hadn't ended up inside his chest by accident.

I had extracted it last night. It was a wicked-looking weapon, a hand's span across at the widest and a foot long or perhaps a little more, with one straight side and one curved, tapering to a long, sharp point. The blade was attached to a pole, the end of which had long ago been broken off. Theo had wrapped it and taken it away, commenting darkly, 'We may be needing this.'

I dragged my thoughts back to the present.

Celia was stirring. Her eyelids fluttered and opened. She looked up at me, anguish in her white face. I took her in my arms, hugging her close. 'It means that someone killed him, my dearest, and I know how hard that must be for you to accept.' I gave her a little shake. 'But surely it must console you to know for sure that he was not in that terrible state of despair from which there is no relief other than the taking of your own life?'

Very slowly she nodded. 'Yes,' she whispered. 'It does console me, of course it does.' She paused, then went on in a tiny voice, 'And we can put him safe and sound in the ground now?'

'Of course,' I soothed. 'Nobody will be able to hurt him any more.'

She relaxed a little at that, as if the concept comforted her. My heart ached with pity. How dreadful it was, to be in such a state that comfort could be derived from such meagre consolation.

I watched my sister over the next few days. Sometimes she appeared serene, as she did the morning we had a visit from Jonathan Carew.

He was a good man. On entering the parlour, he went straight up to Celia, gave her a formal bow and said, 'I offer you my sympathy, Mistress Palfrey, concerning the initial misapprehension that your late husband died by his own hand. The consequences of that misapprehension undoubtedly caused you extreme distress, which I sincerely regret.'

Celia gave a graceful little inclination of her head. 'It was, I have been led to believe, an understandable mistake,' she murmured.

I winced, for I felt we were approaching the dangerous ground of the state of the body when found, the blade driven deep in the chest. My dear sister should not have to contemplate such a thing.

Clearly, the vicar saw the danger too. Straightening up, he smoothly changed the subject and said, 'If you wish me to officiate, then perhaps we might arrange a convenient time for the funeral. St Luke's is not a large church and it may be that you would prefer your husband to be put to rest closer to his place of work and his many friends and colleagues. He was, however, one of my parishioners, and welcome to lie at St Luke's.'

There was a brief silence. Then Celia said, 'I think, your reverence, that Jeromy would like that.'

I left them to their discussion. It wasn't my place to add an opinion, and whatever my sister decided, I would support.

At other times, however, Celia's calm resignation deserted her and she became pale and fretful. She jumped at sudden noises, snapped when Sallie tried to engage her in conversation, complained loudly and hysterically when she thought poor, simple Tock had been watching her as she briefly took the air on her grey mare one fine morning: 'He was *spying* on me, the dirty, filthy swine!'

That was particularly vexing. For one thing, Tock was harmless and Celia knew it, and her accusations were cruel. For another, I'd been trying to persuade her to go outside into the good air for ages, and this was the last thing I'd wanted to happen.

I'm afraid the whole thing descended into a full-out row. When I reminded Celia mildly that Tock was really a boy in a man's body, and no more threat to her than a puppy, she rounded on me and screamed that I was a deluded simpleton and saw only what I wanted to see, burying my head in the sand and turning my face away from unpleasant reality. You'd have thought Tock had dragged her from her horse and tried to ravish her, yet I knew full well (because I quietly checked with Samuel) that all Tock had done was step out from behind the wall to wish her a stumbling, stuttering good day.

I could only conclude that he'd made her jump, and, in her present state, that had been enough to set off the extreme reaction.

Life at Rosewyke wasn't easy just then, for any of us.

The funeral passed off without incident. My sister looked beautiful in her black gown, and the long, fine, translucent veil she wore covered her face and hid her sore eyes from the curious. Jonathan Carew was impressive in his official role, and I resolved once more to make St Luke's my regular place of worship. My parents wouldn't object; in fact my mother, beside me as we listened to Jonathan's powerful and moving words, whispered, 'He's a fine preacher, Gabriel. You ought to give him your support.'

The cakes and ale back at Ferrars were copious and extravagant. Celia had been at the house for much of the time in the preceding days, organizing her servants in the preparations, although I had ridden over to fetch her at the end of each day to bring her back to Rosewyke. She wasn't ready yet to resume life on her own and I wasn't sure when she would be.

A group of Jeromy's former colleagues attended the funeral and the feast. Theo, who was also present, materialized at my side as I stood watching the polite but intense struggle to get at the best of the savoury pies, the dainties and the sweetmeats, and he pointed out to me a tall, stiff-backed, black-clad man with a face like a skull and strangely unblinking eyes, over in the corner of the room with what appeared to be a bodyguard of three heavily built men, each impassive face wearing the same watchful expression.

'That's Nicolaus Quinlie,' Theo murmured in my ear.

I focused on Nicolaus Quinlie's sallow face at quite the wrong moment: just as the cold eyes turned to meet mine. For an instant I seemed to feel a shock of chill, as if something deeply repellent had just appeared before me. The man's utter stillness reminded me of a cobra I'd seen in an Egyptian bazaar, hood flared as it drew itself up to strike.

'He comes well attended,' I said to Theo, shaking off my unease.

'The heavyweights?' Theo smiled. 'Yes, I spotted them too. I was wondering what sort of attack he fears, at the funeral of his late employee.'

'He is rich, they say,' I remarked. 'Rich men always fear for their security.'

'True, true,' Theo said.

I glanced around the room. 'Has he brought any other of his men?'

Theo nodded, silently and unobtrusively indicating a group of four standing in the doorway, and a fair man with a carefully trimmed beard who kept himself a little apart from the throng, murmuring to a dumpy youth with dark, greasy hair down to his shoulders. 'The quartet comprises Quinlie's two senior subordinates and their assistants,' he said in a voice not meant to carry further than me, 'and the man over there is Pius Moran, who I gather was the one who went to fetch Quinlie's precious cargo when Jeromy failed to turn up. The fat lad with him is his nephew Abner, who, despite his lack of intelligence and common sense, Moran seems intent on bringing on as his protégé.'

'You're well informed,' I observed.

'I make it my business so to be,' Theo replied.

'Did he take this block-headed nephew on the mission to Dartmouth?'

'He did.' Theo shot me a glance. 'Why?'

I shrugged. 'I'm not sure.'

There was a thoughtful silence, and then Theo said, 'I sent one of my own men over to Dartmouth back when we were still lacking a name for our dead body.'

'And?'

Theo smiled. 'And nothing. He's a good man – my best – but his orders were only to try to find Jeromy Palfrey. Since that would have been impossible, it wouldn't be fair to say Hodge – my man – had failed me.'

'Did he report no other observations at all?'

'It was he who told me about Pius Moran and his nephew. He thought I might like to know. And . . .' Theo paused. Then his blue eyes widened. 'Now that *is* interesting, now I come to think of it.'

'What is?'

Theo was frowning and shaking his head. 'I can't think why I haven't mentioned it before. It didn't exactly slip my mind; it's more that other things have driven it into the background, so to speak.' He glanced at me and must have picked up my impatience. 'Sorry. It may be nothing much, but Jarman Hodge went down to the warehouse that Quinlie uses in Dartmouth, looking for any word of Jeromy Palfrey. Nobody had seen him – well, that was no surprise since he was lying dead at Old Ferry Quay – and the warehouse owner was cross because he was having to keep Quinlie's costly and valuable cargo for longer than he'd been paid for. Anyway, Hodge overheard one of the men in the warehouse saying something about being very surprised if they ever saw Jeromy Palfrey again after this business. Now Hodge took it to mean that Quinlie would never trust Jeromy with any other important task, but what if the man was referring to something quite different? What if—'

'What if he knew very well they'd never see Jeromy again because they knew he was dead?'

Theo nodded. 'Yes. Exactly.'

'And your man definitely heard the man in the warehouse refer to *this business*?'

Theo waved an impatient hand. 'I can't swear to the precise wording, and I don't suppose Jarman Hodge could either, but it was something very like that.'

I tried to clarify my thoughts. 'Jeromy Palfrey was meant to collect the precious cargo of silk, but he never got to Dartmouth.'

'We don't know that,' Theo interrupted. 'He might have been intercepted after he reached Dartmouth and either brought back or returned of his own volition.' He paused. 'It's definite he was killed where he was found?'

I was on the point of saying yes when I stopped. *Was* it definite? Or could that blade have been driven into him elsewhere – in Dartmouth, for example – and his body taken to Old Ferry Quay in much the same way he'd been taken from there to Theo's cellar, and thence to the crypt in the empty house?

'Has it rained much in the last three weeks?' I demanded.
'Yes.'

I swore under my breath. 'I think you're right.' I could definitely recall at least a couple of days of persistent rain.

'You're thinking there would be a lot of blood if he died where he was found? But that, because of the rain, even if there was, there will no longer be any sign of it?'

'Yes,' I said heavily, 'that's exactly what I'm thinking.'

It was Theo's turn to curse. 'What a pity we didn't think to look when first we studied the body.'

'Indeed,' I agreed. 'As it is, we can't say for certain whether or not he was killed there.'

'I would bet,' said Theo after a moment, 'that he was.'

I looked at him, smiling. 'And that view is based upon what, exactly?'

He smiled too. 'Oh, nothing very scientific. Just a feeling in my guts.'

I nodded. 'Well, my guts tell me the same, although I think we should keep an open mind.'

'I agree.'

'I think,' I said presently, 'that I shall go to Dartmouth.'

Theo understood without being told what I intended to do. 'I'll ask Jarman Hodge to provide a description of the man he overheard.'

'I'd be grateful.'

I planned to set off for Dartmouth the next morning. I had to give some explanation to Celia, so I told her the truth, or at least some of it: that I was going to question the men at the warehouse where Jeromy was meant to have gone to collect the silk.

Her reaction was not what I had expected. She went very pale, and sat down rather hurriedly on the chair she had just vacated. 'You should – I—' she stammered. Then, in an all but inaudible whisper: 'It's not safe!'

I wasn't sure what she meant. Not safe for whom? Me? Her?

Then something dawned on me, and I mentally kicked myself for not having understood before.

It would explain much; explain, for example, why my sister

was so often pale with fear, why she jumped at sudden noises, why she insisted on keeping a candle burning in her room at night as well as lanterns in the gallery and at the top of the stairs. Her continuing presence in my house, when always before she had restricted her visits to a couple of days, three at most.

Somebody had murdered her husband. For some reason – and I didn't even guess at what it could be – she believed this somebody was going to come after her, too.

'I do not believe you are in danger here,' I said firmly. 'This house has strong doors, two men sleep in rooms off the yard – oh, all right, one of the men is Tock, but he's tough and he's very loyal – and a dog sleeps in the kitchen, and when I am away from home, Sallie is always extra careful about locking and barring the doors.'

She stared at me, eyes wide in her white face. She didn't speak.

'If you're afraid for my safety, then I promise I'll take care,' I went on. Still she kept her silence. 'I have to go, my dearest. I think it's important.'

She turned away. She said simply, 'Very well.'

I was still mystified as I set out but, after thinking it over for the best part of the ride to Kingsbridge, I had come up with no satisfying explanation. So as I turned north-eastwards towards Dartmouth, I put the matter firmly out of my mind and thought instead about my destination.

I have very happy memories of Dartmouth. The *Falco* put in there whenever we were in the region – it was rumoured among the crew that Captain Zeke knew a very accommodating and generous woman nearby – and our many shore runs led to strong ties between the crew and the townsfolk. As if that were not enough, something that happened in August 1592, not long after I'd joined the *Falco* in the early months of that year, gave the town a lifelong place in my affections.

The *Falco* was one of a small group of the Queen's ships selected to sail to the Azores to intercept the Spanish galleons groaning their way home from the New World, laden so heavily that they were low in the water and, of necessity, slow-moving. The first treasure ship we encountered, however, was not Spanish but Portuguese, and her name was the *Madre de Deus*. After a fierce battle that went on most of the day we took her, and when we boarded we could barely believe our luck, for all of her decks were heaped with bounty. Not only gold and silver were in abundance, but also bags of coins and chests of pearls and precious stones, fine cloth and beautifully worked tapestries, ebony and enough spices to supply a score of apothecaries for a year. It was rumoured that there was also a particular parchment originating in the Portuguese colony of Macau, on the Cathay coast, and the rumour said it provided highly secret and very valuable information on the Portuguese trade with Japan and Cathay. So precious was it that apparently it had been hidden in its own cedar-wood case, wrapped carefully inside a length of fine cloth as if it were a priceless necklace. I can't vouch for the truth of that rumour, if there is any, for I never saw the document or its case.

We sailed back to Dartmouth in great heart for although nobody had yet made an accurate tally of our haul, we all knew it was extraordinary; someone said what we were bringing home was worth half as much as England's entire treasury, but I'm sure that was an exaggeration. Anyway, we were full of glee at the thought of the news of our feat reaching the Queen's ears, for she was said to be fiercely proud of her navy and therefore likely to reward us well.

She didn't actually get the chance. News of what we were carrying somehow preceded us back to Dartmouth; the more superstitious among the crew maintained that the ghosts of the many Portuguese sailors we'd killed had turned into dolphins and raced ahead with the tidings, while the more practical blamed the pilot who had met us at the river mouth and hurried on ahead. Either way, we had a welcoming committee: merchants, tradesmen, whores, thieves, lads, lasses and honest townsfolk had all turned out, not, as at first we thought, to cheer us home but to push their way aboard and help themselves.

At first we tried to stop them, but very quickly it became apparent that there were just too many of them. I can hear

Captain Zeke's shout even now: 'Fuck this, lads,' he yelled, 'are we going to stand by and see this rabble fill their pockets when we who did all the hard work stand and watch and end up with bugger-all?'

We weren't.

The officers and the ship's surgeon had to try to set a good example, but the sole effect of that was that we employed a little more discretion than everyone else. I dropped perhaps a dozen solid gold coins inside my boots and slipped a pearl as big as my thumbnail inside my medical bag and when I saw a huge emerald rolling down the deck, dropped from a shop-keeper's bulging fist, I picked it up and put it in my mouth.

By the time order was restored – and I've always suspected nobody was in any great hurry – they reckon that getting on for three-quarters of the treasure had gone.

It was an event that will live long in Dartmouth's memory. What was purloined that day saw the rise to relative security and comfort of many a household, for to those who have little, the acquisition of even a small amount of wealth makes a big difference. While I don't like to imagine the Queen's reaction when told the news – if, that is, anyone was brave enough to tell her – still I can't help feeling pleased at the outcome.

My cheerful memories had entertained me and taken my mind off my journey. Returning to the present, I was pleased to find myself with only a mile or so to go.

EIGHT

Dartmouth looked busy and prosperous in the sunshine. I rode past St Saviour's church and turned on to the Spithead, reflecting that the prosperity of Elizabeth's long reign had fired the townspeople into a fervour of expansion. Everywhere I looked there were signs of recent construction, and the sounds and sights along the quay indicated that many more projects were under way. Ships lined the waterfront, some of them, to judge by the activity, recent arrivals, and some on the point of departure. For a moment the old longing took hold of me. Where had they been? Where were they going? Why wasn't I going too?

I made myself turn away. I had a task to fulfil.

Before I left Rosewyke, a messenger had arrived with a note from Theo. The young man had been hurrying, and was breathing hard through what looked like a recently broken nose: 'Coroner says you're waiting for this,' he panted, shoving the document into my hands. I left him in the kitchen with Sallie, already fussing over him and drawing him a mug of beer.

Theo's note was brief but helpful, not only describing the location of the warehouse that Nicolaus Quinlie habitually used for temporary storage, but also giving Jarman Hodge's succinct description of his warehouseman: *Short and fat; struts about with his chest thrown out like a fighting cock; voice like a hinge needing oil.* I found the warehouse and almost straight away spotted the man I had gone to find. I approached him, leading Hal by the rein, and said I was following up enquiries made by an acquaintance concerning a problem with a cargo. I decided not to be too specific. As I watched the man considering whether or not to be helpful – the small eyes in the fleshy face had a look of avarice – I casually jingled the purse at my belt so that the coins rang together. 'Very well,' he said, glancing swiftly over each shoulder, 'but first we'll get away from interested eavesdroppers. And you can pay for my time with a meal and a couple of mugs of ale.'

I agreed, and he led the way along the quay and up a wide street with inns and taverns of varying quality on either side. We went into the yard of one of the busiest, and I left Hal in the care of a stableman with instructions to see to his care and money to pay for it.

'Right,' said the warehouseman after we had ordered what seemed like a great deal of food and he had taken the first four inches off the top of his mug of ale, 'what is it you want to know?'

I didn't think I could afford to waste time. It was apparent that this fellow had an infinite capacity for food and drink and the funds I had brought with me were limited. 'A while ago, someone came asking whether you had seen a man called Jeromy Palfrey.'

The man twisted on the bench so that he faced me, a suspicious look in his eyes. 'What of it?'

'You remember the occasion?'

He sniffed and spat. 'What if I do?'

'You made an observation concerning the unlikelihood of Jeromy Palfrey returning to the warehouse, or possibly to the town, again after some particular business.'

'What if I did?'

I sighed and reached in my purse. If we were to proceed beyond this man answering my every enquiry with a truculent question, it looked as if it was going to cost me an initial, tongue-loosening payment.

'I'll make it worth your while' – I flipped the coin, which glittered in the dim light – 'if you'll be kind enough to tell me what you meant.'

He made a grab, but my fist closed on the coin before he could even touch it. He grinned at me, revealing a few yellow teeth randomly arrayed around his gums and separated by wide gaps. 'Fair enough,' he said. 'It's only talk, see, and I can't swear to whether it's true. I'm a God-fearing man,' he added piously, 'and won't risk my immortal soul.'

'Of course not,' I murmured.

He shot me a look. 'Well, the talk is that the fellow's gaffer has had enough of him. He's unreliable, he's lazy, he's flashy and he's too keen on making a fine show, for all that he's not too fussy about paying for it, if you understand me.'

I considered that. Much of it I already knew, but the last part came as a surprise. I wondered if Jeromy's failure to pay for his luxuries was because he preferred not to or because he hadn't the means. I knew he came from a wealthy family, however, and he had always been lavish in his spending, so it was probably the former. Rich men can always obtain credit.

So Nicolaus Quinlie had had enough of his brash and decorative employee . . .

'I don't suppose,' I said softly, leaning closer to my informant, 'the rumours went as far as suggesting what action this gaffer intended to take?'

The man toyed with a breadcrumb on the filthy table. 'Might have done,' he said coyly. I flipped the coin again. 'Oh, very well, he did. Or, anyway, that's what they were saying. He was going to . . .' He screwed up his face, apparently in an effort to bring the memory into focus. 'Word is, he'd said he was going to dispose of the man's services, them being a luxury he could no longer afford.' He sat back, leaning against the wall, a smug look on his face.

I cursed silently. The crucial remark was still ambiguous, even if it had just been repeated verbatim from the mouth of the man who had made it.

'So when you were heard to say you'd be surprised if Jeromy Palfrey ever returned again after this business, did you mean because his failure to turn up to collect the cargo would be what finally drove his gaffer to terminate his employment?' I leaned closer, dropping my voice to a whisper. 'Or did you mean something more sinister?'

Just for an instant, the man's fat face took on a savage smile. Then he wiped it away and said self-righteously, 'Oh, I'm sure nobody was talking about anything *sinister*.'

The food had arrived. I watched him set about his greasy, gravy-oozing pie with both hands, cramming large chunks into his greedy mouth. I didn't think he'd been going to say more, but there was no point in doing so now, for I wouldn't have understood.

I had a deal to think about as I rode home. It was true that my trip to Dartmouth hadn't revealed much more than I already knew, but one significant possibility had now been confirmed: that Jeromy might have been living beyond his means. I wondered how I could go about verifying this. He'd have engaged a lawyer, presumably, to take care of his affairs, as men of wealth always did. Perhaps I could make some enquiries, find out who this lawyer had been . . .

Law. Suddenly I remembered something Jonathan Carew had said. *I was to have entered the law, but influences and pressures steered my steps instead into the priesthood.* He had studied canon law – as I understood it, that meant the laws that governed the church – but perhaps his knowledge extended beyond that field. He was intelligent; possessed, I was quite sure, of the true intellectual's curiosity and wide-ranging mind.

He would be, at any rate, a place to begin.

I reached Tavy St Luke's very late in the evening. I was tired, Hal even more so, but I didn't want to wait till morning to speak to Jonathan Carew. No lights shone through the windows of St Luke's, so I went on to the priest's house next door – a modest dwelling, stone-built, slate-roofed, with a small kitchen garden adjoining – and tethered Hal beside the water trough, of which he took immediate and noisy advantage. Then I opened the gate in the low fence, walked up the path and knocked on the door.

It was quickly opened and Jonathan stood there, holding up a lantern and with a frown on his face. 'What's the trouble?' he asked.

'There's no trouble' – not right at this moment, I could have added – 'and I apologize for disturbing you so late.'

'Oh, it's you.' His expression became considerably friendlier. 'Come in.'

I entered the house. A fire burned in the hearth – the drop in temperature as darkness fell was a reminder that we were still quite early in the year – and a high-backed chair was drawn

up into the circle of its warmth, a lamp and a leather-bound
book lying open on a small table beside it. The little table also
bore a pewter cup and a modest flagon of ale. It was ill-
mannered, but I couldn't resist having a quick glance round
the rest of the room. It was simply and sparsely furnished, but
as far as I could tell in the poor light, what items there were
– wooden settle and round table, both burnished to a deep
sheen; bookcase packed with volumes bound in leather like
the one on the little table; a pair of shelves bearing crockery,
glassware and silver – all appeared good quality, well used,
well loved, well-cared-for. In the corner, a narrow stair led up
presumably to the vicar's bedchamber.

It was the house of a man whose needs were small, but
who met those needs with the best that he could afford. It
was a house in which I instantly felt comfortable.

'Sit down' – Jonathan pulled up a second chair – 'and have
a drink.'

It wasn't ale in the flagon but wine. Very good wine.

I let the smooth, rich liquid linger on my tongue in appre-
ciation for some moments before swallowing it. Then I said,
'I believe Jeromy Palfrey might have had financial troubles.
How can I find out?'

Jonathan resumed his seat and took up his own wine. 'He
– or, rather, your sister – would certainly have had money
troubles had he been deemed a suicide, for the law states that,
suicide being a crime, the property of a man who dies by his
own hand is forfeited and handed to the crown.'

'*Really?*' I was horrified. If I'd ever known that dreadful
fact, I'd forgotten it. Thank God the truth had come out.

Jonathan nodded. 'Your sister would have become a pauper.'

'She wouldn't, for I'd have looked after her,' I said quickly.
'I *will* look after her.'

His illuminating smile briefly crossed his face. 'Yes. I'm
sure you will. So,' he went on, 'what leads you to believe
Palfrey was in difficulties?'

'He spent lavishly, he ran a large house with quite a lot of
servants, he was a man who loved the expensive and the
fine-quality.'

'Perhaps he earned a very good wage?'

'He worked for a very rich man. Nicolaus Quinlie didn't acquire all that money by being over-generous with his employees.'

Jonathan nodded, conceding the point. 'He came from a wealthy family.'

'He did,' I agreed, 'but . . .' But what? I knew, somehow, that Jeromy hadn't been supporting himself and Celia on hand-outs from his father. 'I'm fairly sure there was some discord with his family. It's just a vague feeling,' I added, 'and I don't know why I have that impression.'

'Could you, do you think, ask your sister?' Jonathan ventured. Then, as something struck him: 'Were any of Jeromy's kin at the funeral?'

I met his eyes. 'No.'

He nodded. 'We appear to have answered the question.'

'How do we find out for sure?' I demanded as Jonathan topped up my goblet. 'Can I—'

'I imagine,' Jonathan interrupted, 'that the matter will swiftly resolve itself. It is normal for the will to be read quite soon after the funeral, is it not?'

'Of course.' I should have thought that out for myself.

'In which case, the lawyer who has been entrusted with your late brother-in-law's estate will undoubtedly present himself at Rosewyke as soon as he finds out that it is the present abode of your sister.'

I stared at him. I had a very uneasy feeling about what he had just said; it was as if I was already experiencing the anticipated meeting with Jeromy's lawyer and not enjoying it at all.

'Will you do me a favour?' I asked.

'If I can, yes.'

'When this lawyer turns up, may I send word so that you can be present for whatever tidings he brings? Or, if that proves impossible, ask you to advise us once we know what those tidings are?'

'It will be my pleasure,' said Jonathan Carew.

We did not have long to wait. As if he had been waiting for his cue, Jeromy's lawyer arrived at Rosewyke the following afternoon. 'I act for the late Jeromy Palfrey and I seek his widow,' he said as I entered the parlour, into which Sallie had shown him before puffing upstairs to my study to summon me. I'd been trying to make the most of the post-prandial time when Celia normally rested in her room to return to my neglected studies, but it looked as if I wasn't going to get very far today.

'May I know your name, sir?' I asked. The lawyer was short, slightly breathless, bald-headed and clad in fusty black, the fabric smelling as if it was in need of laundering. He had seated himself in the fine oak chair with arms that stood at the end of the large table – my chair, in fact – without being invited, and now he was spreading a wide arc of papers across the table's shiny surface.

'I am Bartolomeo Wolverton,' he said. 'And you, or so I am led to believe, are Gabriel Taverner, Mistress Palfrey's brother.'

'I am.'

Wolverton looked up at me. 'Well?'

'Well what?'

'I said I wish to see Mistress Palfrey. They told me at Ferrars that she was here, and I have come all this way – I live the far side of Plymouth – with the express purpose of speaking to her. Will you kindly summon her, Master Taverner?'

'*Doctor* Taverner,' Sallie corrected brusquely as she came in bearing a tray of refreshments. She shot the lawyer quite a vicious look. It appeared she hadn't taken to him.

Bartolomeo Wolverton pretended he hadn't heard the correction.

I took Sallie aside. 'Would you fetch my sister, please?' I said quietly. 'Warn – er, tell her who wishes to see her.'

Sallie nodded, a knowing expression on her face. 'That I will, doctor,' she hissed back. 'Very wise, if I may say so, not to leave him alone in here.' She glanced round the room. 'You don't know what he might get up to.' She leaned closer. 'Never trust a man of the law, that's what my dear old father used to say.'

It would have amused me, except that, in the case of this particular man of the law, I couldn't help thinking Sallie's dear old father had been quite right.

The lawyer and I waited. He pretended to sort through his documents, I simply stood watching him. I like to tell myself I made him feel uneasy, but I don't suppose I did.

There was a hiss of expensive silk, and Celia entered the parlour. 'Lawyer Wolverton,' she said with a polite smile, extending her hand to him. 'We have not met, I think, but of course I know who you are.'

He half-rose, took her hand in his own white, soft fingers and gave it a perfunctory peck, then sat down again. He was a fat man, and I noticed that his plump thighs were being squeezed tightly by the arms of the chair. It gave me a certain satisfaction. Since he clearly wasn't going to bother, I made quite a ceremony of drawing back another chair for Celia, settling her into it and making sure she was comfortable.

'Now, I am sure you can guess why I am here,' Wolverton said, arranging his documents in a pile and tapping their sides neatly to straighten them.

'Jeromy's will, I imagine,' Celia said, smoothing the fine silk of her midnight-blue gown.

There was a short silence. Wolverton was staring at her with a strange expression. 'The will, yes, indeed,' he murmured.

I had the first, sharp intimation that all was not well.

My sister evidently had no such premonition. 'I am sure my husband left his affairs in good order,' she said. There was a faint note of haughty pride in her voice. I wanted to shout out a warning.

The lawyer dropped his eyes. 'I am rather afraid, Mistress Palfrey, that is not quite the case.'

I was standing behind her and I saw her shoulders stiffen. There was a short pause, and she said, in precisely the same tone, 'Explain, please.'

Wolverton shifted in his chair, and the wood creaked a protest. 'He – Master Palfrey – ah, how to explain?'

'Simply and swiftly,' my sister snapped.

Wolverton was not a man to ignore a challenge, or an implied insult. Raising his head again, his small, dark eyes aimed at Celia like cannon, he said, 'The will makes provision for you, dear lady; very careful and precise provision, indeed, and so in that sense you are correct in assuming that your husband's *intention* was to leave all in good order.' Oh, I didn't like that heavy emphasis on *intention* . . . 'Sadly' – the lawyer's face took on an expression of wildly exaggerated regret worthy of a Shakespeare comedy – '*very* sadly, your husband's desire to leave you adequately – more than adequately – provided for is to no avail, for there is no money.'

At first Celia said nothing. I drew closer, so that I was standing right behind her. I sensed that it was taking all her courage not to scream out a protest, and so restrained the impulse to reach out and touch her. It would serve only to undermine her: this was her battle, and right now there was nothing I could do.

'No money?' she repeated in a whisper.

Oh, dear Lord, I thought. *So the rumour is true.*

'No, dear lady.' Wolverton's narrow mouth stretched in an unctuous smile.

'But—' Her voice cracked and she tried again. 'But I have the house?'

'Again, sadly, no.'

'But—'

'Your late husband did not own Ferrars,' the lawyer said, each word dropping like a stone. 'Moreover, since he has unfortunately fallen rather a long way behind in paying his rent, I am afraid to tell you that eviction is being requested.' He hesitated, head on one side. 'I might say rather it is being *demanded*' – he gave a satisfied little smile at having selected a better word – 'for the owner of the property is eager not to incur further arrears.'

'I will pay him what we owe!' Celia said hotly, and I heard the pride behind the words.

Wolverton regarded her sorrowfully. 'With what, dear lady?'

She looked round wildly, seeking inspiration from the room. 'There *must* be some money – Jeromy worked hard and long, he was a valued employee and he was certainly paid accordingly, and—'

The lawyer leaned forward and patted her hand, clenched into a furious fist on the table. 'Not only had he spent everything,' he said solemnly, 'but – oh, dear me, how I hate to tell you this! So tragic! He was in debt. Rather seriously, I'm afraid.'

She snatched her hand away. 'I don't believe it!'

Wolverton riffled through his carefully arranged documents. 'I have proof,' he said. There was a sudden chill in the room, as if he was reacting to Celia's doubting his word. He held up a piece of paper. 'He had been borrowing increasingly large sums of money for the past eighteen months,' he said gravely. 'I have the details here.' He made as if to hold out the paper, but Celia shook her head.

'I don't want to see it,' she said.

Wolverton replaced the document in the pile.

There was silence in the parlour.

Eventually I said, 'My sister has money of her own.' Our father had told me that he was providing Celia with a modest income; his mistrust of Jeromy Palfrey had not been assuaged, apparently. Now I saw how right he had been. 'What of that?'

The lawyer spread his hands in a gesture of helplessness. 'Your sister was a married woman, Doctor Taverner. Her property became her husband's on her marriage, as did the dowry paid by her father.'

'And it's all gone?'

'It's all gone,' he confirmed.

He reached for his mug and drained it. Then he put his stack of papers back into his leather bag and, prising himself out of my chair, got to his feet.

The interview, it seemed, was over.

Celia wouldn't talk to me. I tried – there was something very important I had to discuss with her – but she refused utterly to say a word. Her pride in tatters, mortified at this terrible window into her late, beloved husband's true nature, she hid herself away in her room and refused to admit me.

So that night I went to Ferrars on my own.

I took the large cart that Samuel and Tock use for the biggest, bulkiest tasks, hitching it up to the patient old mare who always pulls it. I went by the back tracks and nobody saw me. At Ferrars, I asked the senior steward and the housekeeper to help me. I didn't explain, and they didn't ask; that in itself told me that they probably knew a great deal more about what had been going on than my poor sister had done.

It took a long time. I had to be careful not to be too obvious, and quite a lot of calculation and thinking had to be done. I also had to think about storage: I had a place in mind, but its capacity wasn't infinite.

When finally I set off back to Rosewyke, the first light was starting to show in the eastern sky and the cart was so heavily laden that I took pity on the mare and walked.

NINE

So Jeromy had been deep in debt, I thought as I trudged along. He owed rent, he'd have probably run out of credit with everyone he dealt with and his way of living was far from a modest one, even for a man of inexhaustible means. In desperate need of money, did the much-vaunted and extremely valuable cargo of Venetian silk present too irresistible a temptation? Did he decide to cheat Nicolaus Quinlie and help himself to it? He knew the trade; surely he'd have been able to find a buyer. He could have reduced the price a little, in exchange for an agreement not to ask too many questions. It was possible, surely; even likely.

So what had happened? Had he been discovered? Had someone guessed what he'd been plotting and made sure an assailant – more than one, perhaps – lay in wait for him? I pictured him, taken unawares as he crept into the dark, silent warehouse. Caught, bound and silenced by Quinlie's toughs, bustled away to that lonely spot on the river where his body had been found, dumped there on Old Ferry Quay and utterly at the mercy of one of those heavies; possibly even Quinlie himself. Had Quinlie stood over him, told him coldly and dispassionately that nobody cheated a man like him, and then killed him? No more powerful message could have been sent to Quinlie's other employees . . .

I'd be very surprised if we ever see Jeromy Palfrey again after this business.

The words rang in my head again. They'd known, those warehousemen at Dartmouth. Someone had found out what Jeromy had planned to do – I found it hard to think he'd managed any great degree of subtlety – and tipped off Nicolaus Quinlie. He had taken the necessary steps to protect his property and punish the would-be thief.

Punish him terminally.

And afterwards, how easy it would have been for Nicolaus

Quinlie to play the part of the angry and frustrated merchant whose feckless employee had failed to turn up as he'd been ordered, so that someone else had to be despatched to do the job instead.

Later, as I lay in bed sleepless, watching the morning light steadily wax, I worked out that there were two people I needed to speak to that day.

My first mission was to seek out Jonathan Carew, and I told him that the anticipated lawyer's visit had now happened and briefly explained Celia's situation. Jonathan verified that she could expect nothing, including any property or wealth she had brought into the marriage, as the law made anything she owned her husband's property. And he had spent it all.

'And this applies even if he's dead?' I knew it was so but I had to verify it.

'His will would have allowed her to inherit, had she been named as his heir, but from what you tell me there is nothing *to* inherit.'

'Only debts.' A dreadful thought struck me. 'Will she have to pay back his debts?'

'With what?' He smiled wryly. 'That, my friend, is the sole advantage of having nothing: nobody can take from you what you haven't got.' He paused. 'The bailiffs will be searching, however,' he added softly. 'Any – er – any small personal items of little value that your sister may wish to retain might perhaps be fetched, sooner rather than later.'

I met his eyes. 'I understand.' *And I've already taken care of it.*

When I got home, it was to find my father in the morning parlour. He was sitting on the settle, Celia beside him. They were holding hands.

He looked up at me. 'Good day, son,' he said gruffly. 'I'm trying to persuade your sister to come and stay with her mother and me for a while. We've barely seen her, except at the funeral. Your mother dearly wants to cherish her a little.' He turned to Celia, bestowing upon her a look of such love and tenderness that I wondered if it was he, quite as much as my mother, who wanted to do the cherishing.

'I've agreed to go, Gabe,' Celia said. She met my eyes, and hers held what I read as a desperate plea: *Don't tell him about the debts.*

As if I would. She'd tell our parents in her own good time – she'd have no choice – but it wasn't my secret to tell. Minutely I shook my head. I guessed why she'd accepted the invitation to Fernycombe: there, she could still be what until yesterday she had been, the grieving but wealthy widow. Perhaps she needed a little while longer to pretend to herself that that was what she still was.

'Of course you should go,' I said, smiling at her. Then – the words sprang into my head and I realized they were absolutely true – 'I'll miss you.'

Her eyes filled with tears, and she hastily brushed them away.

When she and my father had gone, I set out to see Theo Davey.

Seated in his office, the door firmly shut on his staff, I expounded my theory. 'Jeromy was desperately in need of money, you see,' I concluded, 'so isn't it likely, or at least possible, that he tried to cheat Quinlie and steal the Venetian silk?'

'And Quinlie, if he found out, is not the sort of man to permit his employee to help himself,' Theo said.

'Far from it,' I agreed. 'What do you know of Nicolaus Quinlie?'

'Not very much, for he is a man who values his privacy and, since he gives every appearance of being a law-abiding, honest and decent citizen, the law has no excuse to go poking its nose into his business.' He got up as he spoke, going over to the door. He put his head outside, muttered something to someone in the office beyond, and returned to his desk. Noticing me watching, he said, 'I believe I know someone who can help us.'

Quite soon the door opened again and a nondescript man dressed in worn but clean garments of unobtrusive cut and shade came in. 'Ah, there you are,' Theo said. 'Gabriel, this is Jarman Hodge. He is one of my best agents, two of his most valuable qualities being an endless curiosity for finding things out and the rare ability to keep what he discovers to himself. Jarman, what do you know about Nicolaus Quinlie?'

If Hodge was surprised at the question, he didn't allow it to show. With only a brief pause while he gathered his thoughts, he said, 'He was born into the nobility; an ancient Gloucestershire family, I believe. His father and grandfather were at court, although briefly, and acquired a small degree of status and importance and a great deal of money which was used to promote the family into a place of some importance as merchants. Nicolaus was disinherited by his father – it's said it was at his grandfather's insistence, he being the power in the family at the time – because of his misspent youth. Nicolaus was arrogant and cruel, and the story is that he raped a neighbouring lord's young daughter. He refused to come to heel, they say, insisting she was lying, and in the end the family were left with no choice.' He paused. 'There were other complaints, too. He was ever ruthless in acquiring what he desired, viewing it as his right by virtue of his family's position and wealth and not caring overmuch how he went about it. His family, it's said, don't know the half of what he's been up to in the long years since they kicked him out.' He frowned. 'There are dark tales told about Nicolaus Quinlie, but he's too clever to allow any of them to become more than tales. There was the woman he was meant to marry, for instance. She was high-born and her father was related to one of the late Queen's favourites, or so I believe. She died, and Quinlie browbeat her family into allowing him to pay for a very elaborate tomb.'

'Surely that would suggest he has a heart?' I protested.

Hodge looked at me, eyes cool, face expressionless. 'Perhaps. Except nobody quite knows *how* she died.'

The implication being, I had to conclude, that somehow Nicolaus Quinlie had been responsible . . .

'Oh, and he breeds mastiffs to supply the bear-baiting pits of London,' Hodge concluded. 'He keeps a pack for personal defence, including one big brute of a dog that rarely leaves his side.'

There was silence as Hodge finished speaking. Quinlie, I reflected, was far from the respectable silk merchant he purported to be. Whether his deviation from this image went as far as murder, I couldn't have said, although I could have made a good guess.

Theo was speaking to Hodge, and I made myself listen.

'. . . think it may be possible Jeromy Palfrey tried to cheat him of the silk, and was killed and disposed of,' he was saying quietly.

Jarman Hodge seemed to know what was expected of him without Theo having to explain. He nodded. 'I'd best get on with it then,' he said offhandedly. With a nod to each of us, he slipped quietly out of the room.

I stared after him. 'Will he be all right?' I asked. 'Surely what you ask of him is dangerous?'

Theo smiled. 'He can take care of himself,' he replied. 'Now, I do hope you won't think me rude, doctor, but since there doesn't seem much more to be said or done until Hodge reports his findings, I have quite a lot of work I should be getting on with.'

I took my cue and left.

Rosewyke seemed quiet without Celia in residence. It wasn't that she'd made a lot of noise – far from it, since she'd spent a lot of her time in her own quarters – but, even in her grief, she'd contributed some sort of lively, vibrant spirit to the place that I found I missed. Nevertheless, her absence was welcome in one sense, as now I could return to my neglected studies without feeling guilty.

I wasn't going to be permitted to study for long, however. In the middle of the afternoon, when I was deep in Andreas Vesalius's treatise on dissection in which he repeatedly stressed the importance of observation as a physician's tool, I was interrupted by Sallie's brusque tap on my study door. 'You've got a visitor, doctor,' she said, and I could tell by her very tone of voice that, whoever it was, my housekeeper didn't approve. 'I've *said* you're busy and not to be disturbed,' she added, 'but some people won't take no for an answer.'

Reluctantly I laid Vesalius aside and put down my quill. 'Very well, Sallie, I'm coming.'

I followed her down the stairs into the hall, where she indicated the parlour with a disapproving jerk of the head before disappearing into her own domain. The kitchen door closed emphatically behind her.

I went on into the parlour.

I'm not sure who I was expecting, although I certainly hadn't envisaged a woman. Not such a one, anyway, as she who stood in the middle of the parlour, staring around her and perfectly at her ease.

She was strikingly attractive. She was dark: her skin had the healthy, tanned look of someone who spends a lot of time out of doors, and what I could see of the hair beneath the modest white headdress and hat was black and glossy. I'd have put her down as a native of more southern climes – Spanish, Italian – but for her eyes. These were bright, large and clear, and a rare shade of very pale blue with a hint of silvery grey. Her nose was strong and straight, her chin firm, and her wide mouth was beginning to curve into a smile.

'Have you seen enough, or would you like me to take off my cloak?' she said in a low-pitched voice. Even as she spoke, her hands went up to unfasten the clasp at her neck and she flicked back the wide folds of her high-collared cloak. She was tall, her waist was small beneath a generous bosom and her neck rose elegantly from square, strong shoulders. She wore a tightly fitting black bodice over a full skirt made of fine wool, deep brownish-red in colour.

'Please, sit down,' I said, stepping forward and pulling out a chair. She sank gracefully on to it, spreading her skirts. 'How may I help you?'

Her smile widened. 'Maybe it's I who can help you, doctor.'

I stared into her shining eyes. 'I don't believe I know who you are.'

'I very much doubt it,' she agreed. 'I'm called Judyth. I am on my way home after a visit to Josiah Thorn, who summoned me to attend a tricky delivery up at Buckland. I'm a midwife,' she added helpfully, in case I hadn't worked it out for myself.

Josiah Thorn. Why did I know that name? But that was something to ponder later. 'Do you want my assistance?' I asked. Something flashed swiftly in her eyes. 'Not that I can imagine any circumstances in which you might have need of it,' I went on hastily, 'since you have probably brought far more babies into this world than I.' I didn't add that this was the case with every midwife in the land, since to date my sum total of solo deliveries stood at nil. I'd observed and assisted on many occasions, of course, during my training, but that, I was quite sure, was a very different matter from being in charge and alone.

Judyth was studying me. 'No thanks, doctor, that's not why I'm here. As I just said, *I've* come to help *you*.'

'Yes, so you did.' I drew up another chair and sat down beside her. 'In what way?'

'I felt it was my duty to speak to you,' she said calmly. 'You are, I understand, making enquiries into the discovery of a body at the beginning of the month down by Old Ferry Quay.'

It was a statement and not a question, but I said, 'Yes I am,' anyway.

'I have some information for you.'

I felt my senses grow alert. Was it possible she'd seen Nicolaus Quinlie, or, at the least, his thugs? Observed them dumping Jeromy's body? Killing him? It seemed too good to be true.

'Go on.'

'One night round about then I was in the vicinity of Old Ferry Quay. I'd been delivering a baby in a small hamlet further upriver, and I was making my way home along the track that runs along the top of the bank, approaching the place where the steep path down to the river emerges. I didn't realize there was any significance in what I saw, because then, of course, I hadn't heard about the body being discovered at the quay.'

'What *did* you see?'

'A man, cloaked and hooded, making his way along in the shadows as if he didn't want to be seen.'

'*One* man?'

She hesitated. 'I'm not sure. I stopped and concealed myself

– it wasn't that I was frightened exactly, only that, in general, I find discretion is preferable to over-confidence. But I managed to get a good view of this man, and I think I might have heard him muttering. Unless he was talking to himself, that suggests he had at least one companion, even if I didn't see him.'

Quinlie's men? There was no way I could be certain. 'Are you able to describe further the man you saw?' I demanded.

'I . . .' She hesitated, frowning. 'I had the impression he was a foreigner, although I can't really say what made me think so.'

Did Quinlie's gang of thugs include any foreigners? It was a question to ask Jarman Hodge. 'Perhaps—' I began.

But then her face lit up. 'Oh, I believe I may be able to help after all,' she said. 'But, please, do not make too much of this, for, as I said, it was only a swift impression.'

'I won't,' I said.

Again, something flashed in her eyes. Then she said, 'It seemed to me that he was wearing a mask, for the features of his face – what I could see of it – did not look quite human. The nose . . . it was beak-like. And I seem to remember that there was a particular scent, a perfume, in the air. Not something that occurs naturally in the early May countryside, but something alien, unusual . . . Pepper, cloves, perhaps?'

'Like a pomander?'

She shook her head. 'Not exactly, for why should a pomander be the unique possession of a foreigner? There was something else, a sharp sort of smell . . .' Her fine dark eyebrows drew together as she frowned. 'I'm sorry. I can't bring it to mind.' She raised both hands, palm uppermost, in a graceful gesture that made me think of dancing.

'No matter.' I found I was smiling, and hastily straightened my face. 'I appreciate your coming here to tell me as much as you have done, for undoubtedly it will prove extremely helpful.'

'You have a suspicion, then, concerning who was responsible for that poor young man's death?'

'A suspicion, yes,' I agreed, 'but as yet we – they – are a long way from proving it.'

She nodded. 'I see.' Then, after a pause, 'I've heard he was in some way connected to you? Not a close friend, I trust, for to lose one such is a great sorrow to the heart.'

'No,' I said, still thinking about the shady foreigner and the mysterious smell and not concentrating on what I was saying. 'No, he wasn't a friend, he was my brother-in-law.'

She was getting to her feet: a smooth, elegant movement in which she didn't use her hands to help her but relied solely on her strong legs and back. She gave me an enquiring look, and I thought I saw the shadow of a swift, amused smile. Then just as quickly her expression straightened. 'I will leave you to your work, doctor,' she said. 'I am sure I have disturbed you long enough.'

She was already gliding towards the door. 'Won't you take refreshments?' I offered belatedly. 'We have—'

'No, thank you,' she said firmly. 'I have another call to make, and the night promises to be long since I shall be attending one of my mothers whose labours habitually last a day and a half and more.' She turned, giving me an unreadable glance over her shoulder. 'I'll call you if I need you.'

She knows, I thought as I watched her swing up into the saddle of her chestnut gelding and ride away. *Somehow she has picked up the fact that, when it comes to obstetrics, I am a novice whose help she wouldn't send for if I was the last doctor in Devon.*

Was she a mind-reader? It was both an exciting and a scary thought.

I put it from my mind, contemplating instead the news that Judyth had brought: good news, without a doubt. Now we had a witness to what had happened on the night Jeromy was murdered, surely we were that much closer to establishing who was responsible. I glanced up into the sky, deciding it was too late to pay a visit to Theo. I would tell him in the morning.

For now, I would return to Vesalius and his views on dissection.

As I bounded back up the stairs, I remembered where I'd heard the name Josiah Thorn before. Black Carlotta had asked if I knew him, and when I said I didn't, had added mysteriously, *maybe you should*. I'd been making enquiries about the unpleasant offerings left on my doorstep, and this Doctor

Thorn, it appeared, might be involved. Or not: as I recalled it, when I asked Black Carlotta if she thought he had been responsible, she had replied enigmatically. *I don't think any such thing*, she said. *I'm just asking, do you know him?*

I stopped halfway up the stairs. It was true that there hadn't been any more offerings since the beheaded blindworm, but that didn't necessarily mean the perpetrator had done with me.

Now the name of Doctor Josiah Thorn had cropped up again, albeit in a very different context. Perhaps it was time for me to make his acquaintance.

TEN

B efore I could either set off for Buckland to present myself to Josiah Thorn or go down to Theo's house to tell him about the sinister foreigner, however, my own duties summoned me. Not to assist Judyth with her patient's long labour, however – and the thought of her seeking my help was indeed risible – but to treat a small boy who had fallen off the back of a cart and knocked himself out.

It was not until the early evening of the following day that I finally went to see Theo. He was in his office, and Jarman Hodge was with him.

'You come at an opportune time,' Theo greeted me. 'Hodge here has just got back. Jarman? Go on, please, with your report.'

'Like I was just saying,' Jarman Hodge began, 'I didn't reckon there was much point in returning to the warehouse, since both the doctor here and I have already spoken to the warehouseman who made that remark about the dead man, and it didn't seem likely he had anything to add. I considered cornering some of the other men who work there and I spied out the comings and goings at the warehouse for a while.' He paused, clearly thinking. 'There was . . . a mood among them. I reckon they were scared. Maybe they'd had a warning not to speak to strangers, not to discuss Quinlie's private business with outsiders. I can't say. But what I did observe was that there was no sign of the fat man with the fighting-cock walk. And,' he added while Theo and I were still digesting that, 'they've tightened up security.'

'Because Quinlie doesn't want to risk anyone else breaking in and robbing him like Jeromy did!' I exclaimed.

Jarman Hodge gave me a look. 'Or maybe because too many people have been lurking around asking questions.'

I shook my head in an attempt to clear my thoughts. This

whole affair was turning into a dense tangle and I was finding it difficult to see through it with any sort of clarity. 'There's something else,' I said after a moment and I told Theo and Hodge about Judyth's report of the mysterious foreigner.

They both stared at me. Then Theo said kindly, 'It's not much to go on, is it, Gabriel? He could have been anybody.'

'But she saw him, right there at the top of the path that leads up to the road from Old Ferry Quay!' I protested.

'And exactly who is this woman?' he asked.

'Her name's Judyth and she's a midwife. That explains what a woman was doing out alone late at night on the track by the river,' I said before anyone could ask, 'since she was on her way home from delivering a baby.'

Theo looked enquiringly at Jarman Hodge. 'Judyth . . . Penwarden, I believe,' Jarman said. 'Came up to the area from Cornwall, they say. Used to work out of Morwellham Quay but she had an argument with a local doctor there and lost, and now she's based just outside Blaxton, near where the ferry runs across the Tavy.'

Mentally I placed the location. 'That would put her exactly where she said she was if she'd been returning home from a hamlet further upriver!'

Jarman Hodge looked at me. 'It would,' he agreed.

'So what are we to do to find this stranger?' I demanded. Theo and Hodge exchanged a glance. 'It's very important – crucial – that we do,' I insisted. 'He could very well be a witness to Jeromy's murder, if not actively involved.'

'We're not saying he's unimportant,' Theo said pacifically. 'It's just – just—'

'A bit of a vague description,' supplied Hodge. 'You can't even be sure this sighting was on the night Jeromy Palfrey died, since we don't know exactly when that was.'

He was right, of course, and I had to admit it, if only to myself. 'Nicolaus Quinlie has dealings with many foreigners,' I said, with more confidence than I felt. 'It seems we can't prove or disprove the theory that Jeromy tried to steal Quinlie's Venetian silk, but what if he made an approach to one of Quinlie's richer clients and attempted to make a deal direct with him, cutting out Quinlie?'

Both Theo's and Hodge's politely disbelieving expressions suggested they thought I was floundering in deep water, about to go under. I was inclined to agree with them.

'As a hypothesis, it has a certain value,' Theo said carefully. 'But as to how you're going to set about verifying it . . .' He gave an eloquent shrug.

I noted he'd said *you*, not *we*.

It looked as if I was on my own with this particular line of enquiry.

I set off for Rosewyke. It was deep twilight, and the law-abiding villagers of Withybere had retired inside their houses and closed their doors. I could smell the woodsmoke of their fires. We were still in the month of May, and the temperature tended to drop sharply after sunset. I reached the turning for Rosewyke, and Hal automatically headed for home.

But I drew him up.

The idea had burst into my head out of nowhere. I knew I wanted to act upon it, and I also knew that, if I hesitated, good sense would undoubtedly overcome impetuosity and I'd have second thoughts.

I have to do this, I thought.

I turned Hal's head, put heels to his sides and headed down into Plymouth.

Such was Nicolaus Quinlie's fame in the town – in the whole area, probably – that everyone knew where his premises were located. I made my way down to the quay, keeping to the shadows as I led my horse along to the big warehouse at the end. As I approached, I slipped into the mouth of a dark little passage leading up between two neighbouring buildings, securing Hal to an iron tethering ring set in the wall. I took the precaution of turning him – not easy in the narrow space – so that he faced outwards. It was quite possible I might be in a hurry when I left.

The lower floor of the warehouse was one vast storage area, its heavy doors barred and bolted. A little Judas gate had been cut into one of them, and outside it a night watchman patrolled up and down. As I watched from the shadows, he muttered something to his companion, who was stationed further along the quay. It appeared that Nicolaus Quinlie's security measures had been increased here, too, as Jarman Hodge reported was the case in Dartmouth.

It didn't matter to me. I wasn't going to attempt to enter the warehouse.

I drew further into the darkness, looking up at the side of the tall building. Nothing. I edged towards the place where the side wall met the rear wall, and, peering round the corner, saw what I had hoped to see: a narrow stair – little more than a ladder – leading to a low door in the upper storey. The door, I thought, must have been designed to provide access for goods stored on the top floor of the warehouse, and, looking closely, I spotted a big beam jutting out on which there was a pulley, a frayed piece of rope dangling from it.

I sprinted along the rear wall and climbed the perilous stairs. The little door was locked – naturally – and the cumbersome clasp was solid and stout. But I didn't think it was going to defeat me. I reached into the pouch at my belt and took out the small implement I always carry.

One of the first ship's surgeons under whom I learned my craft had shown me how to pick locks. He'd hinted at a degree of criminality in his past, but, since that was true of quite a lot of men serving in the Queen's navy, it wasn't really anything to remark upon. He'd taken a deal of satisfaction when I proved an apt pupil, expressing the opinion that one day I'd be glad of the tuition.

I'd already been glad of it quite a few times, but never more so than tonight.

I closed the low door behind me and stood up, looking about me. There was still a little light in the western sky and it flooded in through the windows, adequate for my purposes. I was in a passage that ran right across the back of the ware-house, in which there were several doors. I began methodically to open them.

The first couple opened readily. A storeroom smelling strongly of hessian; a room in which there was a carpenter's bench and tools and several packing cases, another in the process of being made. The third door was locked.

The precious little implement was still in my hand. I set to work.

It was a large room, with two windows overlooking the quay below. I crossed on soft feet to look out. One watchman stood just below me, the other was leaning against the wall at the corner of the warehouse, over to my right. Both were gazing out indifferently over the water. With a nod of satisfaction, I went back to my perusal of the room. There was a wide oak desk with an ornate chair behind it, its back and arms beautifully carved. Several large, stoutly made chests stood around the walls; one had not been quite closed, its heavy lid propped up by a stack of documents within. The top of the table was strewn with piles of folios, bundled together and tied with tape.

It looked as if I had located Nicolaus Quinlie's office.

Now that I was there, I had no idea how to set about my search. What, indeed, was I hoping to find? The whole escapade seemed impetuous and stupid, and I was tempted to creep away before my presence was discovered.

Still, I thought, *I'm here now. I may as well have a poke around.*

I picked up a pile of the bundles on the table. Holding them so that the dying light fell upon them, I studied them. The documents within were a mass of figures in neat columns, with headings that seemed to pertain to the cargos that Quinlie imported. *Seta reale, indigo and emerald. Viridian. Crimson.* In another document there was a long list of spices, followed by several columns of incomprehensible figures.

I worked my way through everything that was on Quinlie's table. There wasn't anything there that didn't belong in the workplace of a prosperous, hard-working merchant. With an exclamation of disgust – at myself, for having embarked on this ridiculous enterprise – I crossed the room to have a look inside the partly open chest.

I found more of the same: stacks and stacks of neatly tied documents, their dates going back, by the time I was delving around at the bottom of the chest, for a decade and more. As on the table, everything was correct and orderly.

Tucked away in the base of the chest I found a slim bundle

of documents labelled in a different hand from the majority of
the rest. The papers – only a handful – were bound between
leather covers, and the top one had a decoration – a crest
of some sort? – tooled into its surface. Within the indenta-
tions of the design I made out vestiges of gold paint. I picked
up the file and went over to the window to seek what was
left of the twilight.

The top paper had one word written on it, but the letters
were smudged, worn as if with much handling. I held it
right up to my eyes. *Laz-* something, and the word ended
in *to*.

I couldn't think of a word, or words, that it could be. Lazy
something? Lapis lazuli? The latter made slightly more sense,
for the precious blue stone from which ultramarine blue paint
and dyes are made was the sort of commodity in which Quinlie
dealt. I looked at the remaining pieces of paper.

They were only four of them, and all were blank. But the
leather covers had a spine that was wide enough for a great
deal of documents; someone had removed them. Quinlie? I
hurried back to the big table, checking again through the tied
bundles. There was nothing bearing any similarity to *Laz . . .
to*. Had he taken the documents home, to work on them in
greater privacy?

I'd had enough. I removed the top page of the *Laz . . .
to* bundle and slipped it inside my tunic, then put the leather-
bound file back where I had found it, replacing everything as
neatly as I could and leaving the lid of the chest at the same
angle. Then I left.

I negotiated the ladder-like stairs without trouble and crept
back up the passage, peering out to see where the watchmen
were before hurrying along to where I'd left Hal. I led him
out on to the quay and mounted, and was on my way before
anyone had time to call out and demand to know what I thought
I was doing.

Once I was away from the waterfront, where there is rarely
a time when everyone is asleep and all is silent, Plymouth had
more or less retired for the night. I had eight or nine miles to
cover and I was already tired. Once Hal and I were past the
lightly populated fringes of the town and the countryside

opened up before us, I clicked encouragingly to him and he quickened his pace.

We were nearly home. I could see Rosewyke up ahead, and I was just remarking to Hal that he'd soon be settling down in his stall when it happened. He'd been moving at a leisurely, comfortable canter and suddenly, as if his legs had been cut from beneath him, he fell. I was thrown clear, and instantly I tried to stand to check whether my horse was hurt. It seemed not, for already he was scrambling to his feet. I stumbled over to him to take hold of his reins, soothe and reassure him, when I sensed a swift movement behind me, accompanied by a sort of whistling sound. Before I could spin round to look, something struck me very hard on the back of the head.

PART TWO

ELEVEN

I don't think I lay insensate for long. When I opened my eyes, groaning with pain, it seemed that the moon had only advanced a few degrees in her course. Very carefully I sat up. Apart from dealing with the agony inside my head, I was very worried that the blow might have set off the terrible dizziness again. I felt around my skull with my fingertips, trying to locate where I'd been hit – the pain seemed to be everywhere at once – and it was with some relief that I came across a large swelling on the back of my head. The blow, thank the good, merciful Lord, hadn't hit the vulnerable spot behind my ear.

I got onto my knees, then up onto my feet. I felt shaky, but not dizzy. I walked very slowly across to Hal, who was grazing unconcernedly beside the track, and, leaning against him, encouraged him to lead me away towards the house.

Who had attacked me? Had someone followed me from Nicolaus Quinlie's warehouse? It seemed unlikely, for I had been very careful, watching out all along the route, and I was almost certain nobody had seen me.

I tripped and almost fell.

Something had caught me across the legs, just above the knee.

A rope had been tied, its ends secured to trees either side of the track up to my house.

Into my mind came images of the various items left on my doorstep. Perhaps this latest attack was nothing to do with my having explored Nicolaus Quinlie's office, but down to somebody closer to home who, disheartened at my showing no sign of packing up and moving away in response to their threats so far, had decided to harm me personally?

It was an uncomfortable thought.

Samuel heard me come into the yard and came out to take Hal, for which I was very grateful. The bump on my head was throbbing in time to my heartbeat and I knew I would have found it very hard to give my horse the attention he deserved. I wished Samuel a curt goodnight – I didn't mention the rope; I'd untied it and left it coiled up in the undergrowth – and went into the house.

Lying in bed a short time later, flooded with relief at no longer being on my feet, I decided that in the morning I would allow nothing to stop me making the long-postponed excursion to locate and speak to Josiah Thorn.

I had tried to seek him out before but failed. This time, riding out the next morning, I was utterly determined. The inhabitants of Buckland again met my enquiries with blank faces, so I tried another approach. 'I need his help,' I said to a woman busy on her vegetable plot. 'I've suffered a blow to the head and I'm told he's an excellent doctor.'

She studied me. 'He's getting on a bit and he doesn't want any new patients,' she said, her doubtful expression suggesting she was torn between defending the man's privacy and the urge to help someone in need.

I kept silent. Sometimes words don't really help.

'Oh, I suppose he wouldn't want to think he'd failed an injured man,' she muttered. 'Up that track, left by the big oak tree and it's the house at the end of the lane.'

Josiah Thorn had impressed me even before I met him. A man who had won the loyalty of the men and women he had treated, to the extent that they pretended not to know his whereabouts when asked by nosy strangers, had to be worth seeking out.

His house was modest, well maintained and isolated. It was up on a slight rise, and beyond it the ground fell away towards the river. Nearer at hand, a little stream bubbled merrily in a narrow, shallow valley. I rode into a cobbled yard, dismounted and tethered Hal, then crossed to the low door in the rear wall of the house and knocked.

I thought I heard a noise: a rustle, as if someone had moved quickly. I spun round. There was nobody there. Nevertheless, I felt my skin crawl, and I would have sworn someone was watching me.

But just then I heard footfalls from within the house and the door creaked grudgingly open, revealing a tall but stooped figure with long dark auburn hair widely streaked with grey beneath a close-fitting cap, dressed in a robe of black wool with embroidered lapels. He had the pale skin that often goes with auburn hair, and it was blotched with what were either age spots or freckles. Keen eyes stared out from bushy eyebrows, and a surprisingly strong voice – for the man was old – said, 'Yes? What do you want?'

It was a moment for truth. 'I'm called Gabriel Taverner,' I replied, 'I live at Rosewyke, on the river near Tavy St Luke, and I practise as a physician.'

Josiah Thorn nodded, a smile playing around his mouth. 'You do, do you?'

'I've spent many years at sea and a few at college in London,' I went on. 'I owe you an apology, sir, for I should have sought you out sooner to advise you of my presence.'

'And that, you believe, would have been sufficient to stop me becoming tetchy because you had taken my patients?'

'I'm not sure I have,' I countered. 'I've—'

The old man's smile had spread. 'You'd better come in,' he said, opening the door more widely. As he stood back, allowing me to walk into his house, he said, 'I was joking, by the way. As far as I'm concerned, you can take every last one of them and I'd thank you for it.' He took my elbow, encouraging me along a low, dark passage and into a sunny room with worn but comfortable furnishings. 'Sit, sit,' he urged, pushing me towards a settle beside the hearth, 'and I'll fetch us a glass of something reviving.'

Over the course of the next hour or so, I learned quite a lot about Josiah Thorn. He gave the impression of a man who spent a lot of his time on his own; from choice, it appeared, but, as with most people in that position, it seemed that when he had the chance to talk, he didn't readily stop.

He told me he was trying to retire, 'only my . . .' There he paused. 'Only others are finding it hard to accept that I really want to.' He failed to explain that enigmatic remark. He was becoming infirm, he said, and it was time to put his own needs first. 'I'm a bit of a cripple,' he said ruefully, grasping his left knee and giving it quite a violent shake, as if its fallibility offended him. 'I've had enough of being summoned at all hours of the day and night and in all weathers to see to people who've been daft enough to cut themselves, knock themselves out, break limbs, catch nasty diseases, have babies and die. I'm—'

I interrupted him; no mean feat, for he had been talking without pause ever since he'd handed me my glass of canary wine and sat down opposite me. 'I know you still deliver babies, sir, for I have made the acquaintance of a midwife whom you recently summoned to assist you.'

His expression softened. 'The lovely Judyth,' he said. 'Yes, indeed. Mind you' – he leaned forward confidingly – 'I'm not above sending for Judyth even when I don't really need her help, just for the pleasure of her company. She's a fine midwife, mark you,' he added reprovingly, as if I'd suggested otherwise. 'Knows her craft remarkably well, and has a very special touch that you rarely see . . . yes, yes, Queen Mab trained that one all right.'

Queen Mab . . .?

'The fairies' midwife,' Josiah Thorn explained. He must have seen I hadn't understood. 'You need to know things like that, doctor, if you intend to practise your skills hereabouts.'

'Quite so,' I murmured.

There was a brief pause. Then he said, 'Why did you leave the sea?' I told him about my head injury and the development of the seasickness that followed it.

He nodded. 'And this blow to the head was where?' I pointed.

He leapt up, swooping down on me and feeling around behind my ear. 'You damaged your organ of balance, like as not,' he murmured, giving the vulnerable spot a bit of a poke that set off the faintest echo of a spinning head. 'Ears aren't just for hearing, you know!'

Abandoning me as quickly as he'd shot across to examine me, he dived for a stack of parchments, pamphlets and bound volumes on a table under the window, rummaged around for a short time and then picked up a slim volume, waving it at me. 'Read this!' he commanded. 'It's a new theory by some

Frenchman – or maybe he's a Spaniard – on the anatomy of the inner ear. It may help, you never know.' He threw the book to me.

'Thank you,' I said. 'I will make sure to return it to you.'

'No need, no need!' he sang. 'I've already read it and, as I keep telling you, I'm going to retire. Ah, yes,' he went on, resuming his seat and throwing an arm along the back of the settle, 'I'm looking forward immeasurably to retirement, even if it does mean no more long nights shoulder to shoulder with the beautiful Judyth.' He shot me a swift and mischievous glance. 'Know what I'm going to do with myself?'

'No, sir.'

'I'm going to spend my days hobbling down to the river and dozing away the hours with a fishing rod in my hand, watching the birdlife.' He gave a happy smile and slurped up the last of his wine. 'That's the life for me.'

'So . . .' This was tricky, but, given the true purpose of my visit, I had to ask. 'So you really don't resent my presence in the area? You wouldn't try to—' I hesitated – 'to do anything to try to persuade me I ought not to settle here?'

Suddenly Josiah Thorn looked wary. 'What do you mean?' he asked, dropping his voice to a whisper.

I took a breath and told him. About the dog faeces, the dead mice, the square of linen soaked in blood, the rotting calf's foot alive with maggots, the rat and the headless blind-worm. To my surprise, he began to smile and a soft chuckle broke out of him.

That made me angry.

So, hardening my voice, I said, 'Those are the milder of the offerings. There has also been a pleasant little bundle comprising the cut-out reproductive organs of a pregnant sow and only last night someone stretched a rope across my route home to trip me up, felling both my horse and me, and, not content with that, they struck me on the back of the head as I tried to get up.' I glared at him. 'You might care to know that my housekeeper was the one who discovered the sow's organs, and she was greatly distressed, and that, although my horse suffered no ill effects for being tripped, I now have a second injury to my head which is right now causing me a great deal of pain.' *And,* I almost added, *seeing you sitting here laughing is tempting me to hit you, too.*

But I didn't. He was older than me and, by his own admission, he was crippled and infirm.

And moreover, even as I'd been ranting at him his amusement had changed to distress.

'Oh, no,' he whispered. 'Not that – not *any*thing like that.'

'You have knowledge of this?' I demanded, leaning towards him. 'You suspect someone of involvement, perhaps?'

He pulled away from me, leaning right back in his seat. 'No,' he repeated, his eyes wide in his suddenly pale face.

'You must tell me!' I urged. 'Do you not think I have a right to know of any suspicions of yours that might help me track down who is responsible?'

But now he was on his feet, grabbing hold of my arm, pulling me to my feet and dragging me back along the passage. He was strong, for an old man, and his grip was hard and tight. He opened the door and all but pushed me out.

I spun round. 'You can't—' I began.

But he had already slammed the door. I heard the sound of bolts being shot home. It seemed he'd left me with no alternative but to give up.

For now.

My mood had worsened by the time I got home. Everywhere I turned, people were there to stand in my way, thwart me, prevent me finding out what I had to know. Angry, my head aching, I flung Hal's reins in Tock's direction as the poor lad came stumbling out to greet me, whatever pleasantry he was going to stammer out stalling on his clumsy tongue.

I stomped through the house and up the stairs to my study, and dragged out from its hiding place in my bookshelf the single sheet of paper I'd extracted from the otherwise empty file in Quinlie's office. Laz . . . to. Lazuli *to* someone? It was the best I could do. And just who, I wondered, had stolen the rest of the documents? And why? Lapis lazuli was expensive, certainly, so was this about theft, on a dangerously large scale?

I sat there for some time. Slowly I became aware that Sallie was calling me. I'd missed the midday meal, so doubtless she was asking me if I wanted food. 'I'm not hungry,' I yelled from where I sat, not bothering to get up and hear what she was saying.

Presently she came puffing into the room. 'Mistress Celia's here,' she announced, managing to sound accusatory even through the panting. '*Some* people,' she added pointedly, 'think it courteous to go down and greet their visitors, especially when it's their own sister.'

Sometimes, I reflected, having Sallie as my housekeeper was like being back in the nursery, with a very strict and demanding nurse.

I crossed the hall and hugged Celia, then took hold of her hands and held her at arm's length so that I could look at her. 'You're looking better for some parental nurturing,' I said, and she smiled. 'Are you coming back here now?' Still holding one of her hands, I led her into the parlour. Sallie, watching, gave a nod of approval and muttered something about fetching a good, warming drink and a bite to eat.

Celia pushed back the hood of her cloak and sat down. She looked up at me. 'I'll come back soon,' she said. 'Very soon,' she amended. 'For one thing, if I go on staying at Fernycombe, I'm going to have to be a bit more sociable.' She grimaced. 'Mother's insisting.'

'It'd do you good,' I said. 'Life goes—'

'Life goes on,' she finished for me. 'Yes, I know. I get told as much several times a day,' she added with a wry smile. 'But now, I need a favour from you.'

'Anything.'

'Come to Ferrars with me.'

'I thought I'd already cleared out everything you want.' I'd dropped my voice to a whisper.

She gave me a very loving smile. 'You did marvellously. But there's something I keep hidden, and so well that you wouldn't have found it unless I'd told you where to look. It's my old jewellery casket, with some rather precious items in it. I'd hate anyone else to have that.'

I didn't need to be asked twice. We paused only for as long as it took to gulp down the spiced ale and little tarts that Sallie had brought, then set off.

* * *

We found my sister's former dwelling cold and deserted. There was nobody there; the servants, I guessed, had all melted away, since there was nobody now to pay their wages, no food in the larder, no master and mistress to minister to. I wondered what had become of Ruth. She, or so I'd thought, had a real affection for Celia. Even that, however, wouldn't be sufficient to keep her in a damp, empty house where there was nothing to eat and which quite soon would be inhabited by strangers. What would be the point?

I waited in the hall while Celia went up to her room to fetch her casket. She was gone for some time, and I was beginning to be concerned – had she been overcome by grief? Had revisiting the room and the very bed she'd shared with her adored husband proved too much? – when I heard her calling me.

I raced up the stairs and through a succession of other rooms into her bedchamber. She was kneeling before the empty hearth, clutching the brass-bound oak casket that my father had given her when she was fourteen and in which she'd kept her treasures ever since. The fireplace had a border of large, decorative tiles – gaudy things, the colours in my view too bright and unsubtle – and the bottom one had been pushed aside to reveal a deep, shadowy space.

I crouched beside her. 'Did you make that very convenient hiding place?'

She shook her head. 'No. It was already here, and I discovered it one day when I dropped my thimble. Look.' She replaced the tile and then reached for some hidden catch on its top edge that released it again.

I peered into the dark cavity, which was about a foot long and half as much wide. 'Was there anything in it?'

'Sadly not, other than spiders' webs and some dead flies.'

She was looking at me wide-eyed, and I couldn't read her expression. 'Your casket!' I exclaimed. 'Is everything there that ought to be?'

'Yes, yes.' She waved an impatient hand. 'But, Gabe, someone else knew about my hiding place.' She reached under the wide folds of her skirts and handed me a bundle of documents.

I took them from her.

I knew straight away what they were, and I guessed who had put them in the cavity. Well, that was pretty obvious. But this new discovery threatened to reveal – or rather confirm – things about Jeromy that it was perhaps best for Celia not to know. Not yet, anyway.

'I wonder what they are,' I said in what I hoped was a suitably casual tone. 'Documents to do with Jeromy's business affairs, probably. Would you like me to have a look?'

I wasn't sure if I'd fooled her. She gave me quite an assessing glance, then nodded. 'Thanks,' she said curtly.

I rode with her back to Fernycombe. After kissing me goodbye, she went upstairs to her room, saying that she wanted to go through her casket on her own. My mother and I exchanged a glance and she raised her eyebrows. 'How do you think she is?' she whispered as soon as we'd heard Celia's door close.

I shrugged. 'I'm not sure. When I look at her and see that expression of misery, it seems she's no better. But, on the other hand, she has more colour in her cheeks, and once or twice I've seen a fleeting glimpse of her old, happy smile.'

My mother nodded. 'Yes. Perplexing isn't it?' She frowned. 'I wish your father was here, because then the three of us could have had a good, long talk, but he won't be home till late tonight and I suppose, as usual, you're in a hurry?'

I had to look away from the hopeful expression in her eyes. I wasn't in a hurry at all – not in the sense she meant, which was my working life – but I was burning with curiosity to examine those documents.

I leaned down and kissed her, hugging her close for a moment. 'I'll come back soon,' I said. 'I promise.'

Back at Rosewyke, I told Sallie I wasn't to be disturbed and raced up to my study, where I closed the door firmly and pointedly behind me. I lit a couple of lamps – it was getting dark now – spread out the thick sheaf of documents on my desk and set about trying to make sense of them.

After quite a long time, I leaned back in my chair and threw my quill on to the floor; I'd had it in my hand primed with ink, in order to make notes on all the things I was going to discover. Only there weren't any, because, as far as I could tell, the documents contained nothing more than details of payments made by Nicolaus Quinlie to a person or organization in Venice. There was nothing suspicious about that since he traded with Venice, and undoubtedly had many contacts there. The whole collection was just about to join my quill on the floor when I suddenly thought, *why* did Jeromy remove them from Quinlie's office and hide them in Celia's secret place? They were undoubtedly the documents from that almost empty file, for the same crest appeared on many of them.

My excitement rising again, I had another look.

The payments went back years. Four times a year, on the Quarter Days, Nicolaus Quinlie paid a substantial sum of money to someone with the initials LN. Did the L stand for that word beginning with Laz? And I was almost certain that the N word would end in -to.

And this had been going on for a quarter of a century . . .

Then I guessed – no, I *knew*, with utter certainty – that Jeromy Palfrey, so good at winkling out other people's secrets, had found out something about his employer, and it was something that Quinlie really didn't want known. Had Jeromy hoped to use the information to put pressure on Quinlie? We knew that Jeromy had overspent wildly and ended up deeply in debt, and, if some of those debts were owed to his stern and unforgiving employer, it must have seemed like a gift from heaven when Jeromy found the documents. How, though, had he known they were so sensitive?

It was all so tentative; so circumstantial. I felt in my bones that I now knew why Jeromy had been murdered, and who had murdered him, but proving it was going to be nigh-on impossible. I doubted that Quinlie had stuck that terrible blade into Jeromy himself; he'd have employed a killer, and undoubtedly an efficient one, who seemed to have disappeared leaving no trace and no clue, and—

Judyth's mysterious foreigner.

Something was rapping at my brain, trying to get my attention. I made a great effort to empty my mind and still my thoughts, in the hope of giving whatever it was a chance to make itself heard.

Nothing happened.

So I tried to give it a little nudge. Sinister stranger, perhaps masked. Hired killer. Venice. Laz . . . to. Payments made for a quarter of a century to some person, or institution, that had to remain anonymous. A secret that had at all costs to be kept, even if that cost was murder.

I thought so hard I made my head ache.

Still nothing.

TWELVE

I slept long, deep and dreamlessly; the result of my disturbed night, the blow to my head and the frustrations and anxieties of the day. After a swift breakfast, I called to Samuel to saddle Hal and rode off to see William. It was more than three weeks since he'd had his injury and, although I'd seen him a couple of times to remove the clamps and the ligatures and generally keep an eye on the healing, now it was time to see if there was any loss of strength in the arm and the hand.

It wasn't the only reason for this morning's visit.

I found William out in the yard. He was watching over the lad who was washing out the dairy, and it was very apparent that he longed to do the job himself. Suppressing my instant thought – *isn't the dairy traditionally the preserve of the farmer's wife?* – I tethered Hal and strode over to him. 'How does it feel?' I asked, indicating his left arm.

'Morning, doctor,' he greeted me, grinning. 'It feels good. It's been driving me mad with the itching, but Black—' He stopped, blushing. 'But I'm told that's a sign of healing.'

'You're told right,' I said shortly. 'If you can leave that boy to his own devices for a short while, I'll have a look.'

We went inside the house and William took off his jerkin and shirt. I inspected the wound – it had been a little inflamed, but now it felt cool, and the faint pinkness had gone – and then I put William through a series of movements, steadily increasing the range. Finally I got him to grip my hand, as hard as he could.

'The arm is still weak,' I said as he dressed again. 'But I don't believe there's any lasting damage. Strength will build up again with use.' I smiled at his radiant face. 'Go and take the broom out of that lad's hands and finish sluicing the dairy.'

He stopped just long enough to express fulsome thanks, then hurried out.

I had been aware, as I tended William, that there were others in the house; in the kitchen at the back, I guessed from the direction of the small sounds. I went through to see if I was right.

Katharine sat at the table and Black Carlotta stood behind her, leaning against the stone sink. I nodded to the old healer, then, addressing Katharine, said, 'William's arm has healed well. It will now be beneficial for him to use it, but don't let him do too much, and send for me if it pains him unduly.' I glanced again at Black Carlotta as I turned to leave. 'Good day to you both.'

I hadn't gone very far along the track when I heard someone call, 'Oi!'

I reined in Hal and waited.

'You can sit up there if you like,' Black Carlotta panted as she caught me up, 'but we'll hear each other better if we're walking side by side.'

I dismounted. I didn't speak.

After a while she said, 'I admit I've glanced at William's arm once or twice, although that's all I've done. He said the wound itched like the devil and I told him not to scratch it or he'd have you to answer to, and so should I.'

'And you told him the itching meant it was healing.'

She shot me a glance. 'Aye, that too.'

We walked on for several paces. Then she said, 'I wasn't there this morning to see your patient, if that's what you're thinking.'

'I wasn't thinking anything,' I said mildly.

'Katharine's with child. She'd been bleeding – only a few spots, but, given what happened last time, she was beside herself – and William came for me in a panic at first light.'

'Is she all right?' I asked swiftly.

Black Carlotta smiled. 'She is. Far as I can tell, anyway. I told her to have a restful few days' – that explained the fact that William had taken over supervision of the dairy – 'and I said I'd send someone else along to speak to her.'

'Judyth,' I murmured.

'Aye,' she agreed. 'Met her, have you?'

'Yes.'

'She couldn't be in better hands than Judyth's,' Black Carlotta observed.

'Trained by Queen Mab,' I said.

Again she shot me that assessing look. 'Didn't think they knew about Queen Mab in London or on the Queen's ships.'

'They don't.' I paused. Then, since this was precisely what I'd wanted to discuss with Black Carlotta if, as I'd hoped, I found her at the farm: 'I've been to see Josiah Thorn.'

'Ah.' There was a pause. 'Told him your woes, did you?'

'I did.'

She nodded. 'Then you'll have no more reeking objects left at your door. Unless' – again, that sharp look – 'you've attracted the anger of someone else.'

'What does Josiah Thorn know?' I demanded. 'How can you be so sure that my having told him will make it stop?'

'Not my secret to tell, doctor.' Firmly she closed her mouth. I didn't know her well – I didn't know her at all – but I realized that pressing her would get me nowhere.

There was nothing else we had to say to each other. I wished her good day, mounted Hal and, kicking him to a trot and then a canter, rode away.

The next day – it was Saturday – I had a visit from Theophilus Davey. As I went outside to greet him and invite him in, he said, 'I'm not stopping – family dinner with my mother-in-law.' He made a rueful face. 'I just wanted to say that I think Jarman Hodge and I may have caused you offence when we didn't pay much heed to your story of the mysterious foreigner, and I wanted to apologize.'

'No apology necessary,' I said with a smile, deliberately putting to the back of my mind how cross they'd made me at the time.

'And also,' Theo went on, 'maybe it wasn't so unlikely after all, given that it seems that the murder weapon wasn't made anywhere hereabouts.'

'No?'

He shook his head. 'No. I've had a couple of men look at it who reckon they know about such things, and they say it's of foreign manufacture.'

And Nicolaus Quinlie was a merchant who traded with distant lands, in particular, Venice.

I met Theo's eyes. 'A hired killer would use a weapon with which he was familiar. One made, perhaps, in his own land.'

Theo nodded. 'It's no sort of proof,' he said quickly, 'but it may be something we ought to consider.'

'There's something else to consider.' I was thinking of the documents I'd found tucked away in Celia's secret hiding place. Theo frowned briefly, and I remembered he'd said he was pressed for time. 'But I won't detain you now. May I come to see you on Monday?'

'Of course.' He touched a hand to his cap. 'Until Monday, then.' He put heels to his horse's sides and set off back down the track.

I had thought that by deliberately *not* trying to puzzle out the tantalizing and elusive little thought that was niggling at me I might allow it room to surface, but it hadn't worked. In the morning, I rode over to Fernycombe as arranged to attend service with my parents, brother and sister, after which we were all to dine together before Celia returned to Rosewyke with me. The vicar was renowned for his sermons, in which, in the thundering, blood-soaked language of the more violent parts of the Old Testament, he used stories from those colourful books to illustrate his somewhat heavy-handed comments and strictures on contemporary life. Today his choice was the story of Moses and the horrors wrought upon Egypt by God in his determination to win freedom for his people and demonstrate just how far his powers exceeded those of the puny Egyptian gods.

I have to admit to only half-listening. The remainder of my mind was roaming freely, touching now on that deadly weapon, now on my sister's widowhood, now on Judyth's light-filled silvery-blue eyes.

Boils.

I shot up straight, the movement so violent that my elbow jerked into my father, sitting stiff and attentive beside me. He shot me an angry scowl, and I muttered an apology.

Why, I wondered, hadn't the realization dawned as soon as

the vicar started talking about plagues? I could only think it was because in the context of the terrible story of the ten catastrophes the word has a slightly different meaning, one we all know well enough not to give it much thought.

It was only when we arrived at number six, the plague of boils, that understanding came. Perhaps, without my noticing, the very mention of boils had roused my attention, since I see so many of them. From there it was a logical move to think of the frightful boils of plague patients; especially as the vicar kept repeating the word *plague*.

I forced aside the intense frustration that it had taken me so long and threw myself into examining what had come so suddenly to mind.

When I was at sea, we voyaged frequently in the Mediterranean and once went right up into the Adriatic, sailing up its eastern coast and putting in at a couple of islands under the control of the Venetians. I forget now the precise reason, but I seem to recall it was to get an idea of how they had set about fortifying their Dalmatian strongholds. On a shore run I fell into conversation with a doctor; a Venetian who, like me, practised his trade at sea. There was at the time an outbreak of sickness on a ship that had arrived from Constantinople, and we were all worried in case the illness was the plague (it wasn't; it turned out to be food poisoning). This Venetian doctor told me all about how they dealt with the threat of plague in his native city.

'We depend on trade for our very existence,' he explained. 'We cannot afford to turn ships away, yet, for our own survival, we must do our utmost to make sure neither the crew nor the cargo brings the pestilence. Our ambassadors in cities with whom we trade are required to report any outbreaks of sickness in order that our city has due warning. Every ship wishing to enter Venetian territory is stopped by the blockade that marks the boundary of our waters, where all documentation is scrupulously checked. If infection is discovered or even suspected, the ship and everything on board, including the men, is removed to an island in the lagoon and must stay there until the danger period is past.'

In answer to my questions, the Venetian had gone on to

describe his work as a plague doctor. 'The disease is an abomination,' he said simply. 'The fortunate ones die within the day. The unlucky writhe in a white-hot heat of agony for perhaps as much as a week. The huge boil-like buboes are the worst torment, for they cause bleeding beneath the skin and whole areas of the body – the armpit, the groin – turn purple and then black. Fever mounts, the sufferer becomes incoherent and death is the only end.'

And how, I asked, did he protect himself from infection?

'Before I venture among the desperate, suffering victims I put on a heavy, moisture-repellent cloak and gloves, and I pick up my cane,' he told me. 'The cloak and the gloves are for my protection; the cane is to keep the healthy at a distance, for, while I still wear my protective garments, the deadly plague miasmas crawl upon me and it is not safe to approach.'

And, finally, he told me how he covered his head and face.

'I wear a hood, of the same fabric as my cloak, and it fits tightly so as to cover my hair and my flesh. On my face I wear a mask, with crystal eyepieces to look through and a long beak through which to breathe. The beak – it is nearly as long as my forearm – is stuffed with herbs that counter the polluted air. Various substances are employed, but to speak for myself, I favour cloves, pepper and camphor.' He smiled briefly. 'So far, they have kept me safe, and I pray God they continue to do so.'

'Amen,' I said.

Now, sitting in my father's pew in a Devon church, I shivered in horror at the memory. And I knew, without a doubt, what it was I'd been trying to bring to mind: Judyth's description of her mysterious stranger's mask precisely matched that worn by my long-ago colleague.

The killer had used a weapon of foreign manufacture: almost certainly, it was Venetian. He had disguised himself in the sinister guise of a Venetian plague doctor. And Nicolaus Quinlie's main income derived from trading in Venetian silk.

My mind was racing and it took all my willpower to remain in my seat for the last, endless hour of the service.

*   *   *

The following morning I left my sister, newly reinstalled at Rosewyke, sorting through the multiplicity of objects – furniture, fabric, curtains, rugs, paintings, personal possessions – that I had purloined from Ferrars on her behalf, and rode off to my meeting with Theo. I was shown into his office in the usual offhand way, where I found him in intense conversation with Jarman Hodge.

They broke off as I came in. 'Jarman has been pursuing an investigation of his own,' Theo said, 'and we'll tell you about it directly. But, first, what have *you* to tell *us*?'

As succinctly as I could, and trying not to include my personal opinion and speculation, I explained how I'd searched Nicolaus Quinlie's office – I didn't dwell on the fact that I'd picked the locks and broken in – and found the almost-empty file with the one document, and how the rest of the papers that had been in that file turned up at Ferrars, where only Jeromy could have hidden them. I was about to expound my theory as to what Jeromy had planned to do with them but I'd only got as far as 'Jeromy was deeply in debt and in serious financial trouble . . .' when Theo, nodding his understanding, interrupted me.

'And you reckon he planned to use these documents to put pressure on Quinlie to release him from his debts.' I nodded. 'A very dangerous ploy, with a man of Nicolaus Quinlie's nature,' Theo observed.

'Those papers must contain something of an extremely sensitive nature,' Jarman mused. 'Jeromy would have known what a tough man Quinlie is and so, to believe he had any chance of forcing his hand, the secret must have been one that Quinlie wanted very badly to keep to himself.'

They both looked expectantly at me. 'I have no idea what it is,' I confessed. 'The documents merely record a list of payments made over the last twenty-five years or so to some person or organization, and the only clue to its identity are the letters Laz . . . to.'

Once again, that little chime seemed to go off inside my head. *You know this*, I heard a voice tell me. *Think!*

But there was no time for reflection. Theo had turned to Jarman, and was inviting him to share the fruits of his recent investigation with me.

'I've been making more enquiries about Nicolaus Quinlie's past,' he began, 'and I've found out the name of the young woman he was betrothed to. Her name was Rose Willerton, and she was closely related to the Sidneys.'

'Quinlie was after the backing of a man of power and influence,' Theo put in, 'because even in his youth he had great ambitions, and saw his future as a major figure in England's status as a trading nation.'

I knew I ought to know the relevance of the name Sidney but I couldn't bring it to mind. Jarman, apparently perceiving my bemusement, said, 'Philip Sidney was the son of Lady Mary Dudley, the Earl of Leicester's sister.'

The Earl of Leicester. Robert Dudley, the late Queen's beloved Robin. Ah, yes. In terms of importance in Elizabeth's court, families didn't rank much higher.

'And Philip Sidney's aunt – his father's youngest sister – was called Suzannah,' Theo added; it was apparent that he and Jarman had talked all this over already – 'and she married Sir Ambrose Willerton, and Rose was their only child.'

'So . . .' I paused to work it out. 'Rose and Philip were cousins, and she was . . . well, she was some fairly close relative of Elizabeth's favourite.'

'Yes,' Hodge agreed.

No wonder Nicolaus Quinlie had wanted to marry her. 'What happened?'

'Well, Ambrose Willerton was from an old Catholic family – their estates were in Somerset – and Walsingham suspected he was involved in the Ridolfi Plot, although Ambrose denied it.'

Theo was watching me with a smile. 'I think you're going to have to prod his memory again, Jarman.'

'I was at sea during those turbulent times!' I protested. 'I had far more immediate dangers to worry about.'

'Of course you did,' Theo said soothingly. 'Go on, Jarman.'

'The Ridolfi Plot was an attempt by the Catholics to free Mary, Queen of Scots, and it allegedly had the support of the Spanish,' Hodge said. 'Mary was to be brought to London to supplant Elizabeth.'

'Who was Ridolfi?' I asked.

'He was an Italian banker, and he was said to have put up

a lot of the money. The plot failed, obviously, and the Queen's spymaster got busy rounding up all those he thought had a hand in it. He didn't find enough damning evidence on Ambrose Willerton to bring him to trial, but for some reason the common view was that Willerton had been one of the prime movers, and, as they say, mud sticks.'

'Whereupon Quinlie, whose sole reason for marrying Rose Willerton was presumably because of her formerly important and influential connections, instantly decided he no longer had any use for her.' I glanced at my two companions. 'It was convenient that she died when she did,' I remarked, thinking of the elaborate tomb that Hodge had earlier described.

There was a brief silence. 'Yes, I've been asking around about that, too,' Jarman said. He paused. 'Rose Willerton was buried in Somerset. Not at her family home, but in the village in which Nicolaus Quinlie had recently purchased a costly manor, presumably intending that it would be the marital home. The village is called Bircholt. It's in the west of the county, in the hills below Bristol.'

'The Quantocks, I believe,' Theo put in.

'Probably,' Jarman agreed. 'Pretty place, anyway, and not much more than a couple of days' ride from here if you keep up a good pace.'

Theo knew his man far better than I did. Even as I was still wondering where this would end, he said, 'What did you discover?'

'Only rumours, but interesting ones,' Hodge said softly. 'Such as, that great monument of a tomb has no occupant. That the men who bore Rose Willerton's coffin to her grave all disappeared mysteriously not long afterwards. That nobody ever knew *how* she died, so how can anyone be certain it was from natural causes and Quinlie didn't help that death along? That he was hand in hand with the Devil, who somehow spirited Rose away and she was never seen again.'

'Any truth in the tales?' Theo asked.

Hodge shrugged. 'They're persistent, I'll say that much. Mind you, nobody there had a good word to say for Nicolaus Quinlie. He sold up after Rose's death and came down to Plymouth, and they all reckon it was good riddance.'

'Derogatory stories have a way of attaching themselves to unpopular men,' I observed, 'especially when the men are very wealthy and important.'

'True,' agreed Theo.

'And,' added Jarman, 'when a man's as disliked as Nicolaus Quinlie, men don't hesitate to speak ill of him, perhaps in the hope that in some way he'll finally get the retribution he deserves.' Jarman stared into the distance, his eyes narrowed. 'I pick up a lot of information that way. People see me as an ally when I begin to dig for dirt on an unpopular man. What's it they say? *My enemy's enemy is my friend.*'

I studied him, trying not to make it obvious. Such a colour-less, unobtrusive figure: unmemorable, mild-seeming, yet what a quick and agile brain ticked away inside his head; what a sharp glance looked out from those ordinary-looking eyes. No wonder Theo valued him so highly.

A contemplative silence fell. I thought back over what we'd just learned, realizing how extraordinary it was . . . Was nobody going to speculate further? 'If Rose Willerton isn't in the tomb,' I burst out, 'then where in heaven's name is she? Is she alive, even?'

Jarman Hodge looked coolly at me. 'Couldn't say, doctor. Reckon there's only one man knows the truth of it, and I'm not planning on asking *him.*'

As I rode home, I began to wonder if Jarman's attitude wasn't perhaps the right one. It appeared we'd found out who had killed Jeromy and why. Perhaps we didn't know whose hand had wielded that ghastly blade, but there could be no doubt of whose pay he had been in. Nicolaus Quinlie knew that Jeromy had stolen the sensitive documents, guessed what he planned to do with them and forestalled any such hostile move by having him murdered. The killer had worn the disguise of a Venetian plague doctor, so even if anyone had seen him – as Judyth had – then they'd be none the wiser as to his identity.

Nicolaus Quinlie may or may not have murdered the woman he had promised to marry, but was it up to me to uncover the truth of it? As Jarman had hinted, you went up against Quinlie at your peril. Wouldn't it be wiser to look ahead rather than back into the past? I would be better employed, surely, helping my grieving sister make a new life for herself than persisting in my attempts to tie up every last strand of a mystery that was already a quarter of a century old.

I will put all this behind me, I resolved, *and I'll encourage Celia to do the same.* Jeromy was dead and buried, and his widow must mend her broken heart and look to the future. Perhaps she and I could go on a visit somewhere . . . I could take her to London to show her some of my old haunts, and even to see one or two of Shakespeare's newest offerings. It would take a deal of planning and quite a lot of persuasion, but what was to stop us?

Suddenly eager to put my plan into action, I dug my heels into Hal's sides and raced for home.

THIRTEEN

B
ut the optimistic future I'd been envisaging was not yet to be. I didn't see Celia that day to share my ideas with her, for she left word with Sallie that she was going to work on some sewing for the rest of the evening, would take a tray of supper in her room and have an early night. Then in the morning, a messenger came galloping up to my door, thrusting into my hand a crumpled piece of paper. I unfolded it, knowing even as I did so that something frightful had happened.

'Come immediately,' Theo had written. 'Quinlie found dead.'

The air of urgency had communicated itself to Samuel, for he was preparing Hal even as I raced into the yard. I fastened my leather bag behind the saddle, swung up onto Hal's back and clattered out to join the messenger. Then we were on our way, riding fast and without speaking for Plymouth and Nicolaus Quinlie's warehouse.

Theo was waiting for me at the top of the stairs. I'd been glad of the messenger's presence to show me the way, having entered by a less orthodox route on my only previous visit. Theo looked pale. He nodded to me, muttered his thanks for my swift arrival, then stepped back and allowed me to precede him into Quinlie's office.

There was a farmyard stench in the room.

Nicolaus Quinlie sat in a dignified pose, stiffly upright, hands resting on the beautifully carved arms of his chair, the rich, heavy silk of his elegant black robe glowing with a slight sheen as it fell in wide folds onto the floor. But there the gracious, civilized manner ended.

His wrists had been bound tightly to the chair arms. The top eight inches or so of the lacings of his beautiful velvet doublet had been loosened, and blood splashed out to soak the crisp white chemise.

His head was thrown back. His eyes were wide with agony and horror. His mouth yawned open, the jaws straining at an impossible angle.

A roughly shaped, sharp-edged piece of stone about the size of my clenched fist – granite, I thought, for the light caught glistening sparkles in it – had been shoved into his mouth.

The abomination had been done before death – some time before – and blood had flowed freely. His front teeth had been shattered and at least four more had been knocked out, and now lay on his breast. There were ragged tears at both corners of his mouth. His lower lip had split in a wide gash, and I could see the mashed and bloody gums inside his mouth.

I stepped away from him, in need of just a moment's recovery.

Theo said quietly, 'It's awful, isn't it? I've never seen anything like it.'

'Nor have I.' I was once more leaning over the corpse, now pushing back the doublet and the shirt. 'That stone didn't kill him.' I moved so that Theo could see what I had uncovered. 'It was this.'

The ivory hilt of a knife stuck up out of Nicolaus Quinlie's chest. The killer knew anatomy: the blade of the knife was at just the angle for the tip to have been driven deep into the heart.

Theo stood silent beside me. Then he said, 'Was it torture to make him talk? To reveal some secret?'

He was thinking, I guessed, of those papers that Jeromy had stolen. 'He was very obviously a man who had secrets, I grant you,' I replied. 'But as for making him talk, if the method of torture was that lump of granite, then it would have been counter-productive.'

Theo nodded. 'Eventually, yes, but what if the assailant thrust it in just a little way once or twice, to give Quinlie an idea of what to expect if he didn't provide the information?'

I inspected the ruined mouth more closely. 'I can't be certain, but I suspect this was just one very powerful and determined thrust,' I said. I added softly, 'I think the motive for this was sheer hatred.'

'Can we take him away?' Theo asked after a moment. 'You'll wish to examine the body thoroughly, I guess?'

'I'll do that, but it won't tell me more than I already know.' I straightened up, wiping my bloody hands on a clean fold of Quinlie's shirt.

Theo shook his head. 'I thought we had seen the end of all this,' he muttered. 'But now' – he scowled heavily, shooting the corpse a look of intense dislike – 'now this bugger's going to cause me even more sleepless nights.'

I watched as he summoned four of his men, who cut the cords binding Quinlie's wrists and then manoeuvred his body onto a stretcher. As they lifted him out of his chair there came a squelching sound and a latrine stench: in his terror, Quinlie had soiled himself.

The men bore their burden away, the dead face and the stone covered by a length of cloth. They manhandled it awkwardly through the door and down the stairs, and I looked out of the window to see them emerge onto the street and to the waiting cart. I wished that I'd never have to set eyes on it again, but all too soon, I well knew, I'd be bending over it in Theo's cellar.

'Are you staying?' Theo's voice brought me out of my dismal reverie. 'I don't believe there's any more to be found here – my men and I had a good look round while we were waiting for you.'

I was about to say *No, I'll follow you out*, but something stopped me. 'I think I'll have a poke around, all the same.'

A very brief smile creased Theo's face. 'Maybe you'll spot something you missed the other night, eh?'

I smiled back but didn't speak. It wasn't so far from the truth.

'See you later, then,' Theo said as he headed for the stairs.

I waited till all was quiet. The warehouse below was deserted: no doubt the discovery of the master's brutally mutilated corpse had caused the cessation of all work for the day. I wondered idly who would take over Nicolaus Quinlie's empire now that he was dead. Not that I cared overmuch.

I looked through the documents on his desk. To my ignorant eyes, they were of the same order as those I'd seen before. I went over to the chest, and once more rummaged down to the bottom to find the empty leather-bound folder. I didn't expect to learn anything more from it, and I wasn't really sure why I was even bothering to look at it.

But it wasn't empty any more.

It wasn't full, either, but where there had before been the one page with the crest and the Laz . . . to letters and a handful of blank sheets, now there were three sheets covered in neat writing: black ink and a sloping hand, the letters elegantly written and with quirky, pointed tails to the *g*s, *j*s, *p*s, *q*s and *y*s. Although these were predominantly words whereas the documents Jeromy had taken contained mainly figures, there was enough of an overlap to detect that the same hand had written both. The hand, I strongly suspected, of Nicolaus Quinlie.

I tried to read the words but they were in a language with which I wasn't familiar. It was similar to Latin: Vulgar Latin, perhaps?

Or was it the language of Venice?

I ran my eyes down the close lines of text, searching for understanding. And then suddenly a word jumped out at me: *Lazaretto*.

At Theo's house, I found him speaking quietly to Jarman Hodge in the hall. He looked at me and nodded in the direction of the cellar. 'He's down there,' he said briefly, and I followed him down the steps.

Nicolaus Quinlie's body lay on the trestle where Jeromy's had lain before him. I stepped forward, pushed back my sleeves and began my examination of the body.

After a while I sensed Theo's restlessness. 'What's the matter?' I asked quietly.

'I can't say I liked the man,' he replied, 'but it doesn't seem right, him lying there with that great stone stuck in his mouth. It looks so . . . uncomfortable.' He smiled briefly as if at his own sentiment. 'Can't you remove it?'

'No.' I demonstrated, taking hold of the stone and trying to move it. It didn't shift, being set firm in the jaws like steel in a stone. 'The body takes on a rigour after death and, until it passes, the sinews lock up tight.'

Theo leaned forward to look. 'How long will that take?'

'It varies, but it won't be before a day or two. Its presence, however, serves as an indication of how long a body's been dead, since it sets in a few hours after life is extinguished. In this case, I'd say Quinlie died late last night.'

'Do you think the same hand killed him as stuck that blade into Jeromy Palfrey?'

'I can't say.' I stood back, frowning. 'I had been thinking that perhaps that was the case: Quinlie wanted to rid himself of the threat that Jeromy posed and so paid his mysterious foreigner to kill him, then – let's say, for example, because Quinlie refused to pay him as well or as swiftly as he'd promised – the killer has reason to murder his employer as well.'

'That's plausible,' Theo said. I didn't answer. 'Isn't it?' he prompted.

'It is,' I agreed, 'but something tells me it didn't happen like that. Jeromy's murder was wild and savage; the killer was out of control when he struck. Beside himself with anger. Afraid, perhaps. Panicked. But this . . .' I touched the stone again. 'This suggests to me a cool head. Go to see your victim late at night, when you're unlikely to be disturbed. Gain his confidence. Then tie him to his chair, make him totally helpless, and tell him what you're about to do. Only when you've caused him exquisite agony – prolonged, perhaps – do you strike the skilled and merciful blow that ends his life.' I turned to face him. 'In short, the first was a crime of the heart, the second one of the head.'

Back at Rosewyke, I told Celia, as gently and as diplomatically as I could, what had happened. I hated having to do so; hated having to raise once more the ghost of her beloved dead husband, just when she seemed to be starting to recover a little.

As I'd feared, even as I was speaking I saw the colour leave her face. She sank down onto the settle by the open window, and I thought she was trembling.

'I can't believe it,' she said quietly, her voice soft and controlled. But then her composure broke. Tears welling in her eyes, she said, 'Oh, Gabe, what am I to do? I thought it was *over*!' Then she was weeping in earnest, hands over her face, shoulders shaking, harsh sobs loud in the rural peace.

I went to sit beside her and put my arms round her, and she buried her face against my chest. 'I know, dear heart, how fervently you wish to put your sorrow behind you. Not that you'll ever forget him!' Oh, God, how tactless I'd been! 'You loved him so much, and that will never change, but you are young still, and growing in loveliness, and Jeromy would not wish you waste your life. Why, only yesterday I was thinking I would suggest that we travel together, just you and I, and pay a visit to London. You would love it, Celia, it's a city that has to be seen to be believed, and . . .' But she was stiff and unyielding in my arms and I knew she wasn't listening. Hearing my words, perhaps, but they had no meaning for her. So I hugged her more tightly, dropping a gentle kiss on her soft, fragrant hair.

Presently she was sufficiently recovered to sit up, wipe the tears from her face and turn to look at me. 'So, what have you and the coroner decided about this new death?' she asked. There was a cold, brittle tone in her voice that I couldn't recall ever having heard before. 'Were the two victims killed by the same man?'

I studied her, but her stony expression gave nothing away. *She is fighting to control her grief and her horror*, I thought. I knew I'd had no choice but to tell her, but, in revealing the news of Quinlie's death, of course it meant rekindling all the terrible emotions that had torn through her after Jeromy's.

Best, I decided, to employ the same cool logic that was serving her.

'It seems unlikely,' I replied. I explained, as well as I could without going into too much detail, how one killing appeared to be the result of passion, fear and fury, the other a controlled execution. 'One man can, of course, kill two different men in different ways,' I went on. If, as we'd began to conclude, Jeromy had been murdered by a killer hired by Quinlie, and he'd then killed Quinlie for some reason, his mood could well have been different when carrying out the two acts. The first would have been paid employment, the second something he did on his own behalf, and . . .

No. That was not reasonable. If it had been that way, then the heart and head elements would have been the other way round: he'd have killed Jeromy as a paid assassin, coolly and efficiently, and reserved his passion for the employer who had somehow raised his fury.

I met Celia's red-rimmed eyes and shrugged. 'I don't know,' I confessed.

She nodded. After a moment, she got up and began to pace the room. I had a sudden, frightening sense of anticipation: she wanted to tell me something, and I didn't think I was going to like it.

I've always been close to my sister. Our love for each other is profound, and, although we are very different in character, in habits, in our likes and dislikes and in virtually every other way, there has always been deep understanding between us. I have frequently thought she has acted unwisely, and I dare say she would say the same of me. On occasions, we have known even though apart when the other was troubled or in danger. Quite frequently, I've been thinking of her at the very moment she's been turning her horse into the track leading off the road and preparing to ride up to the house. Possibly it's the same for other siblings; I can't say. But I don't share these things with my brother Nathaniel.

So Celia paced, trying to force herself to speak, and I sat waiting.

'You say – you all say again and again how much I loved him, and how blissfully happy we were,' she began.

'Yes, of course, we know full well that—'

She shot me a silencing look. 'But you should know that quite a lot of acquaintances thought that Jeromy and I weren't happy, and gossiped among themselves about frequent and dramatic rows,' she went on, her voice shaking.

I could hardly believe what I was hearing. It went against everything I'd believed; every proof I thought I'd seen, in the course of the last two years, of a happy marriage.

I said, 'And were these acquaintances correct?'

There was a long pause. Then she nodded.

'Why did you argue?' *O merciful Lord*, I was praying, *let*

*it be something trivial, something I can brush aside and that
won't spoil this cosy image I had made of my sister's life!*

But she said, 'What do you think? We rowed over money:
always, always that's how it would start. There would be
bills that couldn't be paid, and dangerous-looking men
coming to the door and demanding to see him, and I had to
go and be smiling and polite while he hid, shaking and
trembling, and left me to face them. And he'd disappear for
a day, two days at a time' – she was talking swiftly now,
well into her stride, as if, having held this in for so long,
breaking her silence at last was like sluice gates opening on
a mighty river – 'swearing he'd come back with his purse
full of gold, but of course he never did, because the only
way he knew was gambling, and he was a rotten gambler.'
She gave a twisted smile. 'He wasn't really clever or perceptive or swift-thinking enough to be good at cards,' she said
softly. Then, her expression hardening again: 'His friends
all sided with him and said I was the one at fault, because
I demanded too much of him. I was spoilt, and I'd been
pampered by a fond and wealthy father—'

'Father's not wealthy and he never spoiled you!' I protested.

'I *know*, Gabe,' she said wearily. 'I'm telling you what
Jeromy's friends thought. Because they liked him – or they
used to – it was easier to put the blame on me for expecting
a level of comfort and luxury that a young man making his
way in the world couldn't provide.' She looked at me, her
eyes huge in her white face. 'After he was dead, I – I thought
perhaps I'd have a chance.'

'A chance?' I prompted when she didn't continue. 'To do
what?'

'Oh – to settle his debts, go through everything and
discover where I stood, sell off some of the more outlandish
things he'd bought to fill Ferrars and then maybe discover
a simpler, wiser way of living.' Her face twisted in a bitter
smile. 'Of course, I was still an innocent fool back then,
and I had no idea how badly he had gone astray.' Again she
paused, and I had the strongest suspicion – more than that:
it was a certainty – that we were coming to the kernel of
what she wanted to tell me. 'A part of me rejoiced that he

was gone,' she finally admitted in a small voice. 'I didn't think I could have gone on for much longer as we were, for the love seemed to have died, he was not the man I thought he was, and every day it was always money, money, money, and once he was dead I knew I'd be rid of all that, with no more—' Abruptly she stopped. Her voice had risen so that she had almost been shouting, and the echo rang in the room.

'Hush,' I said gently.

She spun round to fix me with a furious stare. 'Now you know what your sister really is like!' she flashed. 'Now you know her for the horrible creature she is! Her husband dead, and horribly so, and she was *glad*!'

'Do not let this guilt eat at you,' I said. 'You—'

I didn't think she heard. 'But, oh, God, it was hard,' she whispered, 'because I had to go on playing the part of the grief-stricken widow mourning the loss of the husband she'd adored, while all the time a tiny part of me wanted to dance because Jeromy was gone and safely in his grave, and everyone was quite sure they knew who had killed him.' Her head drooped on her graceful neck. 'But now you tell me Nicolaus Quinlie has been killed too, so things aren't as simple as they appeared, and the whole business will have to be examined all over again.'

I hesitated. 'It will,' I agreed, 'but I'm sure—'

She had resumed her pacing now, her footsteps a fast and furious rhythm on the wooden floorboards. 'They'll be casting round once more for someone to blame, and, oh, Gabe, I'm convinced all Jeromy's friends who hated me and disapproved of me will get their heads together and—'

She stopped dead.

A growing sense of unreality overcame me as I watched her, unable to take my eyes off her. She ceased her pacing, and it seemed as if, one by one, her tense muscles relaxed. Her expression grew mild, and her lovely face creased into a smile. She took a long breath, then another. She reached down to pick up her work bag and then walked calmly towards the door.

'But people always talk,' she said mildly. 'Now, Gabriel, I

shall go to my room and finish a small sewing task until it is
time for dinner.' She gave me a polite little nod, and was gone.

I stared after her.

For the first time in my life, I didn't understand my sister
at all.

I sat and thought for a long time. I believed I knew what
she'd been about to say, although my mind could scarcely
accept it. She came down to join me for the midday meal,
and we spoke of nothing but trivialities. I barely ate anything.
If she noticed, she didn't comment.

In the afternoon I sent for my horse. I wished I could have
spoken to Theo, but under the circumstances his knowledge
and advice were closed off to me. Instead I rode down to Tavy
St Luke and sought out Jonathan Carew.

He was in his church, in the little vestry. 'May I speak to
you in confidence?' I asked.

He smiled. 'It is what people tend to do.' Then, apparently
picking up my mood, he said, 'Unless it is some serious crime
whose commission I may stop by speaking out, then what
we say remains between us. Although this is not the confes-
sional,' he added. There was, I thought, a hint of warning in
his eyes.

So I told him what Celia had said. And, crucially, what she
hadn't said. 'She forced herself not to continue,' I concluded,
'but I am all but sure she was about to confess her fear that
Jeromy's friends will accuse her of wanting him dead. Not that
she could have killed him,' I added hurriedly, 'for that wasn't
the work of a woman. But a woman can employ someone to
do the job for her.' I watched his still face, and his expression
gave nothing away. 'Surely nobody will take them seriously!'
I tried to laugh, as if at the absurdity of the very idea. 'And
would it not be slander to spread such untruths?'

Jonathan seemed to have to stir himself out of his thoughts
before answering. 'The offence of slander does indeed include
perpetrating untrue derogative comments about a person,' he
agreed. 'To put about that a widow had wished her spendthrift
husband gone would, on the face of it, be dismissible as

malicious gossip, whereas to suggest that she had been responsible for his death – by the engaging of a killer, for example
– would indeed be slanderous, she being innocent of the
accusation.'

'Being innocent – of course she's innocent!' I protested. 'She
loved him very much! Their marriage was a great success!'

But had she loved him? I heard a voice inside my head
demand. *Or had his very nature killed that love? Hadn't she
told me that morning that love seemed to have died?*

Jonathan watched me, a hint of compassion in his expression. 'I'm sure you're right,' he said after a while. 'These
friends of your late brother-in-law will be aware of the law,
or so it is to be hoped, and with any luck what you and your
sister fear will not happen.'

I prayed he was right.

'I trust it is so,' he added softly. He glanced up at me. 'You
know, I expect, what happens to a wife convicted of murdering
her husband.'

I shook my head. He sighed, then told me.

'The murder of a husband by his wife is petty treason, since
it is an example of a superior being killed by a subordinate.
High treason, of course,' he added, 'can only be committed
against the sovereign. For a subordinate to kill a superior is
regarded as betrayal, and it is this element that makes the
crime more serious than ordinary murder, since subordinates
are meant to revere and respect their superiors. For a servant
to kill his master, or a clergyman to kill his prelate, would
also be petty treason.'

I was deeply uneasy at his repetition of *treason*. 'And what
would the punishment be?'

He glanced at me, and I saw he was reluctant to answer.
But he did. 'A man would be drawn and hanged, but not, as
with high treason, quartered. A woman would be burned at the
stake.' I gasped. 'Sometimes,' he hurried on, 'more often than
not, perhaps, a compassionate executioner might strangle
the victim before the kindling is lit and the faggots pick up the
flames.'

If he'd hoped by mentioning this to lessen the horror of
what he'd just said, he didn't succeed.

'But sometimes he might not,' I said softly.

He didn't answer.

Then I thanked him and left.

I couldn't let my sister suffer that fate; couldn't let her as much as run the risk of it. I would protect her.

Whatever it took.

FOURTEEN

I t was almost dark when I got back to Rosewyke. I hadn't appreciated how late it was; the events of the day had obsessed me to the cost of virtually everything else.

I let Hal amble along, my mind busy, content to let him find his own way up the road and onto the track leading to the house. I wasn't therefore paying nearly enough attention, which was why, when suddenly he shied, he very nearly shot me out of the saddle.

Then in the fading light I saw what he had seen.

A figure lay across the track, and another crouched over it. I swiftly dismounted and ran over, and realized that the larger figure – a man dressed in dark robes – had the head of the smaller figure – a girl, about fourteen, with shaggily cut hair and a ragged gown – in his lap. He was murmuring, beads and cross in one hand as with the other he gently stroked the wild, tangled hair off the girl's forehead.

Not murmuring: praying.

His prayers were in Latin and they were not in any form that Jonathan Carew would have used.

Such was his absorption in the girl that he didn't notice me until I was almost upon him, whereupon he gave a great start, muttering something that sounded like an apology. He resumed his praying, but now the words were ones that I heard quite frequently.

'Is she dead?' I knelt down beside him.

'Very nearly,' he whispered back. 'Her spirit is – she gave me a sign that she—' He broke off, and I sensed his fear.

'It's all right,' I said very quietly. I guessed that, in the girl's extremity of need, he had reverted to the religion in which he had grown up. To judge by the fluency of his praying, he might well have been a priest.

Now, when he was doing his utmost to help the dying girl's soul, wasn't the time to argue over whose religion was the right one.

I said, although I was sure from the sounds the girl was making and the great pool of blood soaking into the priest's robe what the answer would be, 'Is there nothing that can be done? I'm a physician.' It sounded to my own ears as if I was boasting, suggesting I was a better judge of life and death than he, but in the circumstances I had no choice.

He shook his head.

I made a gesture as if to say, *carry on*.

He said, 'Thank you.' Then, switching back to Latin, he continued with his prayers. I watched as he touched the girl's eyes, lips and hands with something from a tiny bottle; I guessed he was administering extreme unction.

Some time later he gently closed the girl's wide eyes, laid her head gently on the ground and stood up. He was very thin and appeared tall. 'She has gone,' he said. 'God rest her soul.'

'Amen,' I said. I didn't think there was any need to check that life was extinct. If I was right and he was indeed a priest – I didn't doubt it now – then he'd be more than capable of judging that himself. Besides, experienced in death as I was, I was pretty sure I'd just witnessed life leaving her. After a moment, I said, 'What happened?'

He raised his shoulders in an eloquent shrug. 'I do not know. I was on the road and I heard her moaning in pain. I ran to help her, finding her lying on the ground and mortally wounded.'

'And she had been hit on the head?'

'Yes. She . . .' He paused, apparently searching for the words. 'She had fallen. That tree.' He nodded to his right, towards one of the huge oaks that guard the end of the track up to the house; its pair stood opposite. It had a branch jutting out perhaps five or six feet off the ground. 'She had a roll of . . .' Again he paused, but this time, giving up, he indicated a pile of fine rope looped beside the track.

She had been up a tree. With a rope. On the point, perhaps, of tying it right across my homebound path, at the height my neck would be as I rode my big horse. Having failed to kill me by tripping Hal and then hitting me, had she now resolved to try something more drastic? It looked like it.

'Did she speak?' I asked after a moment.

'She tried, but her words made no sense.'

'And she hit her head as she fell? On a stone, perhaps? A rock sticking out of the ground?'

He shrugged. 'I have not looked. It seems that is probably the case.'

Now that he was speaking at greater length, I noticed that he had an accent. It put me in mind of the south . . . was it Spanish, perhaps?

And I thought of Judyth's foreigner.

Judyth had described a mask of some sort, and a strange smell. The man standing before me, looking down with anguish-filled eyes at the dead girl lying at his feet, neither wore nor carried a mask, nor anything that might, in poor light, have been mistaken for one: a deep-brimmed hat pulled low over his face, for example. I breathed in through my nose, trying to see if I could detect an unusual smell. There was the sort of musty aroma that comes from garments too long worn, and an underlying smell of sweat. That was all.

But the man was saying something, and I made myself pay attention. '. . . know who she is?'

'I don't, I'm afraid. At least, I don't believe I do.' I went to crouch once more beside the girl, studying her more closely. The rough-cut hair was reddish-brown, the dirty face freckled. Freckles . . .

'We cannot leave her here,' my companion was saying. 'Is there a dwelling where she can be laid out?'

I nodded up the track. 'My house is nearby. I'll take her there.'

He stood watching me, frowning with concern. 'Do you wish me to help?'

I smiled. 'No.' I leaned closer. 'I think it's better if you go quietly on your way and we pretend we never met, don't you?'

His hooded eyes widened for an instant before he managed to control the reaction. 'But I—'

'I imagine you have come here to seek like-minded friends,' I interrupted. 'I'm hoping very much that you're not planning to make trouble, because then I might regret what I'm doing. But I discovered you in an act of kindness, caring for that poor girl even though, kneeling out on the track as you were, you risked your own safety.'

I wasn't sure if he understood what I was trying to say. I

wasn't sure I understood myself. He looked at me for a long moment, then nodded. The next moment he had hitched up his long robe and was striding away.

I picked up the girl – her body was skinny and light – and carried her up the track to the house, and Hal paced behind us. Inside one of the yard buildings I made a bier for her out of planks laid on trestles and carefully put her down on it, covering her with a length of cloth. Then I left her.

At first light I roused Samuel and told him to take a message to my wounded farmer, William. He gave me a sharp look, then hurried away. I went back inside to break the news to Sallie that there was a body in the outhouse and advise her to work somewhere else for the time being.

Samuel returned. He had delivered my message.

I didn't have long to wait. Black Carlotta arrived as the day progressed to mid-morning.

I went down the track to greet her. 'Thank you for coming.'

She nodded. 'Message said it was urgent.'

'Yes. I very much wanted to find you. I reckoned you'd be a regular visitor to Katharine just now, so trying to contact you at the farm seemed a good idea.'

'You reckoned right.'

'She's well?'

'She is.'

We had reached the yard. I led her to the little outhouse, indicating the body. 'I believe,' I said, 'that you may know who this is.'

She folded back the cloth and studied the still form. She made a small sound of distress, putting out a gentle hand to touch the smooth flesh of the face. Like the priest had done last night, she murmured some words, although I suspected hers were of yet another faith, and one considerably older than the priest's or mine.

Presently she replaced the cloth and stepped back. She strode out of the outhouse, and I followed.

'Back of her skull's stove in.'

I nodded. 'Yes. She tumbled from a tree and had the misfortune to hit the back of her head on a stone lying in the grass.'

I still had to check, but it was surely the only explanation. 'You know her.'

'Aye. Her name's Gelyan Thorn.'

My instinct had been right. Black Carlotta had sent me to Josiah Thorn to find out who had been behind the objects left on my doorstep, so it was only logical that the culprit must have some connection with him.

But she'd been a relation.

'His granddaughter?'

'Aye. She was a wild child, that one. Josiah took her in when her father – Josiah's boy – died ten years back. Her mother died having her, see, so once her father went she was all alone.' She shook her head. 'Josiah did his best but he never understood her. Mind, she was very strange in many ways – reckoned she could hear the trees and the flowers talking, and used to rescue dead animals and try to breathe life back into them. Josiah asked me to help, and I took the girl under my wing a bit, tried to encourage her out of her worst flights of fancy and get her to do something useful with herself, although I never made much of an impression.' She smiled wryly. 'Reckon Gelyan never even realized I was there much of the time, she was that wound up in whatever went on in that odd head of hers.'

'Did she believe I was usurping her grandfather?' I asked.

'Probably. He'd have tried to tell her it wasn't so, that he was pleased to retire and didn't want any more patients, but once Gelyan made her mind up about something there weren't no shifting her.' She sighed.

'You tried to steer me towards Josiah to help Gelyan, didn't you?' She looked at me. 'You probably thought that once he knew what she was doing, he'd put a stop to the worst excesses of her behaviour. Such as leaving dog faeces on people's doorsteps,' I added ruefully.

She sighed again. 'I expect I did.' She glanced back at the outhouse. 'Not that it did any good.'

'I'll go and break the news to him,' I said heavily.

'Want me to come with you?'

'No, I'll manage.'

She smiled thinly. 'Used to breaking bad tidings, I'll warrant.'

'Indeed.'

'I'll look in on him later,' she said. Then she nodded at me, spun on her heel and strode away.

Josiah Thorn's grief at hearing of his granddaughter's death was, it seemed to me, tinged with not a little relief. I sat him down, made him a hot, restorative drink and, as he blew on it and began to slurp it up, I waited to see if he wanted to talk.

He did. He told me how his son had died, leaving him no option but to take in the orphaned little girl, even though he knew he was too old – 'and too selfish' he admitted – for the challenge of a wayward child. He talked for some time, fell silent for a while, then said, 'I know what she was up to regarding you, doctor. After you came to see me I took her to task, and she admitted it. No, she didn't admit it, she boasted of it. She told me with great pleasure and pride how she'd left those revolting things for you to find and she listed them all, every last one' – he repeated the list – 'each time with the sole intention of driving you away. I'm sorry, doctor. I did my best with her, but the job was too hard.'

Then he carefully put down his empty mug, dropped his face in his hands and wept.

I stayed with him till his distress had turned to resignation, then I left him. Riding home, I reflected that the carefully repeated list of Gelyan's offerings had not included the bloody heap of sow's reproductive organs. Somebody else had left that.

And he hadn't mentioned the tying of trip ropes across my path. That, I guessed, was something she'd have kept to herself.

I retired early that night, worn out by the day. I slept deeply for several hours but then woke in the profound pre-dawn darkness. There were two things nagging at me: first, I was feeling guilty about having let that priest walk away. What if he was even now housed with some local family of clandestine but determined Catholics? What if another traitorous plot was being hatched? What if he was no mere priest but a member of the powerfully intelligent Jesuit order; one of those brave men who risked a terrible death to come into this land to persuade men back to what they believed to be the one true faith?

It was true that this particular danger had threatened most acutely while Mary, Queen of Scots was still alive, for she had been the rallying point for all those who wanted a Catholic back on the throne of England. During the 1570s and 80s the Jesuit missions had been relentless, only ceasing – or so we'd all hoped – when Mary was executed in February 1587. After the defeat of the Spanish the following year, the last years of Elizabeth's reign had been tranquil; or so it had seemed.

But now Elizabeth was dead. Mary's son was now our king, and, for all that we were told James Stuart was staunchly Protestant, would there be factions convinced that an instinct towards his mother's faith must lurk within him, only waiting for resurrection? If ever there was a time for the Jesuit menace to begin again, then surely, with Elizabeth dead and James yet to be crowned, it was now.

After quite some time, I told myself it was no use worrying: I'd let the priest go, and that was that. I'd had a good enough reason at the time, so would have to be content to assume I'd do the same thing again.

Then I turned my mind to the second matter.

I'd been dreaming, I think – the images had been vague – of my Venetian doctor; the man who had told me about the plague and how they'd tried to combat it in his city. And in the dream he, or someone, had said *lazaretto*. It seemed as if my sleeping mind had merged the present – those papers of Nicolaus Quinlie's – and the past: my plague doctor.

I puzzled about it, trying to detect what the dream had been trying to tell me. If anything . . . Then, giving up on sleep, I lit a candle and quietly, on bare feet, walked along to my study. I closed the door, put the flame to a couple more candles, then went to the shelf where I keep my journals.

I kept a private journal for the majority of my time at sea. The successive leather-bound volumes, filled with my handwriting, my sketches, my diagrams and even a few maps, numbered twenty-five and more. I kept a meticulous list of the patients I'd treated; of the new and experimental methods I'd read about, copied from others, been told of by strange medicine men in the far-flung reaches of the world and adopted for my own use. I noted carefully which ones worked, jotting down my observations of how they affected the patient. I wrote down everything, and I'd kept every single journal.

It took a while to find the one I'd been using during that visit to the Dalmatian Islands, but eventually I held it in my hand. I went to my desk, sat down, pulled the candles close and began to flip through the pages.

Presently I found, written in my own hand, what I'd been searching for.

The Island of Korčula on the Dalmatian Coast
(called by the Venetians Curzola),
12th April 1594

Today I fell into conversation with a plague doctor of Venice. He had much to tell me, the terrible disease having attacked his city the previous summer, not for the first time, and persisting in its malice well into the present year. It is a scourge straight out of hell, and the sufferings of the victims are harrowing: he described moaning, wailing, foul air filled with the stench of burning bodies; those yet living lie three or four to a bed, for on the plague islands overcrowding quickly becomes acute as the newly sick and the dying outnumber those already released into the mercy of death. I queried what he meant by plague islands, and he answered that many years ago the city had established upon Santa Maria di Nazareth, one of the islands in the lagoon, a quarantine station and hospital for those arriving by sea who are suspected of infection. This island in time became known as Lazaretto Vecchio, or the Old Plague Island, and, a few years later and driven by dire necessity, a second such island, Lazaretto Nuovo or New Plague Island, was also created. Thus in the present outbreak, the islands stand ready for use, although, as my colleague in medicine told me, already they are far, far too inadequate for the task that is asked of them and

But I stopped reading then, for I had found what I sought.

* * *

I managed to sleep, and woke as the early sunlight came softly into my room. Last night, when I'd made my great discovery, the elation had made me over-confident and I'd imagined flying out today and finding the answers to everything that had tormented me for so long. Now, in the practical light of the new day, I realized it wasn't going to be so simple.

For the last twenty-five years and more, Quinlie had made regular payments to one or both of the plague islands in Venice's lagoon. Why, or for whom they had been intended, I had no idea. Was he another of the Old Catholics, appeasing his conscience as he bent the knee before this new version of God by sending support to some nun- or monk-run charitable foundation? For all I knew, any number of England's resolute Catholics might be doing precisely that. Or not . . .

I was finishing my porridge and wondering what to do with my new knowledge when Celia joined me. 'You're late this morning,' she said, mild disapproval in her tone. '*I* breakfasted some time ago.'

I was on the point of apologizing but stopped. This, after all, was my house. Within it, I decided, it was my business what time I rose.

'Will you come over to Ferrars with me?' Celia asked. Before I could reply, she went on, 'Ruth came to see me. She has been very kindly keeping an eye on the house, going over most days, and she'd been there yesterday to fetch one or two personal items she'd only just remembered about. She says someone's been there.'

'Apart from us?' I grinned.

'This isn't a joke, Gabe. Ruth is quite certain someone's been searching through the house, and very recently too, because whatever it was that alerted her, she didn't notice it the previous time she was there, and I need to see for myself.'

It was the last thing I wanted to do. 'But why? We've taken everything you wanted, haven't we?'

'That's not the point,' she said crushingly. 'Ferrars might not belong to me any more' – *it never did, either to you or that scoundrel of a husband of yours*, I wanted to say – 'but nevertheless it was my home, and I still have a considerable attachment to it. The idea that some opportunist burglar has broken in and helped himself to items that once I treasured is *very* hard to bear.' She gave me the look she's been giving me since we were children: the one that says, *Get the better of that!*

I didn't think I could. 'Very well,' I said with a sigh. 'But I can't afford to take long over it.'

Someone had been inside the house: Ruth was quite right. One small pane of a scullery window at the back of the house had been broken, and the broken glass was perfectly situated for a hand to reach in and unfasten the catch. There was a suggestion of muddy boot prints leading into the kitchen. I followed my sister as she strode through the many rooms of the brash and vulgar house that had once been her home, waiting for her to speak.

'It's very odd,' she said eventually. We were in her bed-chamber. 'I *know* someone's been through the rooms – don't ask me how I know, Gabe, I just do – and I think they've examined practically everything, but I can't find anything missing.'

I had crossed the room to throw back the hearth rug, and now I knelt down and levered the loose tile away. The hidden cavity gaped before me, just as empty as we'd left it. Had whoever searched the house been trying to find what Jeromy had hidden in there? There was no way of knowing, but I had a strong sense that was exactly what had happened. The question was, with Nicolaus Quinlie dead, who could it have been? Ruth had been going to Ferrars daily, or so it appeared, and she had only yesterday noticed the evidence of an intruder. Theo Davey had summoned me to Quinlie's warehouse two days ago, which meant the intruder had broken in to Ferrars *after* Quinlie was killed.

Who was it?

I was finishing a late midday meal – Celia had gone back to her room and her sewing – when there was a knock at the door. Sallie hurried off to answer it – she believes it's not proper for a doctor to be summoned personally to callers – and returned a few moments later accompanied by Jarman Hodge.

'May I speak to you, doctor? In private,' he added, shooting a glance at Sallie's avid face.

'Of course.' I led the way out of the kitchen and across the hall to the library. Sallie, I guessed, thought Jarman was a patient come to consult the doctor on a medical matter, and there was no need for her to discover otherwise.

'I've been back to Dartmouth,' Jarman began as I closed the door. 'In the wake of Quinlie's death, see, I wondered if there was anything new to unearth.'

I indicated one of the high-backed chairs set round the big table and he sat down. I settled beside him. 'And was there?'

'Reckon so. Pieter Sparre's dead.'

Pieter Sparre . . . I raked through my recent memories and came up with nothing. 'Who's he?'

Jarman grinned. 'Short, fat warehouseman who struts like a fighting cock, voice like a squeaky hinge?'

'Him! The man who made the comment about not seeing Jeromy any more! He's dead? How?'

'He went missing and was found a day or two later bumping up against the quay. He'd been a bit of a drinker, and most folks' view was that he'd taken a tankard too many and fallen on his way home.'

I knew from the very look of him that there was more. 'But you don't agree.'

'Maybe I do, maybe I don't. I went to see his woman. He lodged with a blowsy old doxy in a tumbledown rooming house down by the port, and she likes a drop of the good stuff as much as he did so perhaps we shouldn't set too much store by what she had to say.'

'Which was?'

He eyed me, a calculating expression on his face. 'She said he was dead scared. In the days just before he disappeared, he'd had a bad fright. I couldn't get to the bottom of it – as I said, she was pissed and ranting about all manner of things – but it seems he'd seen something, and smelt something – it stank of camphor – and it had put the fear of God in him.'

'What did he see?'

Jarman met my eyes. 'According to the woman, he saw a devil lurking in the shadows. A devil with a beak for a face.'

FIFTEEN

I only had a rough idea where Judyth lived and consequently it took me some time to find her house. By Blaxton, Jarman Hodge had said, near where the ferry departed to cross the Tavy. I rode up and down the area around the quay, venturing a little way away from the water, and located several small houses that might have been hers. I knocked at one or two doors and received short shrift. Either people genuinely didn't know of her or else they were reluctant to reveal the whereabouts of a lone woman to a stranger. In retrospect, I reflected ruefully, I should have said I was an anxious husband in dire and urgent need of a midwife for my labouring wife. Finally I came across a neat little cottage set by itself on a low rise above the river bank, and I knew even as I stared at it that I had found her. It was well maintained and very clean: the small diamond-shaped panes of glass in the leaded windows caught the late sun, the solid oak of the door glowed as if someone had polished it, the precise edges of the reed thatch might just that morning have been trimmed with a sharp knife and the vegetable plot looked as if each row of healthy, vibrant plants had been set out with a rule.

I approached, and as I did so I caught sight of a small yard behind the house in which there was a stable with the upper half of its door open. A bay had stuck its head out and was regarding me with interest.

I dismounted, tethered Hal's reins to the post beside the gate and went up the path to the oak door. There was a heavy iron knocker in the form of an angel, its wings spread. I raised it and let it fall with an echoing thump.

Almost immediately I heard swift footfalls and then the door was flung open. 'She's early after all, then, just as I— Oh.' Her eyes widened, and I thought I caught a swift, faint pink blush on her cheeks. Then she smiled. 'Not Walter Murdo come to tell me his wife's waters have broken, then, but our new physician,' she said softly. 'Come in, doctor.'

She turned and walked off down the narrow, dark little passage and I followed, shutting the door behind me. She led the way into a tiny, bright room whose westward-facing window admitted a great burst of golden light from the slowly sinking sun. It illuminated an enchanting space: a settle stood beside the hearth, in which a small fire glowed beneath an iron pot suspended above it; water in the pot steamed gently, and there was a sweet, citrus-tinged smell in the room. A cheerfully coloured rag rug was spread on the flagged floor. Beside it, there was a pale oak table polished to a shine, with two high-backed chairs drawn up to it; on it was a large jug containing a huge bunch of poppies, honeysuckle, foliage and grasses. There was an alcove fitted with shelves on which stood an intriguing selection of objects ranging from leather-bound books and notebooks to roughly made but attractive pots, mugs and bowls. Opposite the settle was a chair which had to be her regular place, for it was made comfortable and cosy with cushions and a soft, thick wool shawl generous enough to serve as a blanket.

Judyth stood, arms folded, watching me. She looked amused.

'Your room is a delight,' I said. 'You have—' I almost said, *You have made so much of so little*, but it would have been an unforgivably patronizing, insulting remark and fortunately I stopped myself just in time. I managed a smile, hoping it would disguise my sudden confusion. 'You have the admirable knack, you women,' I said, 'of turning a house into a home.'

Her mouth turned down at one corner and she raised an eyebrow. I had the disconcerting feeling that she knew exactly what had been running through my mind. 'Your house is quite nice too, doctor,' she said blandly. 'Quite homely, really, but then you do have a housekeeper and a sister in residence.'

I laughed, and all at once felt better. 'I'm sorry,' I said. 'I sense I've been discourteous, and that wasn't my intention.'

Now she smiled properly, her face springing alive into beauty. 'I rather think it is I who have been discourteous,' she murmured. 'Now, sit down, please, and tell me what I can do for you.' She waved a hand towards the settle – I'd been right about the chair being her special seat – and I sank on to it. She made herself comfortable in the chair, bright grey-blue eyes on mine.

I didn't know how to begin, and her alert, intelligent gaze wasn't helping.

'When you came to see me,' I blurted out eventually – the silent scrutiny was making me feel awkward – 'I told you that the dead man found at Old Ferry Quay was my brother-in-law.'

'You did,' she agreed solemnly.

'You said you'd seen a strange beak-masked figure near the place,' I went on.

'Yes.'

This wasn't getting us anywhere. I decided I ought to plunge straight in to the very heart of the matter.

'My sister is devastated by Jeromy's death,' I began. 'She— I love Celia very much,' I heard myself say. 'You won't know because you haven't met her, but she is a delight. She's head-strong and stubborn, she likes her own way, and she's capable of making such a nuisance of herself when she doesn't get it that people – well, her family – tend to give in just for a bit of peace. That doesn't mean she's spoilt and pettish,' I hastened to add, 'it simply underlines that she's a strong, brave woman who knows her own mind.'

Judyth, I noticed, was smiling. She didn't speak.

'Celia's staying with me while she adapts to her life without Jeromy,' I went on, 'and I've therefore had the opportunity to study her closely. I've also managed to encourage her to talk, a little, and she's told me things that have astounded me.'

Judyth's face changed. Her smile vanished and she said sharply, 'What sort of things?'

'Chiefly that she's very afraid,' I said.

'*Afraid?*'

It sounded as if Judyth hadn't expected that. I thought I'd better explain.

'Since her husband died,' I continued, 'certain revelations have occurred, the chief of which is that he was broke.' It seemed best to be blunt. Judyth nodded briefly as if she concurred. 'Under normal circumstances Celia would not, I'm sure, have said a word concerning the – er, the financial troubles they had.

She was devoted to Jeromy, and too loyal a wife to broadcast his shortcomings.' And her loyalty had cost her, I reflected, momentarily hearing her words in my mind: *bills that couldn't be paid and dangerous-looking men coming to the door*. For a proud woman like my sister, how humiliating it must have been. 'When the lawyer visited us and we began to suspect the vast extent of Jeromy's indebtedness,' I hurried on, 'Celia was as shocked as I was. However, finding herself with no means whatsoever, she had no choice but to reveal the truth, and she told me how matters had really stood between the two of them.'

I lowered my eyes briefly. Speaking to Judyth while looking at her, I was discovering, was quite exacting.

'You said she was afraid,' she prompted after a few moments. 'Is her fear because of her lack of means? Please don't imagine I am belittling such a state,' she added swiftly, 'for I know full well that it is indeed something to strike fear in the bravest heart. But—'

But she has you, I thought she had been about to say.

'She has a home with me as long as she requires it,' I said quietly. 'She is, I think, shamed and embittered at the discovery that she has nothing; that her husband had run through his money and hers, and left a queue of debtors baying for his blood.' I had no idea if the latter were true, but it seemed likely.

There was quite a long silence. Then Judyth said softly, 'Why is she afraid?'

We had come to the crux of it. Now I had to share a confidence; now I had to tell this keen-eyed, intelligent and perceptive woman who I barely knew a secret whose potential for damage was so great I didn't even dare think about it.

Did I trust her?

Apparently I did.

'Celia fears the malice of Jeromy's friends,' I heard myself say. 'They cast her in the role of villain. They accused her of being the indulged child of a doting father, and a spoiled, petted woman who demanded very much more from her loving husband than he could reasonably provide. Celia may love rich and costly things,' I admitted frankly, 'but in my experience of Jeromy, his addiction to them was the greater. And our father was certainly not doting and he didn't spoil any of us.'

My voice had risen. Again Judyth smiled, but it was an understanding smile.

'She has got it into her head that these friends of Jeromy may accuse her of involvement in his death,' I said. 'They didn't like her, they knew that she and Jeromy argued about money, and she has allowed those facts to persuade her that these men will begin to spread malicious rumours. She had decided she'd be better off without him, they'll say. She – she made up her mind to act, and she set about ridding herself of him.'

I'd said it. I didn't know if the confession made me feel better or worse. The silence continued and eventually I made myself look at her.

'And just how, I wonder,' she said quietly, 'would anyone imagine a gently raised woman such as Celia, from a loving and nurturing family who had never forced her to fend for herself and who had never had reason to discover the darker paths of this world, would go about hiring someone to kill her husband?'

It was a cool and logical observation, and I wondered why it hadn't occurred to me to ask the same thing. 'So – you don't think these friends would be believed?'

'Of course not,' she said robustly. 'Anyway, have any such rumours been started? Has anyone come near to making such allegations?'

'Not that I know of.'

She shrugged a shoulder, as if to say, *Well, then.*

My unease hadn't really gone away. 'It all seemed so straightforward when we believed Jeromy had killed himself!' I burst out. 'But when that theory was disproved' – *by me*, I could have added – 'happily, another took its place, and it was tentatively concluded that Jeromy's employer had had him killed because – well, because of various offences that we needn't go into.' Her eyebrow went up again but she didn't speak. 'But then Nicolaus Quinlie – the employer – was himself found murdered, so that put paid to *that* theory. I just wish—' I stopped, suddenly unable to go on.

'You wish the real culprit could be located, tried, found guilty and condemned to death,' she finished for me, 'because only then would your dear sister feel safe.'

I stared into her eyes. 'Yes.'

'It is understandable,' she murmured.

'If my sister is accused and convicted of murdering her husband, she'll die, by one of the most horrific methods man has ever devised,' I said quietly. 'I will do anything and everything in my power to prevent that happening.'

There was a long, long pause. Judyth stared intently at me, and I managed to meet her brilliant eyes and not look away. Finally, she appeared to come to a decision. 'In that case,' she said in a low voice, 'I believe I may be able to help.'

The tension that had been knotting my muscles, making my shoulders ache and creating a band of pain around my head, eased. 'Thank you,' I whispered.

She got up and with quiet, efficient movements, set about making a hot drink. She handed it to me, waiting while I blew on it and sipped it. Then I felt a cool hand on my head, exactly at the point from which, since the accident with the packing crate, the pain always begins. Her fingertips slid under my hair, gently making small circles, steadily moving outwards until she was manipulating the scalp right over the side of my head.

The relief was wonderful.

'That's better,' I said gratefully after a while.

'You had a blow to the head.' It wasn't a question.

'Yes.'

She nodded but made no comment. It was as if she was storing the information away for future use. 'Finish your drink,' she said. 'That too will help.'

I did as she commanded, putting the empty mug down on the hearth. Then she said, 'Now, this matter of finding the true killer. You have come to ask, I imagine, if I have recalled any more about the dark stranger I saw on the path above the river.'

'I have,' I agreed. 'I mentioned it to Theophilus Davey – the coroner?'

'I know Master Davey.'

'He listened, but remarked that it was scant information.'

'As indeed it was,' she said.

'Now, however,' I went on, 'another man has died, over in Dartmouth, and his – er, the woman he lived with says he was very scared, ranting about how he'd seen a frightful figure

with a beak for a face that had a particular smell about it, and
I remembered that you too mentioned an odd smell, although
you couldn't be precise about what it was, and I wondered if—'

'It was camphor,' she interrupted. 'Not long after I'd spoken
to you, I had occasion to use some of the resin for a child
with heavy catarrh, and the smell reminded me of the figure
I'd seen.'

'The sighting was that night?' In my eagerness to hear her
confirm it I was leaning forward, almost falling off the settle.
'You saw this mysterious foreigner on the night Jeromy was
killed? It's vital!' I cried. 'Don't you see? If we can place him
where two men died, then surely it must be all but certain that
he's the killer we need to find!'

Still she didn't speak. I had the sudden conviction that, just
as earlier I had tried to decide whether or not to trust her, now
she was doing the selfsame thing about me.

I wanted to demand an answer. I wanted to shake her, make
her say what I so desperately wanted to hear. I made myself
sit back on the settle.

She noticed. I had the impression there wasn't much she
didn't notice.

'I think,' she murmured eventually, 'that there are a few
more things you need to know about Jeromy Palfrey.' She
paused, as if asking herself one final time if she was right to
go ahead, then she said, 'He wasn't just a spendthrift and a
wastrel; he was violent.'

I didn't at first understand.

'Are you sure?' I demanded. 'He never struck me as a man
who was likely to resort to a weapon or the use of his fists,
being far too obsessed with his appearance and not soiling or
damaging his fine clothes, and anyway he was slender and
didn't look particularly strong, so—'

Judyth was staring fixedly at me, almost as if she was willing
me to see the answer for myself.

I felt the anger start, deep down in my guts. I pinned it
down. 'You mean he was violent towards my sister.' Instantly
another question burst out of me; 'Do you *know* Celia?'

'Yes, I do.' The answer, it appeared, was in answer to both
my comment and my question. 'His assaults ranged from

taking her when she didn't want him – sadly, no crime since a wife is her husband's property, and, from what so many of my women confide, all too common – to punching her where the bruises wouldn't show. He also imprisoned her, restricting her life ruthlessly so that he was in total control.'

'When—' My voice broke on the word and I started again. Oh, dear God, I didn't seem to be able to take in what I was hearing. 'When did this start? They seemed to be so very much in love, and from all I hear, she idolized him and he felt much the same.'

'From what you hear,' she echoed. 'Were you not here to witness for yourself?'

'To begin with, no. I was in London, undertaking my studies in medicine. And once I was home again, I just – well, I just assumed Celia was truly as happy as she seemed to be.' Had I been so blind? How had I managed to miss so comprehensively all that was really happening? 'My father never liked Jeromy,' I added savagely. 'Dear God, how right he was.'

'As to when it began, I can't answer that,' Judyth said. 'Celia was extremely reluctant to confide in me, and it wasn't up to me to put pressure on her and persuade her. She had one bully in her life and she didn't need another one.'

'How did she come to tell you even as much as she did?' I asked.

Judyth smiled briefly. 'How do you think, doctor?'

Then, of course, it was obvious, as indeed it had been all along, only I hadn't stopped to work it out.

'I don't know what had gone on in previous years,' she said, 'and whether it had happened before and come to naught, although I imagine it could well have done. If she miscarried in the past, then either she dealt with it herself or she sought the counsel of another midwife. The former, I would say if I had to guess, for undoubtedly she felt deeply ashamed of what her life had become, and her pride made it very, very hard to share her misery with outsiders.'

She paused, staring into the hearth, her expression full of sorrow and compassion, a frown on her smooth forehead. I sensed she was deep in the paths of her memories, and it was not a happy place to be.

As I sat there in Judyth's small, quiet, serene room, my mind fighting to deny what she'd just told me yet knowing it was the truth, I thought of something: I remembered the day Celia had arrived unexpectedly at Rosewyke, fresh from her visit to our parents. I remembered how she'd winced as I helped her down from her grey mare, and how I'd assumed she'd turned her ankle as she landed. I remembered that I'd thought she looked plump from our mother's good cooking and generous portions.

I'd been wrong; as wrong as it was possible to be.

She had winced because I was holding her round the upper body, where recently her cowardly bastard of a husband had been hitting her. *Punching her where the bruises wouldn't show.*

And she was plump because she'd been in the early stages of pregnancy.

I dropped my head in my hands. I felt like weeping.

'Will she conceive again if she remarries?' I asked.

There was a long pause. 'You're the doctor,' Judyth said, not unkindly. 'What do you reckon?'

'*I* don't know!' I snapped. 'For years I was a surgeon in the navy and all my patients were male. I am a novice when it comes to women. To ministering to them as a doctor, I mean.' For some reason I was blushing. Once again, I buried my face in my hands.

I sensed her move, and then she was right in front of me, her hands on mine, gently lowering them. 'I'm sorry,' she whispered. 'You think my remark cruel, and that wasn't my intention.'

'Not cruel.' I managed a very faint smile. 'But you're a midwife, Judyth, and Celia was your patient. Why did she miscarry?'

But Judyth merely stared at me, her light-filled eyes unblinking. 'What goes on between my patients and me is not for sharing, under any circumstances. You, I am quite sure, apply the same rigid rule.'

I nodded. 'Yes, of course. But did . . .' I hesitated, for the question was hard. 'Did she suffer badly?'

She sat back on her heels. 'She did, and I can't pretend otherwise, but Celia is young, she is otherwise healthy, and bodies, as I'm sure you have observed yourself, always try to repair themselves whenever they can.'

Presently she got up and returned to her chair. As if the terrible revelations had lowered the temperature, she wrapped herself in her shawl.

After what seemed a long time, she said, 'I really did see the mysterious foreigner, and he was exactly as I described.'

I raised my head and stared at her. 'And you'll testify to that? You'll confirm you saw this man, very close to where Jeromy was found and on the night he died?'

I realized then that nobody actually knew the time, or even the day, of his death.

Even then, I think I knew it was important.

Judyth said softly, 'When you tell a lie, it is always best, I believe, to keep the fiction as close to the truth as possible.' Now her gaze bored into me, as if she was demanding something of me . . . 'As I just said, I *did* see such a figure, but it wasn't at that time and it wasn't on the track above Old Ferry Quay.'

For an instant, the courage and resolve in her strong face wavered. Then she raised her chin, squared her shoulders and said firmly, 'I said I'd seen the foreigner there because I wanted to protect Celia.'

I shook my head, trying to order my wild thoughts. 'To *protect* her? But why? Because—?'

She made a small sound of impatience. 'You're forgetting what I knew!' she said vehemently. 'You came to me today wanting me to testify to the existence of a likely perpetrator of the murder of Jeromy Palfrey, and to swear that he was present at the murder scene at the appropriate time, because your sister is afraid suspicion will fall upon her because she and Jeromy quarrelled about money. Dear God above, don't you see, doctor? Knowing what I did about their life, I was terrified that suspicion would fall on her for a very different reason, one which, you must surely agree, is far more powerful a motive for her wanting to be rid of him!'

'She didn't do it!' I cried. 'As you said before, how on earth would Celia set about hiring a murderer? It's quite impossible even to contemplate it, and—'

'Of course it is.' Her voice, calm now, broke across my fury. 'But, just in case anyone should suggest it, I thought it best to be prepared. To have our defences in place, on the off chance they might be required.'

Our defences.

I could have kissed her for that.

Hal picked up my urgency and took off for Rosewyke as if he were a young and excitable colt once more. Both of us were hot and sweaty by the time we clattered into the yard and Samuel gave me one of his looks as I handed him the reins and told him to rub Hal down.

I paused only to splash my face and hands at the yard pump before hurrying inside.

I strode through the hall and took the stairs in giant leaps. I raced along the gallery and, after only a cursory tap, opened the door and went into her anteroom.

She was sitting with her sewing in her lap, but I had the strongest impression she had sewn barely a stitch. She looked up and I saw a flash of something – apprehension? anxiety? – cross her face before she adopted an expression of distaste.

'You stink of horse sweat,' she said.

Ah. She'd gone on the offensive. Interesting.

'I've been riding hard.' I paused. Affecting an aloof disinterest, she had returned to her sewing.

'I've been to see someone who, I've just discovered, knows you rather better than I've been led to believe.'

She gave an obviously false, forced laugh. 'You're going to have to narrow it down, Gabe,' she said lightly. 'I do have quite a lot of friends and acquaintances.'

I went to stand over her as she sat in the prettily cushioned chair beside the window.

'I'm not speaking of a friend or acquaintance,' I said quietly. 'I'm speaking of the woman who attended you when you lost the baby.'

Her face went white. 'How did you know . . .' she hissed. Then, taking a moment to recover from the shock, she said more calmly, 'I do not wish to speak of that.'

I didn't blame her. From the little Judyth had said, it was

surely something Celia would be trying her utmost to forget. I was sorry I couldn't let her. 'Judyth is on your side,' I said. 'She is a compassionate and brave woman, and she's . . .' But it wasn't the moment to say, *She's prepared to lie for you in order to provide a credible suspect for Jeromy's murder.* 'She told me some dreadful things,' I said instead, crouching down and softening my tone, 'and I want – it would be helpful if you could tell me about them yourself.'

She stared at me. Her eyes were hard. 'Why?'

'Because I'm trying to help you!' I cried. 'Dear God, Celia, do you think I can't see how terrible all this is for you? For reasons of your own, you seem to have been pretending that you were very happily married to a man who I now know was a spendthrift and a gambler, and who, if what I've just learned is anywhere near accurate, was a great deal more than that. I understand that it's partly pride, because having insisted on marrying Jeromy it must be very hard to admit he's not what you thought he was, even to yourself and never mind to anyone else. But—'

'I can't tell Father,' she whispered. 'He'll despise me, he'll say, *I told you so, I told you not to marry him*, and he'll tell me I brought it all on myself.'

I took hold of her hands. Her accusations against our poor father were so unjust, so patently wrong, that I didn't know where to begin in denouncing them. So I just held her hands for a while in the hope that she'd hear what she'd just said and see for herself.

'Well,' she said eventually, 'perhaps he won't *despise* me.'

'He loves you, Celia,' I said gently. 'All he'll feel, if and when he ever hears the full truth, is a full heart and a huge sympathy.' He'd also want to kill Jeromy, but fortunately that wouldn't be necessary as someone had already done it.

After a while she disentangled her hands – smiling at me as if to make sure I didn't take the action as any sort of rejection – and stood up. She walked across to the window, staring out at the gently rising land over to the east, and said, 'All right. You'd better tell me what you want to know.'

'I want to know the truth,' I said. I went over to the fireplace, opposite her. It seemed best to put a little distance between us. 'You told me earlier that you were very afraid Jeromy's friends might accuse you of wanting to get rid of him, but the only reason you gave was because they thought you were too demanding and forced him to spend too much on you and get into debt.'

Very slowly she nodded. 'Yes,' she whispered.

'Now,' I said firmly, 'tell me the rest.'

She bowed her head, and I couldn't see her face. She didn't speak for a long time. Then, in a tiny voice, she said, 'He wasn't an easy man to live with.'

I leaned my shoulder against the fireplace. I had the feeling this would take time, and it seemed wise to make myself comfortable. 'Go on.'

'He was – volatile, almost from the start of our marriage,' Celia said. 'I hadn't appreciated that he drank, because he was very careful that I shouldn't find out. Not before the wedding, anyway.' She gave a harsh laugh. 'Afterwards, once I was his wife, it didn't matter. And anyway, he'd have found it impossible to conceal from me the extent of his dependence on alcohol.' She paused, staring past me into the hearth. 'Once he was drunk, you just couldn't reason with him or even talk to him. He would just shout, and then shout louder, and turn everything I tried to say so that I was the one in the wrong, even when it was he who had just fallen into the house with his garments awry, his face flushed and a big patch of urine on the front of his hose where he'd been unable to contain himself, and . . .' Her voice had risen and she was all but ranting. With a very obvious effort she managed to take hold of herself. When she resumed, her voice was calmer. 'Then he would begin to flail around, his actions wild and uncontrolled so that things got broken and *that* was my fault too, and he'd say, "*Now* look at what you've made me do!" and he'd accuse me of being a shrew of a wife who was both penny-pinching and wildly extravagant.' Before I could protest she waved a hand and said wearily, 'I know, Gabe. It's impossible to be both, but according to Jeromy I was extravagant when it came to my own needs and penny-pinching when it came to his.'

I tried not to let my fury sound in my voice. I took a couple of breaths, and then said, 'What caused him to behave like that? The drink, yes, I realize that would make him lose all sense, but why did he drink so much?'

'Because he had come to the conclusion that he could never be happy.' She thought for a while. 'Jeromy loved nice things. He craved luxury and a life that others envied, and his aim was a gorgeous, colourful, flamboyant house and a wife whom other men would covet for her looks, her breeding and her wealth.' A harsh note had entered her voice, and she paused. When she resumed, she sounded blandly calm and emotionless once more.

It was, I guessed, the only way she could tell her terrible tale.

'Jeromy wanted the life of a very wealthy man and he drank because he couldn't have it,' she said. 'Sadly for him, he wasn't very bright and he wasn't keen on hard work. Not a good combination.' She turned to me. 'There was nothing inside him, Gabe. There was a lot of *surface* – he was handsome, affable, he was a good host and a friend whom others were always glad to see – but, if you looked hard, you suddenly saw that there was nothing but emptiness behind the blue eyes.'

Abruptly she spun away from the window and began a slow pacing to and fro across the room. 'He decided he wanted to marry me as, apparently, I fulfilled his requirements in a wife,' she said after a moment. 'He went to see Father and, when Father was less than enthusiastic, Jeromy became all the more determined. He made up his mind that he would impress that upstart Benedict Taverner and his haughty family, and he'd have done virtually anything to persuade them he was good enough to wed their precious Celia. He bought clothes, a house—' She broke off. 'No, he didn't buy it, did he?' She smiled grimly. 'He rented it, whilst allowing it to be generally believed that he'd bought the best because only that would do for his prize bride.' Slowly she shook her head. 'He furnished it to the highest level of luxury and comfort, and filled it with hangings and draperies of the finest Venetian silk, and heaven only knows what it all cost.'

'Did he have no money from his father when he married?' I asked. I was pretty sure his family didn't want anything to do with him, but I felt I should check.

She shook her head. 'His father paid him a modest allowance provided he kept well away from the family's ancestral home. But, given the way Jeromy spent money, it was so small as to be irrelevant.'

'So he borrowed.'

'Yes. He borrowed. He cadged from everybody, but quite soon his friends and acquaintances grew wise to the fact that he never paid them back, so he had to look elsewhere. Besides, the sums he now needed were far beyond what you could ask of a friend.' She had resumed her pacing. 'It was some three or four months before the wedding that he first approached Nicolaus Quinlie. To his amazement, Quinlie was only too willing to comply, and Jeromy was too stupid ask himself why.' Again she gave that brief, harsh laugh. 'Before he realized what was happening, Nicolaus Quinlie had ensnared him. Oh, dear sweet Lord, Gabe,' she cried wildly, 'Jeromy didn't even understand that he'd be charged a fee! He told me that the first time Quinlie explained, telling him he didn't owe a hundred pounds or whatever it was but a hundred plus a fee amounting to twenty per cent, making it a hundred and twenty, he thought he was joking!'

I almost felt sorry for the poor fool. Almost.

'So what did he do?'

'When the moment came that Quinlie finally ran out of patience and demanded the first repayment of the debt, Jeromy of course couldn't produce it. A couple of Quinlie's heavies grabbed him off the street when he was staggering home drunk from the tavern one night and took him before their master. They beat him up a bit on the way, to get his attention and let him know this was serious. They were careful not to hit him on his face but on his torso, so he managed to hide the bruises,' she said, adding in a soft voice, 'and when I did spot one and ask about it, he said he'd fallen off his horse and forgotten to tell me. He—' But whatever she'd been about to say she bit back.

Firmly crushing my instinct to pity Jeromy, I said, 'And what did Quinlie suggest?'

'He offered him a way out. He proposed an entry into his criminal and vicious secret world and, because Jeromy had absolutely no hope of repaying the debt, he accepted.'

'What did Quinlie get him to do?'

She considered her answer for a few moments. 'Jeromy was potentially very useful to him because his background gave him access to the homes and the social lives of the wealthy aristocracy of the area: the old money. Jeromy might have been cast out by his own family' – like Nicolaus Quinlie before him, I thought, although for less reason – 'but his kin were – are – old money personified, so of course Jeromy was free to come and go within that exclusive clan.' She glanced at me, anticipating what I was about to say. 'His stiff-necked family didn't advertise the fact that Jeromy was no longer one of them. They'd put the word about that Jeromy was a fine, courageous young man intent on proving he could make his way in the world independently, with no help from his family, and it was in both his and his father's interests to keep the truth quiet.'

She came up close to me to pause on the other side of the fireplace, looking down at the ashes of the last fire. 'Jeromy's job was to find out people's vulnerable spots. Younger sons with gambling debts; a haughty lord's lady who had caught the pox thanks to her husband's frequenting of the dockside brothels; a flamboyant local character who rode a Plymouth whore too hard and killed her; a man of the church who buggered little boys. The nature of the work, as you might expect, brought out Jeromy's worst side, and his enthusiasm grew as he and Nicolaus Quinlie discovered he had a real talent for it.' Slowly she shook her head. 'He could sniff out vice and guilt and misery at ten paces, and he truly thought that was something to be proud of.'

She didn't seem to be able to meet my eyes.

'He led a clandestine life,' she resumed. 'Ferrars, situated as it was – is – on the high ground above the river and close to the old, largely disused Old Ferry Quay, was most conveniently suited to what he'd become. It's not far out of Plymouth and Jeromy visited the town a lot, on Quinlie's secret business, as well as travelling to other towns and ports on both honest business and to meet those from whom he was extracting money. All the time spent in lowly sinks and taverns, of course, was just perfect for a drinker like him. His work seeking out targets for extortion on Nicolaus Quinlie's behalf took him to low dives, taverns, brothels and gambling dens. And those were only the ones he admitted,' she said with a laugh. 'God only knows what other filth he sullied himself with. Until the—' She stopped abruptly. 'He had to make absolutely sure I didn't find out, which was why I became virtually a prisoner at Ferrars, only going out when he was with me. He also had to make sure I didn't accidentally let slip anything revealing to outsiders. But I didn't *know* anything,' she protested, as if I'd accused her, 'not for sure, although, dear Lord, I was beginning to suspect. And, of course, once the suspicions were there, I had to find out.' She laughed shortly, but there wasn't a vestige of humour in it. 'Isn't there some old tale about a wife who's perfectly happy until she disobeys her husband and peeps into the one room in his castle he's forbidden her to enter?'

'Yes, several.'

'Well, that was me. Not that I was perfectly happy – far from it. But my desire to know just *drove* me, and I found out things, awful things, and after I knew I almost wished I didn't.' She risked a quick look in my direction, as rapidly turning away again. 'I think he realized I was asking questions where I shouldn't, and he made up his mind to keep me scared of him; so scared that I wouldn't dare talk, even if I did find out anything.'

I couldn't bear any more. I moved over to her, taking her in my arms. She was stiff, unbending. I said, 'Celia, I'm so very sorry. You were going through all this, and I didn't realize. I didn't notice anything was wrong!'

She pulled away from me. 'Because I didn't *let* you!' she shouted. 'Dear God, Gabe, I have some pride! I'd insisted on marrying a vicious, drunken fool without a penny to his name, purely because he had a handsome face, good clothes and pretty manners – even though my own dear father did his best to persuade me not to! Can't you imagine how I'd have felt, forced to crawl back, admit I'd made a frightful mistake and throw myself on Father's mercy?'

'Father wouldn't have seen it like that and you know it!' I flashed back. 'We went through all this just now! He loves you very much, Celia, just as Mother does and I do, and

Nathaniel too, although you'd never know it, but that doesn't mean even he wouldn't support you and defend you if called upon to do so. None of us would have made you suffer more than you already had done, and as for Father, he—'

'But *I* saw it like that,' she said very softly. She didn't seem to have taken in anything I'd just said, beyond the first sentence. 'I'd set a trap for myself, Gabe, all on my own, and crawling back in ignominy to Father was more than I could bear.'

'But—'

She disentangled herself – I'd grabbed hold of her again – and now, with great dignity, she walked across the room to the door of her bedchamber. 'I don't want to talk any more,' she said firmly. Then she let herself out and closed the door behind her.

I was left alone in the pretty little anteroom. I had the awful feeling that there was more – worse – to come; she hadn't even begun to tell me about Jeromy's violence.

SIXTEEN

I strode along the gallery and into my study, flinging myself into my chair with such a fury of frustrated energy that it tipped backwards and all but threw me to the floor.

I was very afraid for my sister. What she had just told me surely increased the likelihood of some friend of Jeromy beginning to put it around that she had wanted him out of the way. And she and I hadn't even touched upon what Judyth had revealed: dear Lord above, how that would add fuel to the flames if it were to become known.

I had to act; had to do something, for sitting there worrying at questions to which nobody would give me answers was driving me to distraction. The surest way of making sure she wasn't accused – or, God forbid, convicted – of a crime she hadn't committed was to identify the real perpetrator and ensure he was brought to justice. How in God's name was I to proceed with that quest?

I sat there for some time, and gradually my frantic thoughts calmed. I began to feel better, and decided that to dissipate some energy I would collect Flynn and take him out into the good fresh air. Sometimes I'd found that the rhythmic act of walking put the mind into a relaxed state bordering on a trance, and then ideas that hadn't cropped up before could make their presence felt.

It was worth a try.

We went out of the side gate and set off across the fields, heading east towards the higher ground. We walked – well, I walked and Flynn ran – for miles. Whether or not my mind entered a relaxed state I couldn't say. If it did, nothing remotely useful emerged. We had gone round in a wide half-circle, coming back along the path that passes Rosewyke on its way to the river, and we were at the spot where the track branches off to the house when Flynn suddenly dashed off towards the grass beneath the oak tree on the right. Impatient to get on home, I called to him, but, unusually for him, he ignored me. I called again, shouting this time, but his only response was a brief glance at me over his shoulder and an ingratiating waggle of his stern.

I went over to see what he had found.

We were, as far as I could recall, at the place where Gelyan Thorn had fallen out of the tree. With an exclamation, I knelt down; I'd forgotten my resolve to feel around in the grass to see if I could locate the stone on which she had crushed her skull.

Flynn had found it for me. It was a large, irregularly shaped piece of granite such as ploughmen regularly turn up and leave at the field margins. It was not embedded in the earth but lay on the grass, the upward-pointing corner stained with blood.

Poor Gelyan. What evil chance, to fall in such a way that the most vulnerable part of her body landed on so damaging an object. It looked as if the theory concerning her death was the right one. I would make sure to tell Theo, although from his reaction when I'd told him of the circumstances, it appeared he'd never been in much doubt.

So intense had been my concentration that I only now became aware of Flynn, who had abandoned the bloody stone as soon as he'd drawn my attention to it and was now nose-down in the grass some ten or twelve yards over to the left, on the strip of verge beside the track. He was giving little yelps of excitement, front paws scrabbling and sending up clods of earth and clumps of grass.

I got up and ran over to him, taking hold of him by the scruff of the neck and firmly pulling him off. It took some doing, for he is a big dog and he was intent on whatever it was he'd found. 'It's all right, Flynn, I see it. Leave it now.'

Training overcame instinct and, obedient dog that he was, he did as I commanded. The trembling in his body and the soft, anxious whining in his throat told me how hard it was to do so.

I'd known, even as I hurried to get him away from his discovery, what it was. I'd smelt it: that ghastly, unmistakable stench of rotting flesh. In the grass beside the track lay a pair of dead rabbits, skinned, the flesh crawling with maggots and the bodies bloated to double the size.

I sat back on my heels. I knew, then, what had happened: the knowledge came like a sudden flame in a dark room.

These rabbits were what Gelyan had come to deliver. It was precisely the sort of offering in which she had specialized, and formed the latest – the last – in her inventive list of objects designed to repulse and disgust. She had come along as it grew dark, intending to creep up to the house when we had all retired for the night and leave her rabbits on the doorstep. She would have . . .

If she had come to deposit the rabbits, what had she been doing up the tree? Had she intended to tie the rope that would have thrown me violently from my horse *and* leave the skinned rabbits?

Or had the assumption that she'd been about to set that potentially lethal trap been wrong?

My thoughts were racing now. *Did* she fall on that conveniently placed stone as she tumbled out of the tree? But if I was right and it hadn't been Gelyan who had planned to tie it, why would she have been up the tree in the first place?

She had planned to do no such thing, any more than she had been responsible for that first rope that tripped Hal and threw me. Old Josiah Thorn had chuckled when I related the list of earlier offerings, but when I got to the rope across the track he had paled and whispered, *Not that – not anything like that.*

He had known what I now realized: Gelyan had been determined and full of resentment against me but she would never have done something so dangerous.

If she hadn't climbed the tree to tie the rope, then she hadn't died by striking her head as she fell. If that had been the case, then there was another explanation: someone had picked up that heavy, wickedly pointed piece of stone and wielded it to stave in her skull.

Somebody else had also come to Rosewyke that night, found her in the way and dispatched her, for the furtive Jesuit to find as she lay dying.

Someone else whose attacks on me were escalating in violence and who, but for Gelyan's unwitting intervention, might well have succeeded in setting up that taut rope precisely at neck height.

Celia stood at the window in her bedroom and watched Gabriel march off up the track, the big black dog running to and fro in an ecstasy of delight, nose deep in the fascinating smells of the grass verges on either side. She wondered where he was going, how long he would be. She didn't really care about his destination, but having him out of the house made her feel as if a heavy load had been removed from her shoulders. *I know he is trying to help me*, she thought, *and, indeed, I don't know what I would do without him. But the strain of his presence is almost more than I can bear . . .*

She wandered back into the anteroom. Oh, but he'd made her so welcome! He – or more likely Sallie – had gone to so much trouble to prepare these two rooms for her, and she was grateful to the depths of her being. Sometimes, though, she longed to be anywhere but here. Longed to be anywhere that people didn't keep *looking* at her and asking her questions she couldn't answer.

She resumed her comfortable chair beside the window and picked up her sewing. Threaded a different-coloured silk through the eye of her needle. Began to stitch. And presently, as it so often did, the steady, even stitching calmed her. Drove back – for a time, anyway – the images of horror.

She heard footsteps on the track. The sandy, stony ground crunched. Crunch, crunch, crunch; whoever it was, they strode smartly. Then there came a resounding knock on the big oak door.

Celia brought herself back to the present. Took a breath to steady herself – the images had broken down her defences – and stretched.

The knocking came again, louder now.

Where was Sallie? Why hadn't she gone to see who it was?

The knocking sounded again.

Hadn't Samuel noticed they had a visitor? But then she remembered: both Samuel and Tock had gone off to take a bull calf to the cattle market.

Celia suppressed a sigh, pushed the needle into the silk and put down her sewing. It appeared it was up to her to see who had come calling.

She walked along the gallery and down the stairs. *It's probably some patient*, she thought. *I'd better be courteous to him or her.* Gabriel, she had noticed, wasn't exactly inundated with the sick and the injured demanding his services.

She crossed the hall and pulled open the heavy door.

A man stood on the step. He was tall and extremely thin, the long line of him exaggerated by the dark garments: he wore a fine wool cloak in an indeterminate shade of greyish-brown, and beneath it could be seen the skirts of a black robe. His face was drawn, with hollows beneath the cheekbones. His eyes were heavily hooded, and in the shade from his soft-brimmed hat it was difficult to make out their colour. On seeing her, he swept off the hat and bowed, all in one smooth movement. 'My apologies for disturbing you, madam,' he said in a low voice with a marked accent. 'I seek the doctor.'

'He is not here at present,' Celia replied. She hesitated. She was wary, for some reason she could not begin to fathom, and found that she wanted to tell this man to go away and come back later. But he'd just said he needed a doctor, and she owed Gabriel so much . . . She opened the door more widely and said, 'Please, come in. I'm sure my brother won't be long.'

The man bowed again and said, still bent over, 'Thank you, my lady. Most kind.'

Where do I take him? Celia wondered wildly. Parlour? Little morning parlour? Kitchen? No, not the kitchen. She bit back a laugh. It wasn't funny, not at all – this might well be a new patient, and a wealthy one as well, for that wool cloak was good quality, and she knew she must do her best to impress him. She led the way across the hall and into the library.

It was a good choice, she reflected as the man gazed round, his hat in his hands. As with all the rooms in Gabriel's lovely house, the proportions were good. Gabriel had furnished it with taste, and the furniture – table, four high-backed chairs, chests – was of fine English oak. The wide fireplace – empty now – had a granite surround and was framed by beautiful wooden panelling.

'Please, be seated.' Celia pulled out a chair. 'May I fetch you—'

The man made a swift, elegant gesture of refusal. As he did so, the skirt of his cloak fell away and she saw something hanging from his cord belt. It was a string of small, round wooden beads, interspersed at regular intervals with slightly larger ones. Here and there among the dull wood glittered a touch of gold.

Noticing her eyes on the beads, the man twitched his cloak so that it covered them.

Celia suppressed a gasp. *It surely cannot be a rosary!*

She didn't know precisely what happened to people seen carrying rosaries. She was sure, however, it wasn't anything good.

Maybe it was just a string of beads . . .

The man said quietly, 'I disturb you, my lady, and I cannot tell you how much I regret that.' She risked a quick glance at his face. He looked fearful, anxious, yet she could see he was trying to disguise it. He rose, with very evident effort, to his feet, supporting himself with a hand on the table. He drew in a sharp breath, his face creasing in distress. *He's in pain too*, she thought. 'I will go, madam,' he murmured, 'and return another time, hoping that my luck will then be better and I shall find the doctor is—'

She made up her mind. So what if he was carrying a rosary? So what if he was indeed what she was beginning to suspect he was? He was ill, or wounded, and he had sought out Gabriel because he desperately needed help. She couldn't bring herself to turn him away.

She put a hand on his shoulder – bony and hard – and gently pushed him back into the chair. 'Sit down,' she said. 'While we wait for my brother, I will fetch you something to eat and drink.'

'No, please, there is no need!' He was half standing again, a hand raised as if in rejection of the offer.

She smiled at him. 'There is every need.' *You are starving,* she could have added. If what she believed was true, he was probably living the life of a fugitive, friendless, homeless, and in all likelihood it was days since he had eaten. 'Wait here,' she added. 'I won't be long.'

*   *   *

The kitchen was empty. She set about loading a tray – mugs, a jug for the ale – and the small noises must have reached Sallie's little room, off the kitchen.

Sallie was tucking strands of stray hair beneath her white cap, straightening her gown, rubbing the drowse from her eyes. 'I'll do that, miss!' she said. 'I fell asleep! I'm that sorry, I shouldn't have done so, and now look at me, letting you do all this!' Gently but firmly she nudged Celia out of the way. 'What is it you want, Miss Celia?'

Celia thought swiftly. If she told the truth, that a suffering patient was awaiting Gabriel in the library, then undoubtedly Sallie would insist on serving him herself. She took her house-keeper's duties very seriously, Celia had observed, and disliked anyone – well, to be precise, Celia – usurping her role.

I should not let her see him, Celia thought. *I am prepared to take the risk – if risk there is – but I must not allow Sallie to do so*. She thought swiftly.

'Something tasty to eat and something restoring to drink, I think, please, Sallie,' she said brightly. 'I have a visitor! One of my friends,' she improvised, 'the wife of a colleague of my late husband – has come to see how I am, and—'

Sallie paused and turned to face her, giving her a wide, happy beam. 'Now isn't that nice!' she exclaimed. 'Considerate and kind, I call it, and I shall prepare something really appetizing!' She returned to her bustling, now at the larder, now poking up the fire and sticking in a poker to heat up. 'Cakes and warmed spiced wine, I think – it may be the month of May, but still there's a nip in the air.' Celia watched her work. 'You want it in the parlour, Miss Celia? Or the library?'

Again Celia considered. 'Neither, Sallie,' she said. 'I shall entertain my friend up in my sitting room, for undoubtedly we shall not wish to be disturbed!' She gave a little giggle, trying to imply that she and the fictitious woman friend might be exchanging a few girlish secrets.

Sallie nodded sagely. 'I quite understand, miss. There' – with a flourish, she smoothed the clean white cloth and added a couple of pretty silver goblets to the tray – 'that's ready now. Go on ahead, miss, and I'll bring this.'

Firmly Celia took the tray from her. 'No, Sallie, don't trouble yourself,' she said, in the sort of tone that allowed no argument. Sallie stood watching her, face expressing surprise. 'In fact,' Celia added, 'why not get out in the sunshine for a while? It's such a beautiful day.'

Sallie nodded slowly, her expression doubtful. 'Well, I suppose I could walk down to the village and arrange for Dorcas to come up and help me with giving the dairy a really thorough scrubbing-out, for it certainly needs it . . .'

'Yes. I should do that.'

Offering no explanation – why, indeed, should she? – Celia murmured her thanks and swept out of the room.

She hurried across to the library. The man leapt to his feet. She said softly, 'Follow me. We shall be more private elsewhere.' Then she led the way up the stairs, along the gallery and into the anteroom to her bedchamber whose door, she was pleased to see, was shut. Her pretty sitting room, colourfully furnished and smelling faintly of roses, was welcoming, and, putting the tray down on her little work table, she drew up a couple of chairs.

He stepped in after her and closed the door.

The house was very quiet. I'd left Flynn out in the yard, muddy and exhausted, lapping up water as if he hadn't seen any for a week. Not finding Sallie in the kitchen, I risked a glance into her room, but it was empty, the bed neatly made, everything in the sort of order Sallie loved. I wandered across the hall and into the parlour, going on through to the library. A chair was out of place, pulled away from the table as if someone had recently sat on it.

Celia, it appeared, was still in her room. I went up to find her.

I reached the top of the stairs and was about to turn in the direction of Celia's side of the upper storey when I heard a noise. It came from the direction of my study. Had Celia gone in there looking for something? What?

Trying to keep as quiet as possible, I tiptoed along the gallery and into my bedchamber. You can reach my study by going on along the gallery and through the small bedroom, but the door to my chamber was ajar and I thought I might be quieter approaching via the connecting door to the study.

I didn't stop to ask myself why I felt such an urge not to be heard.

My desk stands in the wide window, and entering the room via either door means whoever is at the desk has their back to you.

Leaning over my desk, every inch of the tall, thin body exhibiting tension, was a dark-clad figure. Even before some small noise from me alerted him and he spun round, I knew who he was.

'What are you doing?' I asked. I tried to keep my voice calm, reasonable. 'May I be of assistance?'

His gaunt, sallow-skinned face stretched in a smile. 'Oh, how relieved I am to see you!' he exclaimed. 'I had come seeking you on a minor matter, but that is not important.' He waved a slender hand. 'The lady of the house – your sister, I believe?' I nodded. 'She welcomed me most hospitably, insisting on providing refreshments – very good ones! – although I tried to persuade her there was no need, and—'

'What are you doing up here?' I interrupted, my tone a little cooler. I stared pointedly at my desk and the documents spread upon it, then raised my eyes to meet his.

He strode towards me, hands out as if in supplication. 'Doctor, you must forgive what surely appears to be a most discourteous intrusion into your privacy.' I noticed, as I had done before, the foreign accent; the way in which some vowel sounds were lengthened and exaggerated. Dis*cooour*teous. Pre*eeev*acy. 'But your sister was taken ill, and, knowing of course that you are a doctor, I have hurried in here, much against my natural instinct, to see if I may not find some remedy to restore her among your supplies, a—'

I had stopped listening. Already turning, hurrying towards the gallery, I said urgently, 'Where is she? In her room?'

'*Sí, sí* – yes, on her bed, I thought it best to—'

I ignored his anxious explanations and ran along the gallery, through Celia's anteroom and into her bedchamber. She was lying on her side on the bed, a warm coverlet over her, one hand under her cheek. She looked as if she was heavily asleep.

I picked up her wrist. Her pulse was steady. Her colour was good, and I bent over her to check her breathing. My face close to hers, I smelt something—

And then I felt such a blow to the back of my head, where neck meets skull, that my vision turned black. There was a great burst of pain, and I felt myself falling.

I came to my senses to find myself sitting in my own chair. He must have brought it in from my study. *He is stronger than he looks*, I thought vaguely, *for the chair is solid and heavy.*

My hands lay on the lion heads with which the chair's arms terminate. My wrists were bound to those arms. I tensed my muscles and strained against the cords, but they were very firm.

Ignoring the blaze of pain, I raised my head.

He was standing before me. Meeting my eyes, he said, 'I am very sorry, doctor. You have been kind and considerate towards me, as has your sister, and I am profoundly ashamed to have treated you in this way. I—'

'What have you done to my sister?' I demanded. 'If you have harmed her, you will pay for it with your life.'

'Please, do not concern yourself for her. She is unharmed; merely deeply asleep,' he said quickly.

'You drugged her.' I recalled that smell as I'd bent over her. 'What was it?'

'A concoction of my own,' he replied, 'and – for I see you are still anxious – one I use regularly myself. Please, I say again, she is not harmed.'

'How did you get her to drink it?' Glancing round, I noticed the tray on the little side table, with its goblets, jug, platters.

'I must confess I tricked her,' he admitted. 'I pretended to be feeling unwell, and she came hurrying over to assist. While she was thus distracted, it was a simple matter to reach out my hand and slip the potion into her goblet.'

'A fine way to repay her kindness,' I said coldly.

'Doctor, I know, believe me I know, and I hope you will tender my sincere and heartfelt apologies to her when she wakes.'

That, I thought, was grounds for hope: the priest appeared to anticipate a time when both Celia and I would be free and able to converse normally.

'What do you want?' I asked. 'You're a Jesuit, aren't you? Are you a fugitive? Of course you are!' I answered my own question. 'I have to tell you that although I—'

He held up a hand to stop me. 'Once again, forgive me, doctor, but I'm afraid you really do not understand.'

'Why, then, don't you explain?'

He sighed, turned towards the window and stood staring out over the peaceful fields and woodland. 'Why don't I explain?' he echoed softly. Watching him intently, I thought some of the tension went out of his shoulders. He glanced at me, then returned to his contemplation of the view. 'Perhaps I should, for I owe it to the good doctor here.' He sighed. 'And, after all this time, all these years of secrecy, I yearn to share the tale.'

There was what seemed like a very long pause. Then he began to speak.

'I was born in Venice and raised first by nuns, then monks, and finally given into the care of the Jesuits of the church and school of Santa Maria dell'Umiltà in Dorsoduro. They have quite a presence in the city, as indeed in many places, and support for them throughout the city states began to grow rapidly from the middle of the last century, when they founded one of their great colleges. They are great educators, you know.' He nodded, as if to underline his claim.

'Shouldn't that be *we*, since you are one of them?' I said. He simply smiled.

'The Society of Jesus will educate any boy, whatever his class and no matter how unfortunate his background,' he went on, 'and, indeed, some say that it is among the least advantaged of this harsh world that they find some of their best priests.' He moved away from the window, drawing up Celia's little foot stool and sitting down on it, close in front of me.

'Let me tell you a story,' he said softly, 'of one such disadvantaged boy, alone, grieving, in despair, who had the good fortune to catch the eye of the very man who could help him.'

He paused, perhaps collecting his thoughts. I studied his sallow face, in which his eyes – large and a pale hazel colour, hooded and thickly lashed – burned with whatever intensity drove him. 'This lad of whom I speak was illegitimate; born to a woman who had been impregnated and discarded, as so many are. Far from home, she had nowhere to go when her time came and, since she had no husband and therefore could not go to any place where gently reared ladies are tended, there was no option for her but to throw herself on the charity of the nuns at the paupers' hospital. They did what they had to, and a boy child was delivered, along with many a lecture on the woman's evil ways and the great sin of fornication, for which, as she must appreciate, she was now being punished. Well, she tolerated the punishments and the harsh regime – no kindness there, not for sinners – until she was sufficiently recovered from the brutality of the birth to pick up her child and drag herself away. She had a place to stay – that at least had been provided – but it was in a poor quarter of the town, inhabited by the wicked and the desperate. No place, in short, for one such as her.'

He paused, almost as if to allow me time to comment. I had nothing to say. He had the story-teller's skill, and already I was enthralled.

'The boy grew and, to her amazement, he thrived. She made many sacrifices for him, giving him the better part of every scrap of nourishing food she managed to acquire, and inevitably it followed that her own health suffered. When plague struck the city in 1575, the first few cases growing by the following year into an epidemic that took thousands, she had little strength with which to resist.'

He paused, turning away to gaze out of the window.

'When she first fell sick,' he resumed, 'she was transported, with her little boy, to Lazaretto Nuovo, for that is the island where those suspected of suffering from the deadly disease are taken for assessment. The Venetian authorities are very efficient,' he added, 'for it is also the quarantine island where, in normal times, crews and cargos from ships arriving from plague spots are sent while those in charge decide whether or not infection is present. When it is found to be so, patients are moved to Lazaretto Vecchio, as was the case with the woman of whom I speak.'

He paused again, now staring down at the floorboards beneath his feet. I sensed he wasn't seeing them, for his mind was far away. 'It is a terrible place,' he said quietly. 'A place of pain, torment, anguish, despair, for, once there, barely a soul returns. Back then, at the height of the outbreak, the corpse pits filled up as fast as they could be dug.

'And then, as if all that horror was not enough, a new one came. Rumours began to circulate of a special kind of ghost; a ghoul that belonged to the malevolent company of the *masticatione mortuorum*.'

I tried to translate the Latin. 'The . . . the chewing dead?' Surely I'd misheard.

But he nodded. 'Very good, doctor, although the usual expression in your language is shroud-eater. For those credulous, superstitious fools who believe in such phenomena, it's a particularly dreadful example,' he went on, 'which would have us believe that a certain type of the undead takes up residence in graves – mass graves, obviously, being preferable – where they are heard to make hideous chewing and grinding noises, and who have it within their power to bring death and the impulse to destruction to those who venture too close. In a time of plague, when death seems to leap from one person to the next with such ease and when whole families can be wiped out in a matter of days, it is perhaps understandable for the ignorant to seek a supernatural explanation; although, for myself, I do not believe that a man should ever lose his reasoning power, even in extremis. But I digress.' He flashed me a swift smile. His eyes were wide, and as brilliant as if he had a fever.

'So, there we are on the Venetian plague islands, among the dead and the dying, and out among the mass graves frightful noises are heard. What happens next? Well, the nuns and the monks and the medical men are already at their wits' end as each one tries to perform the work of a dozen, and they have little choice but to try to stem the incipient hysteria. So they investigate the noises and, wanting to put an end to the terrifying tales, they unearth some of the most recently interred. They light upon one corpse – that of a woman – who does indeed seem to have moved, for she has her hands stretched up above her as if trying to dig up through the earth and find the daylight and the air. The holy men and women know they are doing wrong – the shroud-eater, they know, is a malign invention that forms no part of God's world – but they must try to stop the panic. So what do you imagine they do?'

I shook my head. 'I don't know,' I said quietly.

'There is a renowned remedy for putting an end to the antics of the chewing dead, and they employed it. They dragged that woman's body out of the grave, they prised apart her jaws – not hard to do, for there was no stiffening – and they thrust between her teeth a large lump of brick. Someone screamed, there was a great moan of agony, a spurt of blood. The man holding the brick was scared out of his wits, for he believed that the horror stories were true. He thought the dead woman had become reanimated, and he knew that he must at all costs put an end to her, right there and then. He pushed the brick in harder, there was an awful choking sound, a cracking as if of breaking bone, and he let the corpse slide back into the grave.' He stopped, the echo of his words ringing in the silent room. 'There were no more reports of grinding and chewing noises, and it was concluded by the monks, the nuns, the medical men, the sick and the dying that the remedy had worked.'

Images of horror filled my mind. I shook my head, as if to dissipate them, but it did no good.

'The woman's name was Rose Willerton,' he said after what seemed a long time.

Rose Willerton. Yes.

'She had been engaged to be married to Nicolaus Quinlie,' the priest went on softly, 'but when her highly influential family had a spectacular fall from grace, he decided she wasn't the wife for an ambitious man. What, though, could he do? By then he had seduced her, taken her virginity, made her worthless for any other marriage and, as if all that were not bad enough, he had made her pregnant. To abandon her now would harm his reputation even more than marrying her, so instead he decided she must disappear.

'So he told her family she had died. She had been on a visit to see him, to view the house he was preparing for them after their marriage, accompanied by her personal maidservant and a young groom. It was not a long journey there from her father's house, and she had not planned to stay for more than a few hours. She was well chaperoned. But Nicolaus saw his chance and took it. He sent the groom to join his own staff for the midday meal, and told the maid to wait while he showed his fiancée around the grounds of what was to be her home. A little later, he came racing back, in dreadful distress, with the news that Rose had suffered some sort of accident – or perhaps it was a fit – and lay dead in a little copse on the far extremity of the grounds. The maidservant, aghast, wanted to rush to her young mistress's side, but Nicolaus prevented her. "She would not wish you to see her thus," he said firmly, then, in a low voice that only she could hear, added, "And better, I think, for you to start looking to yourself, for surely there will be difficult questions to ask. Such as, why did you not accompany your mistress down the garden, and why were you not present to give whatever help you could, that might just have saved her life? My goodness" – he pretended the thought had just occurred to him – "you'd be dismissed and you'd never find work again! You'd die in abject poverty, outcast and shunned!"'

His tale was so plausible that it had taken me a moment to discover the flaw. 'How can you know this?' I demanded. 'You cannot have been present.'

'No, I was not,' he agreed. 'However, I know the bare bones of the matter. If I add a little conjecture to make my tale flow the better, you will, I am sure, understand my reasons.'

'Go on.'

'The maidservant – she was a mature woman – saw the good sense of that. Meekly bowing her head, she said, "Then I reckon I'd better get on back to her father, and tell him the terrible news."

'"I reckon so too," Nicolaus agreed. He slipped her some coins. "I shall bury her here," he announced, "in a tomb fit for the great lady she was, and so I shall keep her with me always."'

Keep her with me always . . .

'He couldn't bring himself to kill her,' the priest went on. 'He knew he couldn't marry her, yet she carried his child in her womb and, somewhere in his cold and calculating heart, he recognized that he had once had feelings for her. He ran back to where he had left her. He had, it is concluded, incapacitated her in some way; in all likelihood with a drugged drink, for he was known to be very skilled in such matters.' He paused, shooting me a quick glance, as if inviting me to comment on the fact that he had just done the same to Celia. I kept silent. 'Then he proceeded to the next part of his plan: to remove her from his estate, the county, the country, and get her far away; so far that she would never be heard from again, dead to family, friends and the world.'

And Nicolaus Quinlie, I thought, *would have had ships at his disposal even back then, and loyal crews who did not ask too many questions.*

'Did she not protest, I hear you wonder.' The priest's eyes were intent on mine. 'Did she not, once she had arrived at her destination and begun her exile, manage to contact her father, tell him what had happened and where she was, and beg him to rescue her? Ah, I am quite sure she was tempted, many a time, but let us not forget that she was pregnant. She had allowed Nicolaus Quinlie to bed her and impregnate her and she did not dare reveal that to anybody who had known her in her past life, her upright, virtuous and rigid father in particular. No: Rose knew she had sinned – knowledge that was reinforced by every nun, priest and religious she encountered, and they were legion – and she recognized that this was her punishment.'

'She was still alive when they unearthed her, wasn't she?' I felt sure of it.

He spun round to face me. 'I believe she was.'

I nodded. For an instant, I identified with his actions. I might even have done the same in his boots. 'So Nicolaus Quinlie, who was responsible for all her suffering, had to endure the same death.'

'He did.'

'You are, of course, his son.'

He bowed. 'I am. Tobias Willerton.' He gave an ironic bow.

'You were raised and educated by Jesuits and you became one of them,' I began, 'and—'

But he said coolly, 'I am no Jesuit.'

'*What?*' I could scarcely believe it. 'You disguise yourself as one at your peril, then!' I exclaimed. 'Do you not know what is done to Jesuits here? Have you never heard of Edmund Campion?'

He brushed my amazed remarks aside. 'Of course. But as I see it, many Jesuits come to England pretending not to be what they are, so why not the other way round? It's the perfect disguise when I need one since, given recent events, who in their right mind would pretend to be a Jesuit? It's far too risky. And besides,' he added, a sly expression in the shining eyes, 'you have no idea how many doors it opens. I present myself as a stranger, alone, afire with my missionary zeal yet, underneath, very frightened, and the Catholics in this land fling open their doors, their arms and their purses. They take me in, hide me, feed me; give me, in short, whatever I ask for, and all in exchange for the saying of a forbidden mass or two in their pretty little private chapels.'

'That is sacrilege,' I said quietly.

Tobias Willerton smiled. 'I know, doctor. I'll add it to all my other sins.'

He'd been raised by Jesuits, I thought. He'd know exactly how they acted. How they moved, spoke, dressed, prayed. He was observant and clever, and those intelligent, determined and zealous priests had encouraged him; had, albeit unintentionally, made him precisely what he was now.

'It wasn't hard to locate my father,' he was saying, 'since back in Venice he was well known, as was his whereabouts. Once in England I made my way to Plymouth, and quite easily slid into his affections. I like to think that some part of his mind recognized his long-lost son, but that is whimsy. It is far more likely that he was always on the lookout for bright, ruthless young men who were not greatly troubled by their conscience. Over the course of a few months I made myself indispensable to him, and soon he was entrusting me with the sort of painstaking, carefully planned tasks he'd previously had to perform for himself.'

He paused, staring hard at me. 'You cannot have cared for Jeromy Palfrey,' he said.

'Not much.' Why, I wondered, mention Jeromy just then? Then I thought perhaps I knew, although the logic escaped me.

'You left the sow's organs on my doorstep,' I said.

He nodded. 'Indeed I did. I had been watching your house, and observed what was going on.' I frowned, questions buzzing in my mind. 'Jeromy had told Nicolaus that Celia was coming here to stay with you, and, since I had orders to frighten him, I thought the subtlest way to do so would be via his lovely wife.'

'You – the pig's womb was meant to scare Celia?'

'Of course.'

'But—'

Then I understood. When Celia had visited me then, she'd been pregnant. The sow's uterus, ripped open to display the small, pathetic foetuses, had been a warning of the most graphic kind: *Do as I say or the same thing will happen to your wife.*

And Quinlie had urgently needed to regain control over Jeromy, since Jeromy had just unearthed his wealthy and powerful employer's deepest secret.

'What did—' I began.

He didn't let me finish.

'And then there was you.' The bright-eyed stare fixed on me again. 'You were beginning to worry me, doctor, because you're so relentless. As I just implied, I knew about that foolish little girl trying to scare you away with her dog shit and her decapitated blindworm, and I decided to pretend she was getting a little more ruthless. I thought I'd begun to achieve my purpose when I tripped that fine horse of yours, and followed up by knocking you out.'

I made no comment.

'Then, of course, there were the papers: that file that Quinlie kept and in which he detailed all the payments he'd made over the years to the brothers in Venice, to help towards the high running costs of the Lazaretto islands. They have an eye for the ironic, don't they? One has to admire them, really, making Nicolaus Quinlie pay for ever more for what he did, in such an appropriate manner. At the same time, a nice little sop to his conscience – if he had one – and an action that actually did some good. He never knew about me, however; they never told him he had a son.' He paused. 'They kept his identity a secret from me, too. Perhaps they read my nature better than

I imagined, and decided it was too dangerous, for him, for me to know who had fathered me. Anyway, it wasn't important. Information abounds in a place like Venice, and I've always had a talent for extracting secrets. It was relatively easy to find out my mother's name and learn her fate, and after that I took up the challenge of discovering where she'd come from and why she'd ended up in Venice.' His expression clouded, and suddenly he looked desolate. 'I remember my mother very well,' he said softly. 'I was four when the plague came and she fell ill. Old enough to be so frightened that I could scarcely draw breath. Old enough to know, as we approached those islands in the lagoon, what lay ahead. Old enough to recognize the terror on my mother's face when they—' He broke off.

For a while there was utter silence. Then he said, 'It is time for the true fate of Rose Willerton to be known, for she was a courageous, loving, lively woman who paid a very harsh price for the sin of lying with her seducer.' His eyes met mine, and I thought I knew what he was asking.

It could be done, I thought. Presumably the Willerton family still existed, and I believed Jarman Hodge capable of finding out who should be approached. Was this why Tobias had been willing to tell his tale? Because, all along, he had hoped for my help?

As if he read my thoughts, he said gently, 'I cannot do it myself, doctor. I killed the man who begat me, and, even assuming you don't repeat my confession – in which case it would only be your word against mine – Nicolaus Quinlie's missing papers will condemn me.' He knew I would ask, and he supplied the answer before I did so. 'The papers demonstrate the link between Quinlie and the brothers in Venice. Were anyone to follow that link and set out for Venice, it would not take them very long to pick up the end of the thread that leads to me.' Before I could protest, for it seemed unlikely, he said firmly, 'Doctor, I followed the trail the other way. Armed with no more than my wits, kept in deliberate ignorance about my origins by the brothers who raised me, I managed to uncover the whole tragic tale. I do not rate my own intelligence so highly as to think no other man could do the same.'

He had paused by the window and was once again staring out. 'So, doctor. Will you do what I ask?' He spun round, the hazel eyes searching mine.

I nodded.

Briefly he closed his eyes, and I heard him mutter something. I didn't think it was a prayer. 'Then all my hard work and the long, long road that led to this moment have been worthwhile,' he said quietly. His face twisted in an ironic smile. 'I have done well, haven't I? Both my real father and the fathers who raised me would be proud of what I managed to find out, don't you think?'

I hadn't expected to find him pathetic, but just then I did.

I think even Tobias Willerton had noticed now that it was a while since I'd said more than a word. I'd tried to carry on talking, not wanting him to realize I had something else on my mind, but I'd found it hard.

I keep a small and very sharp knife in a sheath attached to a leather cuff round my left forearm, just above the wrist. It's like a scalpel. The device was taught to me by one of the rougher sailors I once knew.

I couldn't think when I'd ever been more glad of it.

While the priest had been speaking, I had worked the blade out of its sheath and now its thin wooden handle rested in my palm. I edged it along till it was held securely between my thumb and forefinger. Then I began to saw through the rope that bound me. I also sawed into my own flesh, but the sharp pain was less of a worry than the blood dripping on to the floor. If Tobias Willerton should notice it . . .

There was the sound of hurried footsteps outside and, after a cursory knock, Sallie came bursting into the room, talking even as she did so. 'Mistress Celia took up some refreshments for her guest and said she didn't need me so I went off to see Dorcas, but I saw Flynn in the yard and knew you were back, doctor, and I thought I'd ask if you want anything, as I – *Oh!*'

The priest had spun round to face her, sweeping out the folds of his cloak to hide me. 'The cakes were delicious,' he began, his tone smooth and soothing. 'We enjoyed them very much.'

'But – but what's going on?' Sallie spluttered.

The distraction gave me precious time, and at last the rope gave way. Hastily I cut the ropes on my right wrist, then leapt up and threw myself at Tobias Willerton.

He saw, or perhaps sensed, the assault. He seemed to flick his long, lean body like a whip, out of my grasp, and then he was off.

Sallie screamed, several times.

'Look after Celia!' I shouted. 'She's in her room!'

Then I thundered after him. Along the gallery, down the stairs, across the hall, pausing for a heartbeat to pick up my sword. Out into the open air, the warm sunshine of a sweet May day.

Tobias must have heard the heavy beat of my footsteps. He glanced over his shoulder and tripped on his long robe, but recovered his footing and raced on.

There was a flash of flying black, and Flynn threw himself on Tobias. He is a big, heavy dog. Tobias had no chance.

I pulled Flynn away, patting his heaving sides, praising him, calming him.

Before Tobias could get up, I was on him. I stood over him, the point of my sword at his throat.

'I understand why you murdered Quinlie,' I panted, fighting for breath, 'but did Gelyan have to die?'

His eyes narrowed. Then he said, 'Ah. The girl.'

'The girl,' I agreed. 'And I imagine we can add Pieter Sparre to your list of victims. Dartmouth warehouseman,' I added tersely. I was not going to be a party to his game of feigned ignorance.

'The Dartmouth fool was too inquisitive by half,' he said. 'As for the girl – I didn't expect anyone to be there. I was trying to recover the papers, which of course was what I came back for today. They're well hidden,' he remarked with a wry smile.

'They are.' I'd put them in my doctor's bag. 'Gelyan saw you, I imagine.'

'She did.'

I waited, but it seemed that was all he had to say on the matter.

'And Jeromy?' I went on. 'Quinlie wanted him dead, but did you have to do it with such savagery?'

He stared up at me for what seemed like several heartbeats. I thought I saw something in his eyes . . . could it have been compassion?

Quietly he said, 'But I didn't kill Jeromy.'

And then I thought I understood.

If he dies, I thought swiftly, *if Tobias dies here and now, nobody will ever know what he just said. If he were to be brought to trial, and could somehow prove it was the truth, then—*

I discovered that I couldn't even begin to think about that.

I put my full weight on the end of my sword and drove it into his throat. He gave a gasp, and a great surge of blood flowed out.

His eyes clouded and I watched as his spirit fled.

The man was a killer. He murdered poor lost Gelyan, he murdered Pieter Sparre, he tortured and killed Quinlie in the most barbaric way. For all that he claimed he didn't want to hurt us, he'd very possibly been about to murder my sister, me and probably my housekeeper too.

And the death I'd just given him had the mercy of speed. Had I done what I should and delivered him up, bound and captive, to the law, then his fate would have been far, far worse. He would have been found guilty of murder: of Gelyan Thorn, Pieter Sparre and Nicolaus Quinlie. Quinlie had been his employer, and that made him Tobias's superior. As if all that wasn't enough, he'd also taken on the guise of a Jesuit priest, and even now he wore the black robe and carried the rosary at his belt. He would have suffered the terrible death of hanging, drawing and quartering, with a vicious, jeering, mocking crowd watching his every agonized spasm.

No. He was better off dead by a swift sword thrust to the throat, performed by a man who knew what he was doing.

I withdrew my sword and wiped it on the grass. I stood looking down at Tobias Willerton.

Rationalize it as best I could, just then the fact that I'd pushed a blade through a man's throat and dispatched him was troubling me.

But I knew I'd get over it.

SEVENTEEN

I buried Tobias Willerton behind the midden. Although I was desperate to get back to Celia – I only had his word for it that the sleeping draught would do no permanent harm – the most pressing need was to get the body out of sight. It wasn't long ago that Tock had laboriously moved the last of the content of the muck heap onto the vegetable beds, and the ground was still quite soft. I dug a hole as fast as I could, put the body into it and covered it over, then shifted a great stack of early prunings on top of it in the hope that I would thus disguise the evidence of newly turned earth.

If anyone from my household saw me and guessed what I was doing, they had the good sense not to say so.

He had probably planned a careful escape, I reflected as I completed my task. Once he had achieved his mission and killed his father, then found and destroyed those incriminating Lazaretto papers that might have led the way back to him, had he worked out the route to some out-of-the-way little port from which he would take ship back to Venice? It seemed likely.

But something was troubling me about that conclusion. There had been an expression in his eyes, just before I killed him. There was – I thought about it. There was resignation in it.

Perhaps killing Nicolaus Quinlie was what had really mattered. That deed done, and by such an appropriately brutal method, maybe the son whom Quinlie hadn't even known about hadn't really cared much what happened to him . . .

Finished at last, I washed my hands and forearms under the yard pump. My left wrist was still bleeding freely, and now encrusted with soil and half-congealed bits of scab. Having sluiced the wound thoroughly, I went inside and through to the library to find my bag and patch myself up. Then I went upstairs.

Sallie was crouching and cooing over Celia, whose eyelids were fluttering. I went to kneel beside her, one hand on my sister's forehead. I turned to my housekeeper. 'Sallie, please fetch some water, as cold as possible, and something sweet to eat.' She nodded and hurried away.

I sat down on the bed, one hand still on Celia's forehead, the fingers of my other hand on her wrist to feel her heartbeat. She felt quite cool and her pulse was steady but slow. *Do not concern yourself for her*, he had said. *She is unharmed; merely deeply asleep.*

I said a silent and fervent prayer that he was right, and that she would recover and be restored to herself.

Presently her eyes opened properly. She looked up, saw me and frowned. 'Your face is dirty,' she observed.

'Yes. I'll go and wash properly in a while. I just wanted to make sure you're all right.'

Her frown deepened. 'There was a man here . . .' Then memory came galloping back. 'Gabe, he's a priest, and he's on the run! I brought him up here to my own quarters, because I didn't want anyone to know about him, and I fetched food and drink for him, and then – and then . . .' She stared up at me in confusion. 'I must have fallen asleep! How very odd!'

'It's a warm day,' I said soothingly. 'And, from the smell of what's left in the jug out there in your anteroom, I'd say you mixed the wine with a good slug of brandy.'

She nodded. 'Oh, dear, what must he have thought of me? I wonder if—' She broke off. 'Where is he?'

'He's gone.'

'Oh.'

'He asked me to thank you.' I sought the words he'd used. 'He said I was to tender his sincere and heartfelt apologies to you when you woke up.'

'His *apologies*?'

My mind raced to come up with a credible explanation but my sister beat me to it. 'Oh, for leaving without saying goodbye, I suppose.' Her face fell and she looked anxious. 'Oh, that poor man! I don't imagine he dares stay in any one place for long. How terrible it must be to live the life of a fugitive. We must pray for him, Gabe. I know he's a – I know what he *is*,' she amended carefully, 'but, all the same, he's a brave man.'

There was no doubt about that. 'We'll keep him in our

prayers, yes, of course.' I took hold of her hand. 'Now, here's Sallie with food and water for you. Sit up, and let's see you tuck it away.'

I rode over to Fernycombe early the next morning.

I had barely slept, worrying all night about how I would go about it; what means I could employ to find out what I needed to know. The one thing I could not do was ask outright.

As I set off up the track, I had decided on a course of action. I just hoped it was the right one.

My mother was outside and came to greet me as I dismounted and handed Hal's reins to a stable lad. 'Father and I were only just talking about you,' she said as we embraced and I kissed her soft cheek. 'Well, you and Celia, really.' She looked over her shoulder as if for lurking eavesdroppers and lowered her voice. 'Are they now convinced that this terrible assassin who murdered that Nicolaus Quinlie was the same man who killed poor Jeromy?'

'It seems likely that's what will be concluded,' I said carefully. I didn't want to tell my mother lies.

'Oh, good,' she breathed, leading me through the grand new porch and into the cool hall. My parents had been having quite a lot of work done to the old house, and now, at last, it appeared it was complete. The Gillards who had built the first dwelling however many centuries ago – in 1150, according to family tradition – would surely not recognize the place, what with its spacious new wing and the entrance moved around to the south. My parents, however, seemed to be delighted. My mother was, at least, and that was probably all that mattered to my father.

'Celia will be able to put it all behind her and settle down to whatever the future holds,' my mother was saying as she poured a mug of ale for me, 'which is what we all want, I'm sure. She won't have a fine house to live in now, I know, but—'

'She can live with me for now.'

'Yes, dear Gabriel, that's all very fine and generous, but she'll marry again, I'm quite sure, and there will be grandchildren.' She shot me a sharp look. It was a perpetual disappointment to her that so far neither her two sons nor her daughter had provided a new baby for the ancient family crib. 'You won't want a gang of little ones at Rosewyke unless they are your own,' she added pointedly.

'We'll see, Mother,' I said mildly. Before she could continue, I said, 'The ale was very welcome, thank you, and well up to your usual standard. Now, is Father about?'

My mother took my empty mug and strode over to the big sink. 'Out in the yard,' she said. She sent me another look, one that said clearly, *You haven't heard the last of this*, and turned away.

My father was coming back from the orchard. He'd been talking to Nathaniel – I saw my elder brother's unmistakable figure striding away – and now, seeing me, his face broke into a smile. I went to meet him.

We covered the usual ground – how was Celia, it'd be good to put this wretched business behind us – and then he said, eyeing me shrewdly, 'Just a social call, is it?'

'Not entirely.'

'Ah.'

'Father, I need to ask you about Grandfather Oldreive's ironmongery collection.'

He met my eyes in a long, slow glance. 'You do, do you?'

'Yes. Will you show it to me please, Father?'

His face lit up, and it occurred to me that I might have just made history as the first person ever to ask to view his precious, and deadly dull, collection.

'It's funny you should mention the collection,' he said as we crossed the yard.

'Why?'

Once again he looked at me, his face puzzled now. 'I'll show you.'

We went out to the furthest of the barns, the one that looked in the most imminent danger of collapse, and went inside. My father went ahead, eager to demonstrate the delights of his great mass of rusty old metal. Every type of implement was there, from plough shares and antique scythes to axes, from carving knives to swords.

'And this,' my father said, pointing to a gap between two

axes where a couple of nails suggested something had once hung, 'is where the voulge used to live.'

'The what?'

'Voulge. It's of foreign manufacture. It was made and used by the—'

'The Venetians,' I supplied.

I've had a couple of men look at it and they say it's of foreign manufacture, Theo had told me. And, I'd thought, Nicolaus Quinlie traded with Venice. We'd surmised, the two of us, that a hired killer would use a weapon from his own land.

We'd been wrong. The link with Venice, however, had stuck in my mind, irrelevant though I now knew it to be . . .

My father frowned slightly. 'No, not the Venetians, the French.'

'The French,' I repeated absently. It didn't matter, not in the least, but I had to keep up the pretence of interest if this was to convince my father.

'Aye, the voulge was a *French* weapon,' he said eagerly, 'comprised of a slightly curved blade attached to the side of a pole. It was the same sort of weapon, and with largely the same function, as a pike,' he went on, warming to his theme. 'The blade was quite broad at the base and good for hacking, but it narrowed to a point at the end for stabbing.' He mimed the action, first lunging forward with his imaginary weapon and then swishing it viciously sideways. 'Sometimes the blade had a hook on the back, which technically meant it was a voulge-guisarme.'

'Of course it was,' I murmured.

My father didn't notice the mild irony.

'It was widespread during the interminable wars with France that stemmed from Henry V's reign,' he explained. 'Agincourt and all those other battles, you know. Of course, similar weapons are still in use – that's the way of it, I've found, that blades go on being modified, or not, as usage slowly and steadily shows what works best. Take the pike, for instance, where you'll find that—'

'And how did this voulge come to be hidden away here in your barn?' I interrupted. My father's lengthy discourses on the development of weapons, tools and other metal implements were well known and usually avoided where possible, and now I had far more important matters on my mind.

He seemed to straighten up.

'My mother's great-great-grandfather Gelbert Oldreive was at Agincourt and he brought home a trophy,' he said with pride. 'He tore it out of the hands of a dying Frenchie who'd tried to kill him with it, only he got in first.'

'And when did you notice it was missing?'

'Now let me see.' He frowned. 'Last week, I think. Or it might have been the week before. I'm not entirely sure. I was hunting for a handle for my scythe, and I reckoned there ought to be something out here in the barn that I could use.'

That was typical of my frugally minded father. It gave him much pleasure to fulfil a need by modifying something he already had instead of purchasing new.

'Perhaps two weeks ago, then,' I mused. It had, I reflected, been rather more than that.

'Somebody's probably borrowed it,' my father said resignedly, 'mentioning nobody in particular, although in heaven's sweet name, I can't guess for what purpose.' He glanced in the direction of Nathaniel's house. 'I'm not a man to make a fuss,' he added in a tone of utter reasonableness, 'and, as I've always said, I don't mind my children borrowing my belongings, but on two conditions: you must ask permission, and you must—'

'Put them back where they belong when we've finished with them.' I completed the sentence. He'd been saying it since I'd been old enough to understand speech.

'Well, it'd be nice if folks listened and obeyed,' he harrumphed. Then, once more eyeing me curiously, he said, 'Why are you so interested? Bit of a coincidence, isn't it, for you to come here asking about my father's old collection just when there's a piece missing?'

I drew a breath. I hated having to lie to him but I didn't think I had any choice. 'I'm very afraid to tell you, Father, but it's possible that someone else stole your voulge; someone outside family and household.'

'But why—'

'It seems it was the weapon that killed Jeromy,' I said

quietly. 'It's hard to see how that could be, but I've seen the blade and it fits the description you just gave me.'

'D'you want me to go with you and confirm it?' he offered. Looking at his suddenly pale face, I guessed it wasn't something he was eager to do.

'Good of you to offer, Father, but there's no need. I don't think there can be much doubt.'

He nodded. Then, after a pause, he said, 'So this man – the one who killed both Jeromy and Nicolaus Quinlie – you think he came here, to Fernycombe, and broke into my barn, searching for a murder weapon?'

'He wouldn't really have had to *break* in,' I said gently. I indicated the loose-fitting door sinking on its hinges. There was a heavy bolt, but it no longer shot home into its socket.

'No, you're right, son,' my father agreed anxiously. 'Oh, dear Lord, I should have done something about that door ages ago – made it secure, somehow – and now look what's happened! My daughter's husband dead, and killed by a weapon stolen from my own barn! This is – this is quite dreadful!' He stared at me, horror in his eyes. 'Can't truthfully say I liked the man,' he added with painful honesty, 'but even so!'

'Don't feel guilty, Father,' I said quickly. 'We can't know why the killer chose to steal a weapon, and from here of all places, and I'm quite sure he'd have used some other method of execution had he not found your barn and its contents.' This was getting very difficult.

But, to my intense relief, he was nodding in agreement. 'Aye, you're right, son. That Quinlie's just as dead as Jeromy, and *he* was done for by a ruddy great stone in his mouth.'

Nicolaus Quinlie had died from a knife thrust, in fact, but I certainly wasn't going to tell my father that. 'There you are, then,' I said, patting his shoulder. 'Put a new lock on the barn door and forget about it.'

We turned to leave. He glanced back inside the barn and grimaced. 'I'll have to find something to fill that space,' he said grimly. 'I don't reckon I'll want that voulge back even if I'm offered it.'

*   *   *

I stayed a while longer, sitting with my parents in the comfort of their kitchen and sharing the midday meal. It was probably the one place in the house that was much as it had been from its earliest days, and whenever I sat there I sensed the presence of the long line of my Oldreive ancestors. It was a comforting place to be, and today I needed comfort very badly.

But I knew I couldn't stay there.

I rode home slowly, turning over and over in my mind what I had to do. But then I was struck all over again at the sheer impossibility of it. Surely I had to be wrong?

But the fact remained that there was only one person who could have taken the voulge, for the fable which I had conjured up for my father was precisely that. I could see, however, why Father had swallowed it, for he could have had none of my dark and frightening suspicions and, as far as he was concerned, it was reasonable enough to postulate that Jeromy's murderer had roamed the locality searching for a weapon and, by a stroke of good fortune, happened across the rickety old barn at Fernycombe where there was a whole collection of potentially deadly blades.

But could my conclusion be right?

I remembered the child, the little tomboy who, despite the constant imprecations of her nurse and her mother to act like a little lady, resisted all suggestions, orders and outright commands. Who withstood the deterrent effect of punishment and went on her merry way, evading attempts to keep her indoors at her needlework and escaping whenever she could to explore the wide acres of her father's land and, on rainy days, the irresistible attraction of a dozen or more barns and outhouses in various stages of dilapidation.

Of course she would have known about Father's collection of old weapons.

She'd gone to stay with them, I remembered. She'd called on me on her way back to Ferrars and I'd gone to take her pack: it was a large pack, I recalled, unusually shaped. She'd stopped me with a sharp word and, observing that she'd appropriated an old pair of my boots, I'd thought with an indulgent smile that there must be others of my former possessions tucked away in that large bundle, and that she didn't want me to know. But it hadn't been any possession of mine she'd taken away from Fernycombe: it had been Father's voulge.

And then what? Had she paid one of the Ferrars servants to do the deed for her? Or – and this, I thought, was more likely – had she entered into the dark network of Quinlie employees and shady agents and found someone willing, for a price, to rid himself of a rival? The other men hadn't liked Jeromy; that had been very plain. Knowing so much more about the whole situation than I could even have guessed at, had she also been aware of that, and used it to achieve the desired end?

I had to find out.

My courage failed and I did not go straight home. I rode instead to Theo's house, where I was asked to wait in the wide hall. Looking around – for the moment I seemed to be alone – I noticed a door slowly opening. Presently the gap was wide enough to reveal a staircase, which I guessed led up to Theo's private quarters.

A lad of about seven or eight was staring at me. He had a bright, interested expression, his father's clear blue eyes and a gap between his top front teeth. 'My father inspects dead bodies,' he whispered importantly. 'Sometimes,' he added, 'there's *blood* on them.'

Another small child appeared beside him: his little sister, I surmised, for there was a strong resemblance. She was quite beautiful, although just now her face was creased in disapproval. 'Blood's dis*gust*ing!' she stared firmly. 'I don't like it!'

The door to the street opened suddenly and Theo's large presence burst into the hall. 'Carolus, back upstairs to your lessons!' he thundered. 'How many times do you have to be told? You're not allowed downstairs in working hours!'

The boy dipped his head in a meek nod and muttered, 'Sorry, Father.' But he glanced at me swiftly and gave me a cheeky grin; his father's loud voice clearly hadn't fazed him in the least. The door closed abruptly and I heard the sound of two pairs of feet scurrying away.

Theo ushered me into his office.

'My elder son Carolus,' Theo said. It appeared he hadn't noticed the little girl. 'My wife wanted to christen him Charlemagne but I persuaded her that might be rather a lot to live up to, so we settled for Carolus.'

'I like it,' I remarked.

Theo grinned. 'The way he's turning out, I sometimes think we'd have done better with Garrulous,' he said. 'Now, to business. I hope you haven't been waiting long.' He had, I'd noticed, the air of a hard-pressed man, his hair standing on end as if he'd been running his hands through it, the lacings of his tunic loose.

Suddenly struck with a powerful sense of alarm, I managed to say in almost my normal voice, 'Is something wrong?' My heart was beating fast and apprehension was making my palms sweat.

'Wrong? You might say that, yes, for a boat ferrying passengers across the river has gone down, at least two are drowned and there are accusations flying about that it was overloaded, and that it's all the captain's fault for squeezing another party of travellers on board because he's too greedy to let safety and good sense prevail.'

I managed to express some suitably sympathetic remarks. I did my utmost to spare a thought for those poor people, panicking as the boat foundered, sinking, drowning. But, God forgive me for my selfishness, the major part of my mind was rejoicing. I'd thought, when I realized Theo was so agitated, that somehow he had discovered what I suspected.

That, even worse, he could prove it.

But, thank God, his holy son and all the saints and angels, it was not so.

When I was quite sure I could speak in the correct, respectful tone, I said, 'I will leave you to your work, Theo. This is a grave matter, and requires your full attention. You don't want me troubling you.'

He looked up from whatever document he had been studying so intently. 'Hm? What's that? Sorry, doctor, I am being discourteous. What did you wish to see me about?'

'Oh – it was merely to ask if there had been any further

developments concerning the deaths of Jeromy Palfrey and Nicolaus Quinlie.'

'Yes, indeed there have. Someone else was killed. That warehouseman over at Dartmouth.'

'Pieter Sparre. Yes, Jarman Hodge came to tell me.'

Now Theo's attention had switched fully to me. It was interesting, I observed, to see the change in his expression. His blue eyes seemed to sharpen somehow, and I could almost sense the powerful brain working, pulling out all the relevant facts and presenting them in an accessible and readily comprehensible manner.

You underestimated Theophilus Davey at your peril, I reflected.

'You have had some more thoughts?' The question was bland enough, but I sensed there was a lively and intense spark of sudden interest behind it.

I would have to be careful.

I shrugged. 'It is hard to comprehend how Pieter Sparre's death fits in with the rest,' I said calmly, 'although, if the testimony of his woman is to be credited, it must indeed fit somehow, for the same mysterious, beak-masked figure was observed.'

Theo stood quite still, watching me.

Was he not going to comment?

The silence became awkward. 'It seems increasingly likely,' I plunged on, 'that this is a falling-out among thieves, as it were, if we may so name Nicolaus Quinlie's employees.'

'No accusations of theft, doctor,' Theo remarked.

'No, indeed not.' I forced a smile. 'I used the wrong analogy. I remain convinced, however, that we are right in our belief that Quinlie, needing urgently to rid himself of the nuisance that Jeromy threatened to become, found an assassin – the beak-masked foreigner – to do the job, and that some dispute between this man and Quinlie led to Quinlie's own murder. As to the warehouseman' – I was thinking on my feet, not having given anywhere near enough consideration to the matter before now – 'I can only suggest that the killer believed Sparre had seen something, or suspected something, and so must be dispatched before he could share it. Sparre was, we know, a nosy man.

It was he, after all, who made that comment about them not being likely to see Jeromy over in Dartmouth again after *this business.*'

Slowly Theo nodded. 'A nosy man,' he repeated slowly.

I thought it best to keep my mouth shut.

After a while, Theo said, 'So, doctor, are we to conclude that this clever and all but invisible assassin killed three times – by three different methods, I might add – and, business concluded, has now vanished back to wherever he came from?'

'Well, there have been no more killings,' I said, trying to sound reasonable. 'And no more sightings of him, so in all likelihood he has fled.'

Theo gave me a very penetrating look. Or perhaps it was that my guilty conscience interpreted it that way.

'No,' he said, drawing out the word.

'Many ships leave Plymouth every day, and countless more from ports up and down the coast.' *Careful*, I warned myself. If I pushed the point too hard, it would make him suspicious.

I watched him intently. What did I mean, *make* him suspicious? He already was.

It seemed to me I stood there for hours, but it can surely have been less than a minute. Then, with an abrupt movement, Theo raised a hand towards me, palm outwards. 'Be on your way, doctor.' There was a rough edge in his voice that I hadn't heard before. 'You're right, I'm sure, when you imply that I'm not going to catch this killer.' The intense blue eyes felt like knife points, but I made myself hold steady and not turn away. He waved his hand again, impatiently now. 'Leave me, please. I have other matters to attend to.'

It was a dismissal; a very plain one.

I hurried out of his house and mounted my horse. I was sorry – more than I wanted to admit – for what I'd just done. I had begun to look upon Theo as a friend; a very welcome friend, a man who I liked and admired.

I hoped very much that it would be in my power to repair the rift that had suddenly opened up between us.

EIGHTEEN

Then there was nothing left but to face her.

Evening was drawing on as I got home. The sun was setting, lighting the sky in the west with stripes of vivid red and orange, and the land looked calm, peaceful and utterly beautiful. I stood for a moment before I went inside, drinking it in, letting its balm comfort me. I knew I was going to need comfort.

Sallie was in the kitchen, and I asked her to draw up a jug of good wine. She did so, putting it on the tray with two of the prettiest glasses. 'Going to spoil her a little, are you, Doctor Gabriel?' She nodded, answering her own question. 'That's right, that's best now, for she's had a bad time these past weeks and the best way to put the roses in her cheeks again is to feed her, give her fine wine, let her rest and let her sleep. Oh, and give her kindness and love, of course.' She blushed and turned away, as if embarrassed to have displayed such emotion.

'I intend to give her all those things, Sallie, and perhaps the love and the kindness most of all,' I replied gently.

She looked up briefly and smiled.

'You wouldn't object if she took up permanent residence here?'

She looked indignant. 'Not up to me to mind, doctor, but in any case I certainly wouldn't.'

I glanced quickly at her, but her expression was innocent.

I took the tray from her and went upstairs to confront my sister.

'It seems the coroner is content to conclude that Jeromy was killed by the same man who murdered Nicolaus Quinlie,' I began as we settled in chairs either side of the fireplace, glasses in our hands.

I heard her swift intake of breath. 'Has – is it likely this man will be found and put on trial?'

'Not likely at all,' I said.

I was watching her closely, and I was sure I saw her slump a little with relief.

'There is no possibility,' I went on, 'that, under harsh questioning, he will convince his accusers that, while he killed Quinlie and, indeed, others, he is innocent of the charge of murdering Jeromy.'

Her head shot up and she stared at me like a frightened animal. 'But – but *of course* this violent man killed Jeromy!' she protested. 'He – he must have done, who else could possibly have . . .' Her voice trailed off.

I leaned forward, clutching both her hands in mine. 'Dearest, you must believe me when I tell you there is no possible chance of this man coming to trial.'

'Has he gone away, then?' she asked in a small voice.

'Far, far away,' I said. 'And he will never come back.'

She was holding my hands as if they were a rope and she was in deep water. Her eyes bored into mine. 'Why don't you tell me?' I whispered. 'There's only me to hear, and you must know I will never repeat it.'

She did not reply for some moments. Then she said, so quietly that I could scarcely hear, 'Yes. Yes, I do know that.'

'Would it not be a relief to share it at last?'

She closed her eyes briefly, and a spasm of pain crossed her lovely face. 'Oh, Gabe, you have no idea!'

'But I have,' I said swiftly. 'Truly, my dear heart, I have.'

She was staring at me again. 'You'll hate me,' she whispered.

I smiled. 'I could never do that.'

'Thank you.'

'So,' I prompted. 'I'd very much like to know the truth.'

And this is the story she told me.

It had taken Celia only a short time to understand that her impetuous marriage to the flamboyant, handsome and charming Jeromy had been a mistake.

It had begun so well, and she had been so happy she thought she would burst. The exciting weeks and days leading up to the wedding had been so wonderful, and the aquamarine silk which her bridegroom had presented her for her bridal gown was the most gorgeous fabric she had ever seen. Just to touch its expensive, luxurious smoothness had been a talisman; as if this costly present from the man she was to marry vouch-safed all the other good things that were to come. And the house! Let her family sniff and say it was all a little brash, and should a man demonstrate his wealth with such flagrant disregard for refinement and taste? Celia didn't care. Ferrars was going to be hers, hers and Jeromy's, and if the furnishings were too grand, if the hangings were so voluminous that they drooped in pools on the floor, if the huge bed with its purple silk hangings was a little vulgar and more suited to a king than a country gentleman and his wife, then that was too bad.

Her wedding day had passed in a whirl. Preparations; dressing herself in that gorgeous gown; arranging her hair and her veil, and the fresh, fragrant flowers that held it in place. Looking at herself in the glass and knowing she had never looked lovelier; walking into the church and seeing the same knowledge in Jeromy's eyes. Speaking the solemn words; striding out into the sunshine on Jeromy's arm, to face the greetings and the congratulations of friends and kin, the wedding breakfast back at Fernycombe.

Going to Ferrars with her husband. Going home, for the first time as man and wife. Ripping off each other's garments in their impatience; falling across that great bed, in far too much of a hurry to pull back the sumptuous bedclothes and slide in beneath them. Lying, spent, sweating and panting, in a wonderful tangle of limbs, amazement filling her that this act that made it a marriage, this wedding-night moment that women spoke of in whispers, that both her mother and her nurse had warned her about as *something a wife must endure*, should turn out to be so incredibly pleasurable!

In her innocence and delight, it had not occurred to her to wonder how Jeromy, as new to marriage as she was, should have such skill; should know unerringly how to bring his young and totally inexperienced wife to orgasm, only a short while after he had taken her virginity and made her bleed. She had imagined, if she'd thought about it at all, that this was what always happened; had not known that many women went right through their lives without experiencing that unique delight, and that, even for couples whose private married life was reliably satisfying, it took time and knowledge to develop the skill.

Jeromy, of course, was no virgin. Jeromy had been introduced to sexual intercourse when he was a precociously aware fourteen-year-old, by a handsome, wealthy and voluptuous widow in her late twenties. He'd been frequenting whorehouses since he was fifteen.

She could not afterwards have said precisely when the shadow began. With the first occasion when he didn't come home when he said he would, and responded to her gentle queries with angry words? With the slow, awful realization that he liked to gamble, and had absolutely no skill at it? With the horrible understanding that he liked a drink; no, not *a* drink, but many drinks? As many as he could force down his throat before he vomited, fell over, pissed himself, passed out, sank into bed in a dishevelled, stinking, ungainly, ugly mess.

But the trouble was that drunkenness did not straight away bring insensibility. First there would be that awful time to endure while he tried to take her. While he lumbered up on top of her, pushed up her luxurious pale silk nightgown, thrust apart her legs and tried, tried, tried, tried to force his limp and disobliging penis into her.

And when it failed, as inevitably it did, always it was her fault. 'You don't want me, you frigid bitch!' he yelled, face scarlet and wet with sweat, spittle dribbling from his loose lips. 'I come home tired after a long, hard day, wanting my wife, wanting the comfort of her body which it is her *duty* to open to me, and what do I get but a cold, unmoving statue that lies there, lips firmly together, head turned away, disapproval and rejection radiating from *every single part*?' He gasped, as if horrified at his own words. 'Is it any wonder you rob me of my manhood?'

That was the first time he hit her: a swinging backhanded blow with a clenched fist that knocked her head sideways so hard that she heard her neck snap and thought, in the initial, frantic, agony-filled instant, that he'd killed her.

Sometimes later she'd wished that he had.

*   *   *

Life went on. Jeromy was absent from home with increasing frequency, and without those blessed periods of respite, Celia believed she might have taken her own life and saved him the trouble.

For he *was* killing her; slowly but surely, he was taking from her every joy, every moment of sweetness; taking the very will to keep trying to stay alive.

On many occasions she almost ran back to her parents, or to Gabriel. But she couldn't; her pride was too strong. She had forced her dear father to permit the marriage, despite his misgivings and despite the fact that he had tried so hard to make her change her mind. How could she now go back like a beaten dog and beg for sanctuary? How could she tell them all that she'd been wrong and they'd been right, and Jeromy was a nightmare? A good-looking, elegant devil in rich man's clothes?

She couldn't.

She thought she was with child, but it came to naught. Her feelings were mixed but overall she was relieved, for at that time Jeromy's gambling debts had begun to worry even him, and she did not believe he was in a state to greet the news of a baby with any pleasure.

Time passed.

Then she discovered she was pregnant again.

She was very, very afraid, for now Jeromy was becoming increasingly violent. Nicolaus Quinlie had begun to tighten the screws on him, demanding the return of his loans. Jeromy was by now deeply, hopelessly in debt, running out of people from whom to borrow, beg, extort or steal money, increasingly desperate. Too cowardly to take it out on anyone who would fight back – he had neither the skill with his fists nor the courage to pick a quarrel with one of Quinlie's toughs, although not a few of them would gladly have taken him on – he went instead for the soft option and got drunk, then expended on his wife the violence he wanted so much to throw at Nicolaus Quinlie.

Driven by a terrified anxiety, both for herself and, even more, for the child she carried, Celia realized she had to act; to make plans to defend herself. It was risky, perhaps, to ride, especially astride, as she liked to do. Or so people told her, Jeromy in particular, who had all but forbidden her to leave the house on her own and would have been angry in the extreme if he'd known what she planned to do.

But Jeromy was not at home. Jeromy had gone to Exeter.

Before he left she had approached him meekly and asked his permission to visit her brother during his absence. 'I am lonely without you, dear husband,' she said, 'and Gabriel's company lessens the pain of missing you.'

She thought she'd gone too far. But Jeromy, loving himself as he loved no other being on earth, had long ago convinced himself of his own irresistibility. As if bestowing upon her some kingly gift, he flicked his fingers in her face and said, 'You may go, and the grooms will take you in the litter. That brother of yours will see that I do things in style!'

The grand remark was somewhat undermined by a drunken, wine-smelling belch.

She didn't go in the litter. She couldn't have done, for there weren't the servants to bear her. Jeromy spoke pompously of *grooms*, but there was only one now, and he was a skinny, weedy-looking boy. The household had gradually been reduced to the barest skeleton of staff but, if Jeromy noticed, he didn't comment.

She didn't go to Rosewyke; not initially, anyway. She took her grey mare, rode as she always did and went to Fernycombe, where her parents, delighted to see her, fed her and cosseted her.

She knew there was a hoard of old blades and weapons in one of the barns. Unlike Nathaniel or Gabriel – the one preoccupied with learning everything there was to know about being a farmer and the other having left home young and, even when still there, taking precious little interest in the farm or anything in it – she had lived at Fernycombe all her life until her marriage. Ever curious, ever adventurous, her fertile imagination full of stories in which she was a soldier, a sailor, a pirate, an explorer, she had spent her childhood nosing around.

She crept into the old, dilapidated barn one quiet afternoon when nobody was about and made her choice. She didn't believe her father would miss it. As far as she knew, he rarely went out there. If he did notice it had gone, he would probably think Nathaniel or one of the farm hands had borrowed it.

How likely was it that he would suspect his pretty, elegant, beautifully dressed and happily married daughter?

She visited Gabriel on her way home to Ferrars. She didn't like the deceit, but she had to go there in case Jeromy checked up. She spent the afternoon with her brother, and made quite sure that his housekeeper and outdoor servants saw her, too. There had been a moment of horror when Gabriel had reached up to untie her pack, for she had wrapped the stolen weapon in a blanket and the moment he touched it, he would know it wasn't the sort of object a lady normally carried with her.

But happily the moment had passed, and she was safe.

He'd hurt her a lot when he held her waist to help her down from her mare. Her ribs were blue-black with bruises, for Jeromy had given her quite a beating the day before he left for Exeter. She couldn't remember why; often – usually – there wasn't really a why.

Gabriel noticed she had put on weight; he didn't say so in as many words, but she knew it all the same. He said she looked pale, and asked her if she was well. She managed to deflect him, telling him quite abruptly that her digestion was suffering after a surfeit of her mother's cooking and generous helpings.

Then Jeromy came home.

More time passed. A week? Two weeks? The memory was vague, for her mind was in turmoil and she was able neither to eat nor sleep.

And his state was the worst she had ever seen.

He was beside himself with a sort of nervous, terrified excitement. He had not a single coin with which to begin the repayment of his huge debts. He had called upon everyone he knew – friend, distant acquaintance, business contact, colleague – trying to raise money, with absolutely no luck. And Quinlie would be sending for him very soon . . .

She thought, but could not be sure, that he was up to something; that, against all odds for he was not a clever or quick-thinking man, he had found – or *thought* he'd found – a way out of his frightful difficulties.

If he had, she realized that she had absolutely no faith that it was going to work.

Despite everything – despite all the harm he had done to her – still she felt a stab of pity for him.

The house was as good as empty. Ruth, the only indoor servant, slept far away in a tiny room off the scullery.

He picked a fight. He always picked a fight, now. Thinking about it later – and how much time she had spent thinking about it – she thought that he was deeply inadequate and, quite unable to face up to it, made himself feel bigger, better, by treating her like a dog. A dog? No, for he *liked* his dogs . . .

She tried to defend herself. Tried to tread the fine, delicate and ultimately unguessable balance between defending herself and not antagonizing him further by letting him *see* that she was.

Impossible.

His fists drove into her breasts, then her stomach. Instantly she doubled over, protecting what curled inside her. So he began on her buttocks, as so often he had done before, pushing her face-down across a chair and thumping, thumping, thumping his fists into her flesh.

She managed to wriggle free. Her backside on fire, she ran around the big, shiny, rectangular table that stood so proud and grand in the brilliant, gaudy room.

He ran after her.

He grabbed her by the upper arm, fingers biting into the skin, tearing the silk of her sleeve. Frantic now, swiftly she turned her head and bit his hand.

He roared in pain. Then, in one fast, powerful movement, he gathered her up and hurtled her against the table.

Its sharp corner drove hard into the soft swell of her belly.

The pain made her pass out.

When she came to, it was dark and she was very, very cold. Shivering. Wet. All wet, lying in a puddle.

But the puddle was warm.

She lay on the floor half under the table, in a flood of her own blood.

*   *   *

Judyth – kind, tactful, strong Judyth – looked after her. Someone must have summoned her. Probably that someone had not been Jeromy.

Judyth told her gently, hugging her all the while, that the force of the table digging into her had ruptured something. Her womb, attacked, distressed, had ejected its contents.

'Will I have another chance?' Celia whispered, face pressed to Judyth's warm breast.

But Judyth said sadly, 'I do not know.'

Judyth was wise, and very observant. She saw the bruising on Celia's body. It was consistent with the cover story – 'I fell down the stairs' – but also there was a deep mark right across Celia's lower belly. In addition to that – as if it were not enough – Celia's buttocks were so badly damaged that there wasn't an inch of unbruised flesh.

Celia recovered. She was grieving; the development of the foetus was sufficiently advanced to show it was a little girl. She had been uncertain, before, as to whether or not she wanted a child. Knowing that child had been a girl somehow made her real; now Celia knew just how much she did want a baby, and the knowledge was a deep, enduring pain.

She began to plot.

And so the story reaches its end.

It is late.

Jeromy has had a good day. He has ensnared a new victim and safe in his keeping is a stout leather bag of coins to give to Nicolaus Quinlie. It may not be much, but Jeromy is pretty confident this is merely the first of many payments as his victim is very rich, has a particularly nasty, dirty little secret, and consequently has a very great deal to lose. Jeromy comes swaggering into his house and immediately goes to the sideboard where the drink is stored. He has already had a few celebratory drinks on the way home. 'Why not?' he asks himself aloud. 'I work very hard, I get precious little thanks, and nobody appreciates me!' He is feeling very randy. The house is very quiet, and nobody is about. He calls out to his wife: 'Celia? Celia! Where are you? Come here, wife, I'm desperate for a fuck!'

There is no reply.

He begins to search for her. He searches downstairs. She isn't there. He goes upstairs and finds her in their bedroom, lying down, eyes closed, her feet up on several pillows.

She has been bleeding again.

He stands watching her, swaying slightly.

She opens her eyes. Sees him. Draws up her legs, curling herself tightly, her eyes wide in fright.

'I want,' he says, slowly and deliberately, 'to bed my wife. Take your clothes off.'

But her miscarriage and its aftermath have wounded her, and she's still sore, raw and seeping. 'No. I *can't*!' she whispers urgently.

He launches himself on her, and she manages to fight him off. He grabs at her between her legs, his fingers digging into the tender flesh of her thighs, and she howls in pain. The sounds of her distress seem to egg him on. He pushes her down onto the hard stone floor, so roughly that she bangs her head violently against the flags and briefly sees a dazzle of white lights. Then he is ripping at her undergarments, shoving her knees apart, tearing aside the soft pads she's been using to absorb the blood and thrusting brutal fingers deep inside her. She screams again and he claps his other hand so tightly over her mouth that she can't breathe. She looks into his eyes and knows it's him or her.

Without stopping to think, acting purely from the fierce instinct to survive, she shoots out her right hand, the first and middle finger tight together and ramrod-stiff, and pokes them as hard as she can in his eyes: right first then left, and even as his hands swiftly abandon her vagina and her mouth to defend himself, she attacks again, punching up into the underside of his nose with the heel of her hand and then pushing her bunched fingers with all her force into his open, howling mouth. He retches, gags and rolls off her, one hand to his eyes, the other to his nose, now bleeding profusely, and she shoots out from under him and struggles to her feet. She races out of the bed chamber, risking one swift glance over her shoulder, desperate to keep ahead of him, for she is going to fetch her weapon from where she's hidden it.

She must not attack him in the house.

She gathers her torn gown around her, puts on a cloak and she flees. What will he do if he can't find her? He'll come flying after her. She must ignore the impulse to hide in some secret corner he'll never find and go to a place he knows. She is aware of most of the spots where Jeromy goes to drink: the nearest is the sordid tavern down on Old Ferry Quay. There is no landlord there any more, it's true, but Jeromy and like-minded cronies meet at the deserted tavern when desperation drives them to resort to the fiery and gut-rotting brews that one of their number makes.

He knows the way there all right.

She runs down to it. She goes a little further along the river bank and hides, but she doesn't hide very well – just crouches behind the last of the deserted, dilapidated houses – because she wants him to find her. She must kill him in an out of the way, lonely place where he won't be found.

Where nobody will associate his death with her.

All is very quiet. It's the dead time of the night and even the most desperate night owls are abed. Even if anyone had been in the old tavern, by now they'll have either gone home or passed out. The place is in darkness. She watches as Jeromy arrives and briefly tries the door. It's locked. He walks on.

She must have made some small sound for suddenly she is aware that he knows she's there. She gathers up her courage and clutches it to her. *Be brave*, she tells herself. *For just a little longer, be brave.*

She hears him approach. 'Come out, come out, wherever you are,' he sings. He laughs softly. 'I can see you, you fucking whore,' he whispers.

He comes round behind the house. He leans a shoulder against its ruined wall, nonchalant, elegant, as if he had all the time in the world. He's smiling.

He reaches out and grabs at her.

She lunges upwards, her weapon held firmly in her hand. The big blade rips into the soft flesh of his belly and she thrusts it upwards, finding his heart.

He dies.

He slumps down against the wall.

She leaves the weapon in place, lifting Jeromy's hands and carefully placing them round the shaft. She is soaked in his blood; the cloak especially is beyond remedy. The nightgown is already irrevocably marked, although the brown is fading now. The stains are from her own blood, from when she lost the baby. It's quite ironic, really.

She isn't quite sure why she didn't throw the garment away. She suspects it is because it was the one she wore on her wedding night.

She creeps home, tears up the cloak and puts the bloody pieces on the fire, small fragment by small fragment, until it's consumed. She puts the nightgown in to soak. She washes herself, dresses.

She tidies up the house to remove every last trace of the attempted rape and the ensuing fight. She bathes her cuts and bruises. She decides to wait until they've healed before reporting Jeromy missing. He's often away for days at a time and nobody will question his absence. She'll leave it about a week. Or maybe more.

In her mind she begins the process of thinking herself into the guise of a normal, happily married woman who very slowly begins to be a bit worried because her beloved husband hasn't come home.

And she waits to see what will happen next.

There was a long silence in the pretty room when my sister stopped talking.

In the end it was my sister, not I, who broke it.

'You knew, didn't you?'

I looked up and met her eyes. Her face was calm now. All the tension and distress of the past weeks had gone.

'I knew you'd taken the voulge, yes.'

'The what? Oh, the blade thing. Yes, that was me.' She smiled. Her old smile. 'What a silly thing to say. Of course it was me.' Then, anxious again: 'Does Father know?'

'That it's missing, yes. That you took it, no. He is persuaded that, by some extraordinary chance, the person who killed Jeromy stole the murder weapon from Grandfather Oldreive's collection in Father's barn.'

'Thank you,' she said softly.

'I thought you'd given it to whoever you paid to kill him.'

She looked at me for a long moment. 'Oh, I wouldn't have left it to someone else. I saved that particular task for myself.'

There was, I reflected with a slight chill, a side to my sister that I had never seen before. I had suspected it might be there – suddenly I realized that with total clarity – but now I had proof.

I looked at her. She was frowning slightly, muttering to herself, counting on her fingers. 'What are you doing?'

'Hm? Oh, just working out who I must see. Mother and Father, of course, and I suppose that means Nathaniel too. Ruth, because she was always kind to me. That vicar who did the funeral, and—'

'Why do you wish to see them?'

She gave me the sort of look she perfected when she was five, the one that said so clearly, *Goodness, surely you don't need to ask?*

'Because, dear Gabriel, I am about to turn – what's that wonderful word? Metamose?'

'Metamorphose. It means a complete change of form.'

'Yes, I know. Well, that's what I'm doing. What I've done. Now I have to present myself to the world in my new form.'

I thought I understood. 'Which is?'

'I'm still the sorrowing widow, horrified at the way my dear husband met his end, but my love for him has been somewhat tarnished by the discovery that he was a liar, a cheat, a spend-thrift, and in debt up to his ears.'

I shook my head slowly, amazed. 'You had worked it all out, hadn't you? Every last detail.' I didn't know if I was horrified or deeply impressed.

'Of course I had,' she said shortly. 'I had to survive.'

I couldn't argue with that. And what a battle she'd had.

'I'll see that big blue-eyed bear of a coroner, too,' she was saying. 'He—'

No.

'I shouldn't do that,' I said quietly.

Her eyes shot to meet mine. 'Why not?'

It was, I thought, a moment for absolute honesty. 'Because

Theophilus Davey is a quick-witted and astute man and not easily fooled, even by very beautiful women batting their eyelashes at him.'

'I wouldn't dream of—'

'Don't interrupt. For now, he appears to have reluctantly agreed that the assassin hired by Nicolaus Quinlie to kill Jeromy fell out with his paymaster and killed him too.'

'But that's *good*, Gabe!'

'Yes, I know. But note the use of the word *reluctantly*.'

She thought about it. 'Oh.'

'Oh, indeed.'

'Do you think he'll – er, do anything?'

'There's not a lot he can do, and I think he's aware of it.' We stared at each other. 'Celia, he *knows* something is being kept from him. He may even have guessed what it is, although I don't see why he should.'

She had gone pale, but now her chin jutted out with new strength and determination and she said, 'We must *never* tell.'

There were all sorts of answers to that. In the end, I just smiled slightly and said, 'Well, *I'm* not planning to.'

The days passed and became weeks. Celia set about her campaign and met with great success. She extended her circle to many of the wives of Jeromy's erstwhile business associates, and, from what she told me and from her appearance when she returned from such visits, she was greeted with warmth and kindness. And, I dare say, a good deal of compassion, for by now quite a lot of rumours about Jeromy were starting to circulate and hardly any of them showed him in a good light.

Sometimes I went with her, but more often she went alone. 'I *am* on my own now, Gabe,' she said the first time she made it plain that she'd rather I didn't go with her. 'Other people must accept that and get used to it, as must I, and, very nice as it is to be escorted around the countryside by my big brother, it's not really going to help me stand on my own feet, is it?'

She was right.

In any case, I became increasingly busy with my own work. William at the farm, whose arm I'd saved, must have put in a good word for me here and there, probably adding that although I was London-trained and lived in a big house, I didn't charge more than a family could afford. I think Black Carlotta probably did the same, for on occasion quiet, shy people would turn up on my doorstep, often at twilight, whispering of ailments or wounds that hadn't responded to hedge medicine and asking my opinion, my advice and my help. Often they didn't pay with coins at all – I doubted very much whether they had any – but with beautifully presented gifts of food and drink. On one occasion, I was left a stone jar of some innocent-looking but extremely potent concoction tasting of blackberries that gave me the sort of hangover I hadn't experienced since my days at sea. On another, I was paid with a basket of recently hatched chicks. I didn't mind. I wasn't wealthy by the standards of great men but I had enough, which was more than could be said for most people. And I loved my work.

Celia and I transferred our allegiance to Jonathan Carew, at Tavy St Luke's, only occasionally worshipping at my parents' church if we happened to be taking the Sunday meal at Fernycombe. We enjoyed the Reverend Carew's services. He always provided his congregation with something to think about, although those thoughts were often very far from comfortable ones.

Celia had made her visit to Jonathan Carew quite soon after she'd first mentioned the idea. It was the one time when she returned to Rosewyke looking distressed.

I took her hand and led her into the library, where I'd been reading and making notes. I poured measures of brandy for us both. It was evening now, and I was ready to stop work.

'Was he unsympathetic?' I asked.

'No, quite the opposite.' Tears filled her eyes and she wiped them away.

'What, then?'

She took a generous mouthful of brandy. 'In a minute.' She paused, took another sip and then said, 'He's organized the headstone and it'll arrive in a month or so. We can't put it up for a while yet anyway, he says, as the ground has to settle.'

I waited. I guessed she was talking of practical matters in

order to postpone the moment when she told me what had upset her.

She took a further mouthful of brandy and said, 'He was so kind, Gabe. He said how shocking it was for a young wife to lose a loved husband, and in such a brutal way.' She was speaking very quickly, as if she had to get the words out before she broke down. 'He said I was being very brave and that doing my best to pull myself together and get on with my life was the right thing, even though it was so hard.' She gave a great sob, putting down her glass and burying her face in her hands. 'Oh, Gabe, I feel so guilty! He was so compassionate and gentle with me because he thinks – he thinks – whereas of course I—'

She couldn't go on, which was perhaps just as well.

I got up and went to crouch beside her, taking her hand. 'Was that all he said?'

'Yes. Wasn't it enough?' she cried passionately.

'Sssh,' I soothed her. 'Celia, listen to me. Think what Jonathan said, step by step. He said it was a shock to lose a loved husband.'

'But I didn't love Jeromy!'

'You did once, and very much. It was he who killed your love, not you.'

'But—' She thought about it, then nodded curtly.

'Then he said you were brave, which you most certainly are.'

She managed the ghost of a smile. 'Not perhaps in the way he imagines.'

'In many ways,' I insisted. 'And then he said pulling yourself together and getting on with your life was the right thing to do, and who could argue with that?'

She sat back in the chair and picked up her brandy. 'So – so you're saying I shouldn't feel bad about him? That it was all right for him to be kind to me, even though he'd be horrified if he knew the truth?'

'I am,' I said firmly.

I thought, although didn't say aloud, that the Reverend Carew might very well be kind to my sister even if he did know what she'd done. I had a feeling about him: I sensed there was a great deal more to him than met the eye, and I didn't think it was entirely impossible that his own past had included incidents he would rather put behind him. That he would prefer nobody else knew about.

And, as regards Celia, he wasn't blind or deaf and he certainly wasn't a naive innocent. He'd have heard what was being said about Jeromy, just like everyone else. I thought it was interesting that, in everything he'd said to my sister, he hadn't mentioned grief and heartbreak.

Perhaps he had a better idea of the truth than we thought.

It was a wonderful June. The sun shone with almost too much intensity, the hay crop was one of the best for years, the fields and the vegetable plots gave in such abundance that we knew we'd all be able to put away a good amount of stores for the lean months.

I made good my undertaking to Tobias and travelled up to Somerset to seek his Willerton kin. When Jarman Hodge had first related the sorry tale of the family's disgrace, he had said that, although there hadn't been enough evidence to bring Ambrose to trial, nevertheless he'd been ruined: 'Mud sticks,' had been Jarman's exact words. Well, mud had stuck all right. Ambrose was dead – he had survived for less than a decade after his downfall – and I found his widow, Suzannah, living in a dark, isolated little house with only two ancient servants to look after her. She was crouched with age, sitting hunched beside the fire wrapped in shawls and blankets, for all that the day was warm, but she had retained her wits.

I told her who I was and why I had come. As gently as I could, I told her what had happened to her daughter. I didn't go into details: the terrible tale that Tobias had related was not for a mother's ears. I simply said that she didn't die when Nicolaus Quinlie said she did and wasn't buried in that showy, costly tomb. Instead, she had gone to Venice.

'Venice!' her mother breathed, the old eyes gleaming. 'A very beautiful city, I believe. Oh, she must have loved it! Don't you think? Do you think she was happy?'

I hesitated, trying to remember what Rose's son had said. 'I'm sure she was. She was a brave woman, as well as a lively and a loving one.'

'Yes, yes, indeed she was.' The old woman smiled briefly.

'But you speak of her in the past tense' – she'd noticed, then – 'and so must I assume she is dead?'

'Yes, my lady, I'm afraid she is.'

She wept a little at that, and I did what I could to comfort her. Later, when I got up to leave, she took my hand. 'Thank you for coming,' she said. She added in a whisper, 'I always thought that dreadful man was lying. He built that monstrous edifice, but I just *knew* my girl wasn't lying there.'

I wondered how she could have been so certain. And I thought what it must have cost her, over the long years, to suspect and not to know the truth.

I reached the low door of the dark, little room and turned for a last farewell. Suzannah Willerton was staring at me, tears in her eyes but a smile on her face. 'Rose got away from him, didn't she?'

And all I could say was, 'Yes.'

On the last Sunday in the month, Celia and I sat in church listening to Jonathan preach on the virtues of compassion; on how we should not leap to judge one another, as so often we did, but try to put ourselves in the boots of others, walk a mile and see how it felt to be them.

Good preacher that he was, I found my attention wandering. I'd been up most of the night with an elderly man dying of lung congestion, and I'd be going back to him later in the day. He hadn't long for the world and both he and his large family seemed to find my presence a help, even though there was little I could do for him now.

My wandering glance was arrested by a worn old plaque set in the wall to my right, on which there was a familiar name: Gillard. It was the name of my mother's family. This ancestor was called Henry and he had lived from 1182 to 1240. A life span of fifty-eight years, then. Not bad for his times; not bad, I thought with a smile, for *my* times.

I wondered what his life had been like, this Henry Gillard. He seemed to have moved away from the family home at Fernycombe, or else he'd have been buried in the church there. He must have achieved some sort of fame, to have been accorded a plaque on the church wall . . .

What had he done? What had he seen? What experiences had marked his life? I rummaged through my mind to see if I could recall any great events that had occurred as the twelfth century gave way to the thirteenth, but found nothing. There had undoubtedly been strife, battles, wars. Perhaps Henry Gillard had been like me, his descendant, and had no wish to farm. Perhaps he'd gone to sea. Perhaps he'd been a soldier, and fought, like Gelbert Oldreive, at some great conflict such as Agincourt.

I would never know.

But I found I liked the idea of Henry Gillard as a soldier. He'd been brave, I decided, ruthless, recognizing when it was unavoidable to offer violence, to take a life.

I wondered if he was looking down at his many-greats grandson and granddaughter, sitting in this church on a fine June day. Would he understand? Celia and I had both taken life. We'd had good reason, both of us, although I suppose a man of peace would say we should have found other ways of achieving our ends.

You wouldn't have said that, would you, Henry Gillard? I thought.

Jonathan had finished his sermon, and now we were all kneeling to pray.

I folded my hands and shut my eyes.

A sense of great serenity flowed through me. Was I forgiven, then, for what I'd done? Was Celia too, so calm and demure beside me? Or was it my distant forefather, telling me – and I could almost hear the robust Devon accents – that sometimes a man had no choice, and the important thing was to do what you had to and fulfil your duty and stand by those you loved.

Behind my clasped hands I smiled. Whether it was God or Henry Gillard, someone seemed to be blessing me.

I was quite content with that.

POSTSCRIPT

'Do you think,' my sister whispered in my ear, 'that's Quinlie silk?'

We both stared at the tall, broad-shouldered man riding sedately beneath a light canopy borne by twenty-four splendidly dressed men. He wore gold and cream, the silk smoothly luxurious and decorated with pearls. He was the calm centre of a vast sea of people that entirely covered the street: above, women and children leaned from casement windows in the buildings lining the route. Thousands of faces all turned his way, and the noise of the crowd was like a low, constant hum that rose to a new, fervent pitch of excitement as the man beneath the canopy drew level. Ten paces ahead of him rode a boy of about ten, the young face stiff with concentration. Behind rode a woman, surrounded by maids of honour and a group of about seventy ladies; the sheen of their brilliantly coloured gowns gleamed in the early spring sunshine.

In solemn procession from the Tower to Westminster, preceded by his elder son and followed by his wife, King James was making his ceremonial entry into his capital.

He had been crowned the previous July, but London was rotten with plague at the time and the occasion, from all accounts, little more than an observation of the necessary formalities that made James Stuart King of England. Since nobody was prepared to be in the city unless they had no choice, the elaborate festivities were postponed.

Now the City of London was intent on making a day that would never be forgotten. Seven triumphal arches had been erected, seventy feet high and constructed from wood painted to look like stone; they were the brainchild of men of the theatre – highly skilled stage carpenters, scene builders, playwrights – who knew what they were about when it came to dramatic effect. A pageant had been prepared, in which brief performances were enacted at each of the seven arches in the form of allegories that honoured and flattered the new King and Queen.

I smiled as I considered Celia's question. She'd been joking but, when I stopped to think about it, the possibility that all that huge yardage of the best silk had come from Nicolaus Quinlie's warehouses was quite likely. The late Queen, after all, had been a customer. And, as my late brother-in-law had been wont to say, Quinlie silk was the very best.

We had found ourselves a prime spot on Cheapside, not far from one of the seven arches and at a slight elevation at the top of a flight of steps. As the procession stopped beneath us for the next instalment of the pageant, the King was close enough for us to study him.

He had a look of melancholy, I thought, the long face marked by lines that led downwards. His eyes were hooded, their expression resigned. The light brown beard, masking the mouth and whatever expression it bore, neatly bisected the elaborate lace collar.

The two halves of his body didn't match very well. His broad upper body suggested strength, but his long legs were thin and feeble-looking. As if she read my thoughts, Celia leaned close and said softly, 'They say he insists on thick padding under his garments, for he is terrified of being attacked and hopes so to foil the assassin's blade.'

Perhaps that explained the disparity between his powerful torso and his spindly legs.

'Not much chance of that here,' I whispered back. The royal party seemed to be lined six or seven people deep in servants, maids, guards and sundry other attendants. And, more crucially, the mood in the crowd was benign: Elizabeth's long reign had given the country a taste for peace and prosperity and most people, if asked, would probably have said they didn't as yet have much of an opinion of their new monarch but were very grateful that the handover of power had been accomplished so smoothly. It was extremely unlikely that any disturbance would occur today.

'The Queen looks a little bored,' Celia said in my ear. 'They say she's a frivolous woman not given to deep thought.'

'She's provided the King with two sons and a daughter,' I whispered back. 'That's pretty much all a Queen is required to do.'

Celia gave a slight shrug. 'He'll be back with his scintillating young men as soon as this is over,' she remarked. She shot Queen Anne another scathing look. The Queen was suppressing a yawn. 'I can't say I blame him.'

Celia and I were at the end of our time in London. We had been in the city for a month, throwing ourselves into the excitement fizzing through the air as preparations for the King's official entry were finalized. I'd taken my sister to all the places I'd discovered when I was studying at the King's College of Physicians – well, most of them anyway – and we'd been welcomed and made comfortable by the landlady of my old lodgings, who had provided us with two of her best rooms (clean sheets and tapestries on the wall) at what seemed a reasonable cost, considering the current pressure on accommodation for the King's pageant. We'd worshipped at St Paul's, we'd been up the river to stare at Hampton Court, we'd walked streets full of shops and the stalls of street vendors, we'd stood on quays and looked at ships newly arrived from far-flung ports all across the world. We'd gone to the Globe and seen *A Midsummer Night's Dream,* where we'd joined in the cheerful laughter at hapless, self-important, enchanted Bottom in his ass's head and Celia had fallen instantly in love with the handsome man playing Theseus.

I sensed that this trip to London marked the final stage in my sister's recovery. While I didn't underestimate her suffering, I observed in her a strong resilience; I recognized it because I possessed it myself. In that, we were very similar. Like me, she had the ability to face what had happened – what she had done – and, while not proud of some of her actions, console herself with the thought that, given the same circumstances again, she would do precisely what she'd done the last time. She had made peace with herself, and, more crucially, with God.

Or so I hoped.

It gave me pleasure to watch her absorbing the sights, smells and unique ways of the capital. She'd been amazed, at first;

wide-eyed at the massed spires of the city's twenty-five churches; at the dense thicket of chimneys belching the smoke of a thousand hearths into the sky; at the great lumbering wagons arriving daily to feed the various needs of half a million people and trundling away to bear away the products of London industry to the rest of the country; at acres of bed linen spread out on the grass by the laundresses; at the nausea-inducing stench of the tanneries; at the unimaginable gulf between the rich of the Strand and Holborn and the poor, clinging on to precarious existence in the filthy, overcrowded squalor of the cheaply built tenements up to their ankles in the foul waters of the Fleet Ditch. She had bravely ventured south of the river – and not just to visit the Globe theatre – and felt the dark underside of the city in areas such as Southwark and Bermondsey; haunts of cutpurses, tricksters and worse. She had wandered past bowling alleys and bear-baiting pits, she had seen taverns and brothels, drunkenness and lewd behaviour; men vomiting in the gutter and whores with bodices so low-cut that their breasts were on display.

And she loved every moment. I found myself watching with amazement as my gently reared sister threw herself into exploring the vibrant, dirty, befouled, fascinating city, for a greater contrast to the life of a prosperous farmer's daughter in rural Devon could hardly be imagined. But then I remembered what she'd been through. What she'd done. And I realized, once again, that there was more to Celia than met the eye.

I had left her resting in our rooms the morning after our visit to the Globe to meet my fellow members of the Symposium, our proposed meeting the previous summer having been cancelled, like the celebrations for the new King, because of the plague. I presented my paper expressing my doubts over the universal benefits of blood-letting, to the predictably raucous reception: in summary, disbelief, mockery and the suggestion that I stop being so arrogant and thinking I knew better than a thousand years of medical experience.

But I didn't let my friends change my mind. I had a long way to go with my research, my experiments and my observations, but I knew I was right.

*   *   *

It was time to go home. Celia and I had loved our time in London, and we had made a firm resolve – solemnized by raising our glasses of good French wine on our last night – to return. Celia's eyes were now open to what the rest of the world had to offer, and, as she remarked, our life in the Devon countryside seemed rather *small* by comparison.

Nevertheless, as we set out for home, both of us felt a lift of the heart.

In the course of our long journey, I had plenty of time to think ahead. Celia had intimated that she'd quite like to make her home with me, although she was still considering my parents' offer of her own quarters at Fernycombe. Since Jeromy's death, she had been dividing her time between the two households. Being my sister, she had somehow contrived to make it sound as if accepting my offer would mean she was graciously granting me a very great favour. But I didn't mind; quite the opposite, really. I had liked having her live under my roof even during the awful time just after Jeromy's death; I reckoned I'd like it a great deal more now, when my sister was restored to herself. If, that was, she decided to do so . . .

We were returning to a small but pleasant social network. Celia has a little group of her own, for the kind-hearted women who had supported her after Jeromy died – those wives of his business acquaintances – had not melted away once Celia was over the first shock. A few of them have become true friends, and quite often I return home after a long day to find Rosewyke full of the light-hearted voices of women, sweeping up and down the stairs with a swish of silk, little heels tapping on the floorboards, sounds of laughter and good-hearted teasing echoing to the roof. Sallie, red-faced and shiny-cheeked, is in her element, for the feminine touch she had yearned for was now present.

Perhaps a little *too* present, for me, but I am learning to cope.

In addition, Celia and I have shared friends: Jonathan Carew is a regular visitor, coming once a week or so to dine with us, and we now attend his services as a matter of course. With my sister and me he is ever the urbane, courteous and amusing man of the cloth, keeping the conversation light-hearted and frequently making us laugh. It would be forgivable to imagine this was all there was to him, but I don't believe it. Apart from the impression I gained when I first met him, I have now experienced other moments that invoke my interest: quite often after dinner, Celia retires to bed and leaves Jonathan and me to finish our brandy. Then occasionally – not often, for he is careful – he says something that makes me think all over again, *Who are you really, Jonathan Carew? What is your story?*

I look forward, although without a lot of hope, to finding out.

Our other good friends are Theophilus Davey and his wife Elaine. Theo, I am relieved to realize, seems to have forgiven me for not revealing the whole truth about Jeromy's death. Or perhaps *forgiven* is the wrong word; more likely, he appreciates that he is never going to find out anything more (not from me, anyway) and has sensibly decided that it isn't worth losing a friend purely in order to make a point.

I like to hope so, anyway, for I have become very fond of Theo.

Sometimes he and Elaine bring all three children out to Rosewyke for the day, for the elder two adore playing in the yard, the vegetable patch, the orchard and down the path towards the river, and poor Flynn doesn't get a moment's peace from the instant Carolus and Isabella arrive till they are dragged, protesting, away. The youngest, Benjamin, is overawed by the wide spaces of Rosewyke and prefers to seek out Celia and hold on to her skirts while his elder siblings tear about. I'd wondered, given Celia's recent history, how she would be affected by a small (and very loveable) boy intent on making her his friend. Happily, she seems to appreciate it. She is, I like to think, healing.

Slowly and steadily our journey passed.

Our progress wasn't fast, for, although the weather was good – cold but fine – the days were still relatively short, and there was no need to go on after dusk fell. As a consequence, it took over a fortnight and, by the time we turned into the track up to Rosewyke, we were very glad to be home.

Samuel and Tock came out to take our horses and give them the attention they had earned. Flynn rushed out to lick hands, faces, necks and anything else he could reach. Inside the house, Sallie greeted us peremptorily and instantly rushed off to prepare hot food, mulled ale, a cauldron of near-boiling water with which to wash off the dirt of travel and – luxury of luxury – clean clothes.

Finally, fed, washed, clothed and in all ways restored, Celia and I were sitting either side of the fire in the library. Full darkness had fallen, and the room was softly lit by candles and the flames. We were drinking the last of the spiced ale. Neither of us had spoken for some time, and I sensed she, like me, was sleepy and thinking of bed.

But I had to ask.

'So,' I said in what I thought a suitably casual tone, as if I didn't much care one way or the other, 'what have you decided?'

'About more ale? No thanks, Gabe, I've had enough.'

While it was true I'd half-heartedly offered to get up and fetch more, that wasn't what I meant and she knew it. I decided not to rise to her bait and merely waited.

After a while, she just said, 'Yes. I will.'

Silence fell again. I'd imagined it was all she was going to say. It was enough, for I understood and neither of us have ever been great ones for shows of emotion.

But then, so softly that I almost missed it, she added, 'Thank you.'